D1606188

The Office Wife

Also by Faith Baldwin
in Thorndike Large Print ®

District Nurse
Innocent Bystander
The Rest of My Life With You
That Man is Mine
Rich Girl, Poor Girl
Twenty-Four Hours A Day
"Something Special"
Beauty
Make-Believe
For Richer, For Poorer
Enchanted Oasis
And New Stars Burn
Lonely Man

This Large Print Book carries the
Seal of Approval of N.A.V.H.

The Office Wife

Faith Baldwin

Thorndike Press • Thorndike, Maine

Copyright, 1929, 1930, by Faith Baldwin.

All rights reserved.

All the characters in this novel are imaginary.
                        Faith Baldwin.

Thorndike Large Print ® General Series edition published in 1993 by arrangement with Henry Holt and Company.

Large print edition available in British commonwealth by arrangement with Harold Ober Associates, Inc.

The tree indicium is a trademark of Thorndike Press.

Set in 16 pt. News Plantin by Minnie B. Raven.

Printed in the United States on acid-free, high-opacity paper. ∞

Library of Congress Cataloging in Publication Data

Baldwin, Faith, 1893–
    The office wife / by Faith Baldwin.
        p.   cm.
    ISBN 1-56054-318-3 (alk. paper : lg. print)
    1. Man-woman relationships — United States — Fiction.
    2. Private secretaries — United States — Fiction.
    3. Large type books. I. Title.
    [PS3505.U97O38   1993]
    813'.52—dc20   93-26416

To
RAY LONG

Whose idea it was
This book in grateful recognition

Foreword

The time has passed when the teaching and nursing professions alone were open to women with their living to earn. Nowadays, few doors are closed to the intelligent female of the species, and you will find that most women holding important positions today have come up by the typist-stenographer-private secretary route.

The position of private secretary to a man of breadth, significance and power in his particular line of business is almost a twenty-four hour job. A man is compelled toward the woman he marries by emotion, and a biological need, but he selects his secretary with more care and more intelligence. Also he may change secretaries with more rapidity than he may change wives, and more ease. He demands of the woman in his private office not only alertness, efficiency and the clairvoyant quality of being able to carry out even the orders he does not give, but also a certain amount of charm, of personal attraction. He shares with her an intimate knowledge of himself that not even his closest friend may possess. His life is more or less open to her, she knows his faults and his hesitancies, his fears and psychological twists, as his wife can never know them. Also she sees the determining, weighing and into-action side of him which, if brought into play at home, is used only in the domestic urgencies and is thereby tempered with emotion of one sort or another.

Because the private secretary comes so close to her employer she has set herself a new standard of men. Hundreds of women who may not be at all emotionally involved with the men to whom they give their working hours find, nevertheless, that their personal lives are colored and complicated by their association with these men. They are no longer content, as were their grandmothers, to sit waiting for some man to come along and, in return for certain approved services, support them for life. Nor are they content, as were their mothers, to choose an "eligible" man, one with spirit and the will to advance, and by their smoothing of his domestic path and their intelligent interest, aid him toward that advancement, often "making him" as the phrase runs, yet without taking any of the credit themselves or pointing it out to him.

These women of today have gone a step further than their maternal ancestors. Unconsciously, yet aware of their own ability to get ahead of their own ambitions, they measure the men they meet by the yardstick of the man who has already arrived. They demand tangible success and proved power. And the unfortunate part is that men who are already successful and powerful are generally men who have married in their youth — and married either the parasite woman or some young eager thing anxious to see her man get ahead and putting her shoulder to the domestic wheel with that purpose in mind.

Therefore the young business woman of today is a misfit, and is often discontented with her personal experiences. Therefore she often falls in love, whether consciously or not, with her employer. Therefore she becomes the office wife. And if she has standards of comparison, so, by the same token, has the business man. How many business men wish futilely that their homes could be run as well as their offices and their wives comprehend their needs as swiftly and silently as their secretaries?

This business of the office wife is distinctly a modern problem. It will continue to be so until girls, working among men, cut the cloth to the coat and decide to do as their mothers have done — love and marry the men who are, like themselves, on the lower rungs of the ladder; it will continue to be so until the human equation no longer enters into business mathematics, and until there is utter cleavage between office and home, both for the man who occupies that office and the girl who works in it with him.

There are a great many men who never give their secretaries a personal thought; there are a great many girls who close their desks with sighs of relief and go out to find pleasure and amusement with gay hearted young men of their own sort, and their own class. But these are the exception which prove the rule. The girl whose standards are set by her employer, who has ambitions beyond quitting time, a cookstove and a suburban cottage with the rent paid by a masculine officer worker, has come to stay. And that girl is, for good or for evil, "the office wife."

Contents

Chapter 1

Miss Andrews is Hysterical

Nine stories above Park Avenue the Fellowes Advertising Agency had its headquarters. Through the many open windows the roar of traffic drifted up, subdued to the pulse-beat of a Gargantuan heart, and weaving a minor obligato to the sharp, decisive tapping of typewriter keys. Now and then the sound of a police whistle pierced through, thinned to an elfin note of warning.

The doors of the three elevators gave directly upon the reception room of the agency. They clanged open or shut almost without cessation, receiving or discharging their burdens. People came and went continuously — men, for the most part, the majority of them space-salesmen from the publications, calling to see Larson, the space-buyer, or his assistants. There were young men and elderly men, men with top coats slung over an arm and derbies pushed back from the foreheads, men carrying brief cases, men consulting memorandum books and wearing, almost without exception, that rather stubbornly anxious look overlaid with an aggressive optimism, which is the facial trade-mark of the man who makes his living by selling.

One by one they came up to the girl at the reception room desk, mentioned their names, their appointments, their business or requests, and then sat down to wait their turns while she spoke into the transmitter of her rarely silent instrument. Some fluttered the pages of magazines on the long tables under the reading lights; others smoked lazily or nervously, according to their temperaments and chances of success, reviewing as they did so their selling arguments in their busy, bedevilled minds. One, a slender blond boy, was speaking low and urgently through a telephone which stood on a table beside him. He had the accent of the Harvard man but recently down from his university.

A big man, with a square, rather florid face, and an out-thrusting chin, entered the reception room and approached the girl at the desk. He had an ingratiating smile and a carelessly charming manner.

"Mr. Jameson," he informed her. "My appointment with Mr. Fellowes is for three o'clock."

The girl smiled back, tossed the heavy black bang of bobbed hair from her intelligent, somewhat mocking eyes, and picking up her receiver spoke into it once more.

"Miss Andrews? Mr. Jameson to see Mr. Fellowes."

She replaced the receiver and looked up. "If you'd wait just a moment, Mr. Jameson?"

The big man nodded and, sitting down, took up a newspaper and occupied himself with it with a genial patience.

In the private office of the chief executive of the agency, Lawrence Fellowes, president of the concern and nephew of its late, dynamic founder, looked across his great desk at his secretary who, returning from the telephone in her adjoining office, reported in her quiet, colorless voice:

"Mr. Jameson is waiting."

She tried to smile, mechanically, but her thin face twitched nervously as she stood beside him, her notebook in her hand.

"Five minute," Fellowes told her, adding, "We'll just finish this letter. I want it off by special delivery."

He leaned back in his chair, waiting until she should deliver his message to the reception room clerk. In his relaxed, passive position there was a suggestion of force in leash, of power under control. His gray eyes were dark with concentration but lighted to an impersonally caressing smile as Miss Andrews returned

15

and, sitting down, held notebook and pencil poised.

Fellowes continued his effortless dictation. The tall woman in her blue serge frock followed the sound of his voice with the pencil and, save for that sound, the big office was very still. Writing, she jerked herself back to the sense of the words he was speaking, having lost herself momentarily in the mere cadence of the voice. What an amazing voice, she thought, keenly conscious of her aching head and the difficulty she had in writing — a voice that could infuse warmth, charm, magnetism into dry business phrases.

The room in which they sat was beautiful. It had recently been decorated, under Fellowes' personal supervision, in the best of the modern manner. But there was nothing restless about it, nothing sharp. The chairs were low to the thick-carpeted floor, solid, embracing, cushioned in soft-toned leather. The long couch under the great windows was of no particular period. It simply promised relaxation and kept that promise. The desk at which Fellowes sat was square and massive, of a most beautifully grained, polished wood. A silver bowl, brimming with roses, stood upon it near one lovely bronze, a sexless winged figure, vibrant with dark, gleaming life.

The panelled walls were broken by built-in bookcases, filled to the last inch of space with volumes. And over the stone mantel of a big fireplace there hung one very good etching — that of a row of pines, in black relief against a gray sky, roofed in hills of snow, marked with the delicate tracks of small four-footed creatures.

Miss Andrews lifted her eyes from the page of pothooks. She lifted them as if in answer to an inner compulsion, as if they were dragged from the page, upward, to the very familiar face of the man with whom she had worked for five years. She saw the gray eyes, set under heavy brows, the rather blunt nose, the mouth that though firm was so beautifully modelled, the square cleft chin; saw, too, the thick brown hair, with its rusty glint, and the long, fine hand idle on the polished surface of the desk. And these things she viewed with that heavy pressure at her breast, that troubling of the blood which had grown, this past year, into such proportions that she could no longer ignore it — no longer endure it.

Her lips, repressed by habit into a straight, thinned line, quivered, softened. She dropped her eyes again and stared unseeingly at the sheet upon which she had set no mark for a full moment. Fellowes, withdrawing his gaze

17

from the windows, spoke to her pleasantly:

"Will you read back what you have there, Miss Andrews?"

She turned her pages, read for a paragraph or two, then faltered, stumbling to a full stop, to silence. Then she asked, not looking at him, her voice lowered to a shred of sound:

"I'm afraid — I haven't — inattentive — if you would please repeat the last — Mr. Fellowes?"

Fellowes moved his broad shoulders in the suggestion of a shrug but with no hint of impatience. His glance, chancing to fall upon her hands, saw that they shook. His brows drew together. What on earth was wrong? Quiet, self effacing, efficient, she was the best secretary he had ever had. He had been satisfied with her from the time when, taking his uncle's place in the firm, he had employed her.

Of her personal life he knew little. He rarely exchanged a word with her beyond the daily routine. Did he even know her given name? Of course he did, that was absurd — Janet it was, Janet Andrews. If now and then she absented herself owing to some minor illness he got along as well as possible, scratch secretaries temporarily filling her place. He inquired concerning her daily, with genuine if abstracted interest, and sighed with relief when she returned, quiet and colorless as usual.

He knew that she lived alone; that she went to Cape Cod on her summer vacation; that she must be — how old —? Forty, at a venture.

He was dictating as the swift thoughts flashed through his consciousness. Finishing, he looked at her. She had not written a word. She sat there, watching his mouth, her hands in her lap. And as he stared back, incredulous, she flung her notebook to the floor and surrendered herself — to her own horror no less than to his — to a passion of violent tears.

Fellowes rose quickly and approached her. Standing, he was slightly above middle height, a very well built man, with strength and endurance in the set of his shoulders.

He touched her shoulder and she quivered under it, uncontrollably. Fellowes drew back his hand and spoke, exceedingly uncomfortable and terribly sorry for her.

"Miss Andrews — are you ill? Is anything wrong? May I help?"

She stumbled to her feet, her handkerchief crushed to her eyes. Her inadequate explanation reached him, muffled, broken and frantic with shamed embarrassment.

"I — yes — please forgive me. My head

19

is splitting. I'll be better presently."

He said, quickly, sympathetic, compelled to accept this interpretation of her disturbing symptoms:

"I'm sorry. It's quite all right. Take the remainder of the day and go home and rest and do something for your headache."

The thin blanketed voice answered his in three words.

"You're — so — *good!*"

More than gratitude there. A smothered heat, stifled, oppressive. Fellowes, usually the most poised of men, felt absurdly ill at ease. He said something — anything — anxious only to help her pull herself — and the situation — back to normal.

"Run along. Don't give me another thought. —"

"No, no," she said hastily, a little recovered, "I'll stay. I'll be all right. The letter must go —"

"I'll see to that. Mr. Sanders' secretary can take it for me. I can get along for the rest of the day," he assured her.

"Thank you, Mr. Fellowes."

She went into her own office and he heard the pitiful, unlovely sound of her quiet but obvious sniffling as she took down her well cut coat from the rack and jammed an expensive unbecoming hat over her reddened eyes. A moment later, with no further word spoken between them, he heard the outer door close, that door which she guarded, behind which she sat, alert to keep him from any intrusion.

Fellowes returned to his desk, and relaxed in his chair, his legs stretched straight before him, his hands deep in his pockets.

He frowned, whistled once or twice softly to himself, found his mind framing profanities.

What the devil ailed her?

It was not the first time during the past year that hysteria had flown a warning signal. Latterly she had been close to tears much of the time. If he spoke to her somewhat brusquely, if, as occasionally happened, appointments became confused or messages forgotten, she would cringe as if he had struck her by merely calling minor misdemeanors to her attention — and her pale anxious eyes would fill.

And she fussed over him so of late. Was he tired? Must he work so late? Couldn't she stay on? Should she send out for crackers and milk? Was he coming down with a cold? She'd been far worse than a wife — than *his* wife at any rate — for Linda, superbly healthy herself, thought such discussions better left to doctors and nurses.

Damn it, he couldn't have Andrews around

any more — if he and she were going to get upon each other's nerves at this rate!

Sitting there he came to one of his characteristic quick decisions. He would give her a long leave of absence and, at the end of it, dismiss her. Meantime he would have to break in another secretary, no small task or pleasing thought. And he would find a place for Janet Andrews in another office, one, say, less high powered, operating under less of a nervous tension. But he hated to let her out. She had served him well and loyally. It was difficult to understand the gradual, recent change in her. Yet, was it so difficult?

Fellowes shrugged as if to shake off an irritating burden. He could not have reached his present position in the business world were he not alive to human, as well as business, reactions. There was, therefore, to any thinking man, a natural, even simple, answer to Janet Andrews' present state of mind and emotions. But Fellowes was too decently masculine, too removed from personal, petty vanity, to wish to admit that answer even to himself.

Then, with relief and compunction, he remembered Jameson, cooling his heels in the reception room. He picked up his telephone, was connected with the black-haired clerk, and a moment later Jameson came in.

Fellowes liked Jameson, an amiable bachelor of his own age whom he knew very well socially, and the call was not upon a business matter. Jameson's only business was finding new ways in which to spend his enormous unearned income, and Fellowes was glad to see him today, if only to dismiss the problem of Miss Andrews from his mind for ten minutes.

He greeted his friend, indicated a chair, offered a cigarette case.

"Sit down —, Dick — sorry to have kept you waiting."

" 'Sall right," answered Jameson easily, "My time's my own, thank God —"

"*And* a father in Standard Oil!"

"Quite so. Too bad to barge in on you like this but you're never at home, rarely at the club, and I haven't seen you since Hardy's bachelor dinner."

"That," remarked Fellowes, with feeling, "was some dinner. A complete K.O. for most of us. But at that, Dick, you and I kept our feet, if not our heads, better than the majority."

"What have you been doing? The last plan I heard — at Hardy's dinner — was your solemn assurance that you would be charmed to fly to the South Sea Islands with that imported Viennese blonde who came in as part of the entertainment."

"Don't I remember it! Linda heard it too, afterwards. Tommy Norton heard it — and told his wife. Hence Linda's information. She didn't take it very seriously. No, I've not been to the South Seas. But I have been away a lot. Strictly business. No Strauss waltzes."

"So Linda told me. I mean that you'd been away. She's much less uncomplaining than the average wife of the T.B.M. Very sporting, really. Now what I wanted to see you about is this: a baker's dozen of us are kicking in to buy some property in Virginia. There's a small disused inn on it, which could easily be turned into a hunting club. We propose to put caretakers in, clean it up, hire guides to be on call, and use it week-ends or longer. It won't cost much to get it started and keep it going. I've the approximate figures here. You business men are mad on figures — any kind!" He laid a slip of paper on the desk and leaned back, inhaling his cigarette. "Think it over. Come in with us if you care to. Linda says it will do you good."

Fellowes was smiling.

"She does, does she?"

"I spoke to her about it at Hot Springs last week. Sorry you couldn't join her there. She seemed to enjoy it this year for, though the season was early, there was a good bit doing."

"I was sorry too. I've been infernally busy.

As to your proposal, I can't promise, Dick."

"Take your time, don't turn it down right off the bat," Jameson answered. "By the way I ran into Harry Marsten, at the Springs," he went on, "he told me you were handling his account."

"Working on the campaign now."

"I see." Jameson looked keenly at his friend. "Larry, you look tired," he commented.

"I am tired. Tired of —"

Fellowes broke off and laughed suddenly. If people ever wondered why the employees of this particular agency were so fiercely loyal to their chief, they would have been answered had they heard him laugh like that — with the full laughter of genuine good humor; laughter which took the hearer into confidence, which was amused at itself, as light-hearted as a boy's.

"What's the joke?" asked Jameson grinning in sympathy. Occasionally women told him that Larry Fellowes was the most attractive man of their acquaintance. And Jameson didn't doubt it, despite the usual difference of opinion between the sexes on the subject of masculine attraction. No, he didn't doubt it, though for personal reasons he would have preferred that the ladies exaggerated.

"Joke? Oh, it's on me. It's hell the way a man gets to depend on his secretary, isn't it?

Oh, I forgot — you don't work. You merely cut the coupons and get scissors' cramp. But it so happens that I've sent Miss Andrews home for the rest of the day and contemplate keeping her there indefinitely. She's been — splendid — but it looks as if she has outlived her particular usefulness here."

"I remember her — wasn't she at your place in Southampton one week-end last summer? Tall, thin woman, not bad looking really, if she'd only get wise to herself and take pains to put other people wise, too. What's wrong with her?"

"Nerves," said Fellowes.

"Why don't you get a man?"

"I'd rather not. They're all right for travelling but the work is just a stepping stone to them — means to an end. They don't take the personal interest in it that a woman does."

Jameson smiled, his eyes on the etching over the mantel.

"The trouble with your secretary," he diagnosed smoothly, "is, I should say, too *much* personal interest."

"Now what do you mean by that?" asked Fellowes. His tone was quiet, even mildly indifferent, but his jaw had hardened and his eyes were alert.

Jameson fingered a small, well kept mustache and chuckled faintly.

"Keep your shirt on. I've seen it happen before. I didn't always cut coupons. I once sat in an office and dictated lovely letters to a series of little girls. And these efficient virgins of the type of your Miss-What's-her-name let their work get a strangle hold on them. That is, they think it's the work. Then, when they inevitably discover that it's the man they're working for, instead, they go to pieces. That woman — forty if she's a day, I judge — didn't look to me like the sort who'd have a good time after office hours. I suppose she goes home to a little flat, picks up a cold supper, drifts off to the movies and goes to bed praying for morning and the office. Nerves! No wonder she has them. She has a right to crawl with them! No emotional outlet, my boy, and you or I, or any man knows what that means."

"I don't see it," Fellowes said stubbornly. But he did see it, being no fool, and his heart sank. Why hadn't he faced it before, admitted it to himself? He might have saved the poor woman some decent shreds of reticence.

Later, when Jameson had taken his breezy departure, Fellowes left his office and went into that of Timothy Sanders, the vice-president.

Sanders was a fairly young man who had come up through the copy-writing depart-

27

ment and even now wrote much of the important copy. He was a lean, enthusiastic person, who thought in headlines, remained a bachelor through choice, and whose passions away from work were for bridge and detective novels. He and Fellowes liked each other enormously but came very little into contact outside of the office.

Sanders, it happened, was not at his desk, but his secretary was there alone in the room over in the corner, by the big window. The light streamed in through the big sheet of glass and haloed with an especial tenderness her cropped red-gold head. The effect was charming, and Fellowes responded to it with quick pleasure before he spoke.

"Is Mr. Sanders in the building, Miss Murdock?"

She had not heard him enter, so noiseless had been his tread upon the thick piled carpet. If she was startled she did not betray herself but rose to her feet and faced him quietly, a small girl, extraordinarily pretty.

"He just stepped outside a moment, Mr. Fellowes," she replied. "I can find him for you."

She smiled. Fellowes responded to the smile as he had to the picture she had made — with instant pleasure. He had seen her before of course — but somehow saw her more personally today, alone in the quiet room with her. He said "Thank you" with marked warmth and as she left the room he walked to the windows, looking down on the massed tops of many cars, upon the people hurrying about their pitifully unimportant concerns — unimportant, that is, to the serene blue sky which roofed them in and to the careless shining of late autumn sunlight.

Presently the girl returned with Sanders. Fellowes thanked her again and spoke to his associate.

"Spare me ten minutes, Sandy?"

"Twice that," offered Sanders cheerfully and nodded to his secretary.

"Just a moment," said Fellowes as she turned to go. "When I am through here could you, if Mr. Sanders can spare you, take a letter for me? Miss Andrews has gone home."

The blonde girl smiled and assented in a controlled little voice that was low and warm and very pleasing to the ear. As she went through the doorway and it closed behind her straight little back Fellowes asked suddenly:

"Satisfied with that girl of yours, Sandy?"

"Miss Murdock? Sure. She's all right."

"Been with you long?"

"Six months. She's been three years in the organization though. She came to me from Dick Johnson. Why?"

"Nothing — except that my mind runs on secretaries. I find I shall have to let Miss Andrews go. She's not well — can't stand the gaff. Why," he asked suddenly, a little humanly on guard since Jameson's visit, "why the devil are you grinning like a Cheshire Cat?"

"Can't a fellow smile? Want to take Miss Murdock away from me? I'll wring your neck if you do," threatened Sanders, without savagery. "She knows more about this business than I do."

"That wouldn't be much," Fellowes insulted him, with genuine affection, and Sanders continued to grin, amiably.

"About the Marsten campaign," asked Fellowes, sitting down near the desk, "just what are your reactions? I want to stay down and work on it tonight."

Meantime, Anne Murdock, leaving her office, went down the aisle of the outer room in the open main office, between the rows of desks, back to the copy-writing department in which she had a close friend.

Arriving there, she looked about for her friend, saw her, beckoned and stood leaning against the low railing until the other woman left her desk and hurried up to her. They stood together in a little space of low voiced privacy while the hum and undercurrent of the office

Anne laughed and her small pointed face, with its vivid coloring, lighted up with sheer mischief. "Her people and his hailed from the same county back in the old country. They have a grand time together. I think they get along because they're both red-headed and neither can put anything over on the other."

"You're not far in from red-headed yourself. Well, he's a nice boy," commented Betty — "and he'll go far in his job."

"That's what mother says," Anne told her, and stopped and bit her full lower lip. Over the satin texture of her skin the bright color flooded. And Betty smiled and thought: "so Mrs. Murdock has been backing Ted's bill!"

Her own disaster uppermost in her own mind, she warned low, almost involuntarily: "Don't — don't be hasty, Anne!"

"Not me!" Anne answered, "I like my job so well. I'm too ambitious — too darned ambitious, I guess," she said ruefully, with her lovable little trick of catching herself up, laughing at her own earnestness.

She turned, touched Betty's hand a moment.

"I must get back. The Chief's with Mr. Sanders. He asked me to take a letter later. Andrews has gone home."

"What's wrong?" Betty wanted to know.

"I saw her — she came in the lavatory while

went on all about them.

"First chance I've had to get away," Anne told her breathlessly, "I've been so anxious since you 'phoned last night. Betty, how *is* he?"

Betty Howard, a good-looking woman in her early thirties, smiled, but her dark eyes remained troubled and lightless.

"It's pneumonia, all right. The doctor sent in a nurse. His temperature was pretty high when I 'phoned last —"

"Oh, poor little man!" Anne's eyes were heavy with pity, "but don't worry so — try not to," she begged and then, with an effort at condolence, "youngsters have to go through these things. Mother said last night that Jim, Kathleen and I all had measles at once, and Kathleen went into bronchial pneumonia — she was only a baby, younger than your Billy, and she came through flying."

"I know. But it's so hard," Mrs. Howard said, with a desperation of tone breaking through her control, "I have to do my work and my mind isn't on it. I'm — torn to pieces all day. A woman's a fool to marry," she added suddenly, "a woman with her living to make."

Anne nodded. She made no pretense at disagreement. She knew Betty Howard's commonplace story — the clever girl of more than average talent, working her way through college, finally getting a good position and dreaming of reaching the heights of her chosen profession. Then, after five years, marriage to a man much older than herself, a man struggling to come through the physical and spiritual disaster which his war service had brought him.

Betty had come to the Fellowes agency shortly before her marriage. She had carried on very successfully, dividing her personality, it seemed, with but little effort, between the office and her home. Then had come an enforced period of absence from her desk, before and after the birth of her boy. During that time she had worked at home, driving herself savagely when her body rebelled and her nerve energy had been at its lowest ebb. Then she had returned to the agency, leaving the child with a competent nurse.

But Frank Howard had not long held his own position with an insurance company. His lungs had been weakened and scarred by mustard gas. He was now up at Saranac for an indefinite time and Betty's salary, the income from some freelance article writing she did in her scant leisure, and Frank's disability money just about carried the small separated family from week to week.

Anne thought, observing Betty's haggard face:

"She was so in love with him — still is — that's what happens to you when you turn soft and marry a man on the make, earning little more if as much as yourself."

Her chin went up as if in conscious defiance to an unspoken challenge, and her eyes, of the rare dark blue which deepens to black under emotion, were black now, and her ardent mouth straightened to a firm red line.

Betty murmured:

"Mrs. Holmes — that's the nurse — was to telephone if — if —"

"You'll be home pretty soon," Anne reminded her hastily. She could not bear the dreadful implications in that two lettered word — if — *if?*

A young man, tall, built like a greyhound but with frankly red hair and very merry eyes, passed by, a sheaf of papers in his hand. Seeing Anne, he paused and smiled, very gaily yet with a sort of hungry appeal.

"Remember — eight o'clock!" he reminded her and went on his way, whistling under his breath.

Anne looked after him, rather thoughtfully.

"You see a good deal of Ted O'Hara, don't you?" asked Betty with the pardonable curiosity of a good friend.

"Considerable — we go out — or he comes to the house. Mother's crazy about him

32
33

I was there and washed her face. That's all she ever does to it, poor soul. Her eyes were red and she looked all shot."

Anne shook her bright head, ruddy gold in the sun, pale gold in the shadow.

"I don't know. I see her sometimes, you know. I occasionally eat dinner with her. She lives alone on West Tenth Street. She's an odd woman. And she eats, sleeps and breathes the office."

After a short silence during which each thought her own thoughts, Anne said:

"Well, I'll get back now. I'll ring up tonight and see how Billy is. 'Bye, for now."

When she had gone, with her heartwarming smile, Mrs. Howard returned to her desk and looked out at the office, watching Anne's swift sure progress. How beautifully she carried her small person, thought her friend. She had liked the younger girl so much ever since their first meeting in Mrs. Howard's own department. Anne was so pretty, so vital, so friendly, with a warm, giving, genuine sort of friendliness: and an excellent brain functioned under the clipped lovely hair. She had worked up, well, thoroughly, not too quickly. Her present job was a good one. Forty a week, Betty estimated. Forty dollars a week for a girl with no responsibilities was an excellent salary.

Mrs. Howard glanced at her watch. No news was good news.

Ted O'Hara passed her desk and went out of the railing gate en route to Sanders' office, probably to get another glimpse of Anne. He'd been obviously fathoms deep in love with her since the day he'd first set eyes on her. No one could blame him, mused Mrs. Howard, but a girl was a blind and gallant fool to marry. —

Still if she herself hadn't married she wouldn't have had Billy — Billy and his father, those dear obstacles to the fulfillment of her once ambitious dreams, dreams which if they had become realities would have taken every ounce of her energy, every thought, sublimated every deep emotion.

With an impatient sigh she turned back to her desk. But her mind was not on the work which had gone badly today — it was not concerned deeply with the superior quality of Gala Hosiery. The Stocking Fastidious Women Prefer.

If Andrews were let out, thought Betty fleetingly, would that mean that Anne might be a logical candidate for the position?

Anne was with Fellowes now, in his office. She waited while he attended to a message that had been brought in and, waiting, looked about the room with an appreciation, an excitement which never failed, no matter how often she saw it. In the past six months she had come almost daily to Miss Andrews' office, bringing memoranda from Sanders to Fellowes, and had looked always longingly through the door between, and, once or twice, when Fellowes was not there, she had gone in.

Now she could study the room. It has such beauty she thought. She could spend a year there and never see enough of it. She loved beauty intuitively and wistfully, and it had not much entered into her life. Her own home was comfortable. It was glaringly modern in the employment of electric lights, shining radio and phonograph, and lurid chintzes. But it had no magic. When beauty reached her it did so through the pages of magazines and books, through an occasional theatre or motion picture which tried to capture glamour on stage or screen, through eventful trips into the country — country that was not merely half city, stretches of beach and sea which did not border on asphalt pavements. And now, touching her life a little more closely, had come these recent glimpses into Fellowes' big quiet office with its suggestion of money spent for loveliness, of a busy and ordered life that yet took thought for the things which feed the hunger of the spirit.

Now Fellowes spoke to her in that deep and dangerously magnetic voice, handing her Miss Andrews' notes.

"Do you think you can read these, Miss Murdock?" he asked, "or shall I start over again?"

Anne looked at the pothooks with accustomed eyes.

"It's Gregg," she said, "Yes, I think I can manage, Mr. Fellowes. Will you take up your dictation where you left off?"

Fellowes flashed her a quick appreciative smile. It was rather rare to find a girl who could read another secretary's notes he thought. And thought too, as he dictated smoothly, that it was even rarer — and amazingly pleasant — to be working with so pretty and young a person. His terse, crisp phrases continuing evenly, he saw how easily Anne's pencil kept pace with them. Well, Janet Andrews had been a good worker too, but she'd certainly lacked charm. Somehow the whole room seemed to settle into a becoming and suitable background for the small girl with the red-gold hair and the pointed, ardent face, whose crossed legs and short skirt revealed silken delightful knees. And Fellowes was absurdly conscious that he was taking especial pains with his dictation.

"Thank you," he said, as she rose to go,

"can you get it out at once for me? Special delivery. You might, if Mr. Sanders doesn't need you immediately, use Miss Andrews' office."

A moment later and Anne had settled herself at Janet's orderly desk. The small room was pleasant and well furnished. It had about it a certain air of prestige. Andrews' name was on the glass outer door in discreet gilt letters — Secretary to the President.

A little later Anne laid the letter on Fellowes' desk. He read it through, commented upon her speed and accuracy, signed it and, as she turned to go, asked on a sudden impulse:

"Shall you be busy this evening, Miss Murdock?"

She thought of her engagement with O'Hara; answered immediately:

"No, Mr. Fellowes."

"Miss Andrews' illness leaves me in rather a hole," he confided, ruefully. "I'll arrange things with Mr. Sanders if you can stay and help me for an hour or two?"

He looked up at her swiftly. She stood quite near him, her beautiful little figure quite apparent in the autumn brown frock she wore. Her face did not change as he asked his question, but her round small breasts rose perceptibly with an increased pace in her

breathing. But she replied quietly:
"I'd be glad to, Mr. Fellowes."

She went back into Andrews' office and straightened her letter paper and carbons mechanically. Glad! What an inadequate, almost fatuous word! Her heart was pounding. To work with The Chief, after three years of hoping and planning for such an opportunity, and to work with him through the quiet evening hours, the office hum silent, the lamplight shining on the big desk, shut in with beauty, beauty reflected from panelled walls, beauty in drawn draperies and opening roses —

To work — *with The Chief!*

Well, why shouldn't she . . . permanently? Since her coming into his business she had planned every step to reach this one particular goal. Had cultivated, with consciousness, the uninspiring friendship of Janet Andrews, uninspiring, that is, in itself. Had learned, cleverly and subtly, the great man's secretarial requirements, and some of his personal needs as well. It was on the cards that Andrews would go some day, and Anne had prepared herself to fill that hypothetical vacant place. She had no feeling that in studying Fellowes' demands through the unconscious medium of Miss Andrews she was doing anything unethical. If her chance came to her why shouldn't she take it? She was younger than Andrews;

40

she was well equipped; she was infinitely better looking. People said that appearance, personality didn't count. But Anne knew better, and she was honest about it — with herself. Larry Fellowes was a man, as other men. And a woman in business had need of every weapon she could employ to hold her job, and the man who controlled the job. Well, if she got this job, thought Anne, she'd hold it!

Chapter 2

Miss Murdock Has a Proposal

Miss Andrews returned to the office on the following day, perceptibly nervous beneath her air of schooled repression. Fellowes, who had worked late the previous evening, remaining long after he had let Anne Murdock go, arrived at the office somewhat tardier than was his custom and found Janet at her desk. He spoke to her pleasantly, determined to ignore the scene — and its implications — of the afternoon before.

But she said, timidly enough:

"I — I was so sorry about yesterday."

"That's all right," he told her hastily, "I hope your headache is better?"

It wasn't. But she lied mechanically.

"Oh yes, thank you. But I was worried about the letter to Mr. Goddard."

"Miss Murdock got it out for me," he said, and went on into his room, conscious that after "Miss Murdock," the presence of Miss Andrews was a considerable letdown.

The early morning routine having been disposed of, Janet Andrews drew a deep painful breath and sat tense and erect at her desk, her thin hands idle, staring at the wall upon which she seemed to see an inevitable hand-writing. God alone knew what a hideous night she had put behind her — hours of endless, sleepless, bitter self-reproach and shame. She had always prided herself upon her cool intelligent interest in her work. She had never been able to understand women who took their jobs simply without self-surrender — jobs that were merely agreeable or disagreeable ways of earning a living. She had been proud of her business loyalty and integrity, and of Lawrence Fellowes' reliance upon her. So the five years had passed and, slowly, inexorably, by almost imperceptible degrees, she had come to this agonizing self-knowledge that it was not the work, but the employer which mattered.

All night, weaving her head from side to side upon the crumpled pillows she told herself: "I shall resign — I must —"

But she couldn't face it. Never to see him again! Never to hear his voice! Never to watch the slow deep smile illuminating the gray eyes! Never again to have the usurped right to mother him a little, to watch over him, to guard him. She did not appear at all ridiculous to herself.

She'd dragged herself back to the office

wondering why in God's name this devastating thing had come to her. She'd been far too busy all her life to speculate upon her physiological and psychological problems. She read little — business magazines, the staider periodicals, and the most sedate newspaper. Her young womanhood had been spent in caring for and supporting an invalid father. At his death she adjusted herself to living alone with no difficulty. No one had advised her of the perils she ran into, the dangers of a starving maternal instinct, the warning signals of her forty years. She could meet men graciously enough — in business. Socially she was repressed, a little awkwardly austere. One or two men who might have loved her had come into her life during the period when her father and his demands constituted a burden she could not drop — nor share. She'd been quite pretty in her twenties, a prettiness of good features, abundant vitality and youth. But her vitality had gone into the job, and the youth had passed and the prettiness faded, become pinched. She was extremely critical of "smart" clothes in the office and of cosmetics. She dressed well and plainly, and as Betty Howard had said "washed her face," and let it go at that.

She had a few friends, professional women of her own age, some sober plodders like herself, others of a more volatile nature, a little impatient of "poor Janet's" incapacity for enjoyment.

Anne Murdock was the youngest friend she had and by far the most attractive. Janet disapproved of Anne. She thought her too pretty and, erroneously, too "light," for all her alertness, to be in an office. She should be married to some nice boy, settled in a suburban cottage with a family to raise, and a house to keep, away from the pressure and temptations of the business world. Not that Janet herself had been subjected to temptations. But she liked Anne, was even fond of her, scolded her as she might have a dear younger sister, was glad when Anne found time for her.

But, today, at her desk, staring at the walls, she experienced a sharp stab of jealousy. Anne was twenty-four. Anne had youth, ambition, beauty and a flashing gaiety, a warm ardency of manner. And last night Anne had been with Lawrence Fellowes in the quiet big office taking his dictation, finishing her, Janet's, tasks. No, she could not resign.

But, as she was leaving for the day Fellowes called her to him.

"I am going to give you a leave of absence, Miss Andrews," he told her quickly but most kindly. "I think you need and deserve a rest. You work very hard, your vacations have been inadequate. You will leave us at the end of

45

the week on full pay."

But his deliberate kindness went disregarded. Her eyes were distended and her mouth shook as she asked him hoarsely:

"Does that mean that I am — dismissed?"

He answered, wishing to be honest yet finding her so very pitiful:

"I hope not. I want you to take six weeks. If at the end of that time you are strong again, quite well — ?"

He left the sentence unfinished. Yet she felt as if she had watched him sign her death warrant.

She drew a little nearer, her hands clasped before her in a futile endeavor to still their tremor, the shaking of her entire body.

"I'm all right," she managed. "It was temporary — please — please don't send me away from you," she implored, so desperately unhappy that she did not realize what she was saying.

Fellowes felt ashamed — curiously humiliated as if he had received a wound in the spirit through this sword of revelation. And at the same time, being masculine, he was a little, consciously, angry. At all events her attitude settled things. Had to. He said firmly, sanely:

"You see, Miss Andrews, how quickly you become upset? I am not sending you away.

46

I am giving you a leave of absence with a good chance to recover your health and return to us."

In another moment she would cry. She knew it and he knew it. She said, "Thank you," very low, and walked back to her office. By some stupendous feat of will she managed to get her things together and to crawl wearily home to the little flat.

She'd seen this sort of thing happen before to other women — the tactful granting of leave —

Well, in six weeks' time she would be looking for another job.

When she left, at the end of a terrible week, the fiction was kept up between her and Fellowes. It had to be, to save, at least in public, that haggard face of hers.

"The work?" she wanted to know when she was saying good-by to him. "Good-by," she thought dully, "means 'God be with you.'" But it seemed that He had ceased to be with her.

"I've arranged with Mr. Sanders to borrow Miss Murdock for the time being," he answered.

So she had that to take home with her, the definite knowledge of her supplanting.

When she was gone Fellowes had time and inclination to think about her without that little flash of masculine anger, for the love of a woman one doesn't want affects a man in one of two ways, according to his character and the quality of his vanity — or pride; either it affords him smugness, complacency and a little scorn, or it annoys him. It had annoyed Fellowes.

Yet he thought he understood — a little blindly, as men always understand women. For he knew better than most men the dangers of repression, the need for reckless giving, the bursting of carefully builded dams.

To Anne Murdock he said briefly:

"Mr. Sanders will let me have you for the duration of Miss Andrews' absence."

Anne looked up and smiled. His mind banished Miss Andrews completely and centered upon her successor. What a very pretty girl, he thought, for the twentieth time, as Anne evidenced her willingness to fall in with his plans. And if Sanders didn't like it he contented himself with a good stenographer as substitute and warned Fellowes frankly:

"You won't be able to keep me out of your office while Miss Murdock's with you. She carries forty thousand details of my work in her head that I can't be bothered with. So don't crab if you see me coming in half a dozen times a day."

"I'm sorry, Sandy — and come as often as

48

you want. But I must have competent assistance with this Marsten business, and as far as I can see Miss Murdock is the only person who'll fill the bill at present. I don't want to bring in an outsider. Miss Andrews will come back, you know," he added with no conviction.

Nor was Sanders convinced. But he made no comment.

At the end of her first day with Fellowes Anne went home a little late, rather tired, emminently satisfied and excitedly happy.

Things had gone well. She'd made no mistakes. The Chief had praised her at the close of the day. A good Monday. Why did people call Mondays blue? And Betty Howard, whose boy was well on the road to recovery, had prophesied during a lunch hour snatched together:

"You'll get Andrews' job. She'll never come back."

"Mr. Fellowes says she will," Anne said, arguing against her own ambitions and happiness in a way women have.

"You let that mislead you? When a man gives his secretary a vacation because her nerves are shot there is more in it than meets the eyes. No, he'll never take her back. Men can't be annoyed with nerves in their offices. They have enough of them at home."

49

"Look here," asked Anne suddenly, "I fell into this. I didn't try deliberately to get the job away from her — but — if she doesn't return and I do get it — well, I haven't done anything really underhanded, have I?"

Betty smiled at her, with something of envy for the younger girl's vitality.

"Of course not. It's dog eat dog in this world anyway," Betty told her a little wearily, "and if it's true anywhere that one man's loss is another man's gain it's true in business. It's not your fault," Betty reminded her, "that Andrews went to pieces."

Anne lived in one of those suburbs of New York City which are neither town nor country, a suburb in which every little brick house was its neighbor's twin, a place of backyards and clothes-lines, straggling grass and dusty lilac bushes, a place which in Springtime bloomed with the gallant gaiety of tulips and flowering shrubs — a neat, windy place with a startled and somehow impermanent air.

Anne's house was fifth in a row of ten. The door being open, she heard her mother's voice, with a rich hint of County Clare in it, raised in argument as she entered. Anne grinned to herself, like a small boy.

"Kathleen's at it again," she guessed silently, as she walked in.

The small living room, cheerfully and comfortably furnished with its overstuffed suite and radio and indoor window boxes, was empty. In the far corner, next to the kitchen door, the gate-legged table was laid for four. Later, the dishes cleared, it would be folded up and set against the wall, a strip of embossed leather over it, two brass vases and a brass ashtray set symmetrically upon it.

In the kitchen, Mrs. Murdock was lecturing her youngest child, darting from stove to cupboard, a blue bibbed apron tied about her round waist, every red hair in place above her flushed, animated face, one hand gesticulating with a large tin spoon.

"And that you shall not!" she ultimatumed as Anne entered.

Kathleen was sitting on the kitchen table, swinging her beautiful legs. She was nineteen years old. She had Anne's facial contour and Anne's dark blue eyes, but her hair was dusky black, and her full startling painted mouth was weaker than Anne's and at the moment markedly mutinous.

"What's all the shootin' for?" Anne inquired as she seized her mother about the waist and implanted a hearty kiss under the little lady's left ear.

Kathleen, whose face had brightened at Anne's entrance, produced a package of cigarettes from her sweater-suit coat pocket and

51

reached for a kitchen match. She struck it and a moment later inhaled a lungful of smoke.

"Painted!" commented their mother darkly, "and smoking like a chimney!"

Anne laughed.

"Darling, you do fuss, don't you? Kathleen isn't hurting herself or anyone else by some lipstick and a cigarette now and then, I've been known to indulge in both myself."

"If I'd carried on that way," remarked Mrs. Murdock, "my old mother — rest her soul — would have killed me, and well I'd have deserved it!"

Anne swung herself up beside her sister and regarded her with indulgence. It was impossible to regard her otherwise. Kathleen was so pretty and Anne loved her so much. And she'd been a problem ever since leaving High School. She had refused to take a business course and had spent her days hanging around the Long Island motion picture studios and getting work as an extra. Her father raged, and her mother stormed, and Anne stood as involuntary buffer between her sister and their parents. And now —

"She's going into the chorus, no less!" announced Mrs. Murdock, much as if she had said, "She's going to murder her invalid great aunt!"

Anne looked at her sister. Kathleen nodded,

52

and tossed her chin a little.

"The Sky Girl," she explained, "at the Forty-Fifth Street Theatre. Got in through Lola — the girl I met over at the studio. Watch my step, Anne, I'll soon be glorified by Ziegfeld."

"Golly, that's great!" said Anne. There was no sanity in putting obstacles in Kathleen's way. She was more than stubborn, she was determined, and Anne had reasoned for some time that the more she was opposed the more set she'd be upon her own way. Besides, as far as Anne was concerned, the stage, provided you liked it and were suited temperamentally and otherwise for it, was a perfectly good way of earning a living.

She said as much to her mother.

Mrs. Murdock sniffed.

"Kathleen, get off that table and carry these things in for me," she commanded. And Kathleen complied, smiling a little. She knew very well that Anne was the barometer by which their mother judged the domestic weather. If Anne put the seal of her approval upon Kathleen's ambitions, Mrs. Murdock would, in time, set her seal there also.

"That's your father!" exclaimed Mrs. Murdock unnecessarily as a car rattled into the side drive.

He came in presently, a tall man with dark,

graying hair and an intelligent, irritable face. He was shop foreman for one of the outlying districts of the Gas Company. He had worked for the company since youth and had reached the limits of his capability. For, practical and competent though he was, he lacked education. He growled at the increased cost of living, but his salary, three thousand a year, was to him a large one. He had bought and paid for the little brick house on the usual "terms," had purchased in the same manner the radio, the phonograph, most of the furniture, the vacuum cleaner and the second-hand car in which he went to and from work. He had married Molly, his Irish-American wife, nearly thirty years ago, and they had been inarticulately happy and harried all their hard working partnership.

Molly Murdock was an ambitious woman. She had prodded and pushed her husband to his present position, and now could do no more for him. She loved him, scolded him and mothered him as she did her children. She shared the children with him as far as his rather saturnine temperament permitted, and exacted that they respect him and obey him in as far as they were temperamently capable of so doing. Murdock had a hair-trigger temper, was markedly fretful, suffering as he did from chronic dyspepsia for which he took quarts of patent medicine and was, naturally, a man who enjoyed a grievance. But he was a good husband, a devoted, if peppery, parent and a valuable, if sour-humored, employee.

As far as he was concerned Mrs. Murdock's task of getting the family up in the world was finished. So she had turned her many powers of persuasion toward her children. She was immensely proud of them. Anne was her unfailing standby, Anne was impulsive, a little reckless and in her her mother saw a warmth of nature, a giving sort of spirit which occasionally caused her worry, but not too much. Kathleen was Mrs. Murdock's torment, her despair and her secret idol. No good would ever come of that wild girl! she deplored — but only to herself — and refusing really to believe her own harsh maternal prophecy. As for Jim, the only son, he was a reporter on a tabloid, and lived with his wife and babies in the Bronx. Jim had done well. He was a fine boy his mother assured herself with justification, and if he had ever given her anxiety, well, boys will be boys, she admitted comfortably. She was not quite modern enough to admit also that girls will be girls.

She advised Kathleen, passing her on her way back into the kitchen:

"Say nothing to your father yet — let him have his good hot supper."

Later they sat down to the filling, if un-variegated, meal of the average American family — a good cut of meat, scalloped potatoes, a canned vegetable, pie and coffee, bread, butter, pickles and jam. And, contrary to expert opinion, Anne and Kathleen, nour-ished upon this diet, retained their loveliest legacy from their mother — their glowing fine-textured skins.

"Sit still, Mother, I'll bring in the dessert," Anne told her.

"And why should I be sitting still? Sure you've had enough to do at the office this day without coming home and serving supper!" said Mrs. Murdock indignantly.

Murdock read his evening paper during the meal in the almost complete silence which he maintained on such occasions. Kathleen jumped up three or four times to twirl the dials of the radio and snatch some dance music from the compliant ether. During dinner as the melodies reached them from the dining room of a great hotel she tapped her slim feet and swayed her pretty shoulders as she ate.

"Quit weaving around like that!" her father ordered. "Must you be wasting your time dancing even at the table?"

"Is Ted coming tonight?" Mrs. Murdock asked Anne hastily.

"I think so. Why don't you wear your new

foulard?" Anne asked her mother gravely.

"Hush up with you!" Mrs. Murdock began, somewhat gratified, and Kathleen said, generously:

"You can have the living room, Anne, I'm going to the movies with Laura and May. Dad, you can read your old paper in the kitchen. You know you like it better anyway."

"Is *that* so?" But he smiled. He couldn't resist it. A feeling of contentment, of well-being invaded him. He was rested, his hunger was appeased, and after all the music had sounded rather cheerful. Great things, radios. "Where's my tonic, now?" he demanded, remembering his sacred custom.

The bottle found, and the dose taken, he lighted his pipe and tilted his chair off its front legs, thumbs hooked into armpits.

"What's the news, girls?"

Anne said, quite quietly, but her eyes danced, betraying her:

"Miss Andrews is away on leave. I'm doing Mr. Fellowes' work."

"Will she be coming back at all?" asked her mother, keenly.

"He says so," Anne answered, noncommittally.

"And how does Mr. Sanders take it?" her mother pursued.

"All right, but I'll have part of his work

to do, too," Anne answered. She chuckled faintly. Absurd how these important busy men grew to lean upon girls like herself — absurd — yet somehow significant.

Kathleen looked toward her mother and a lovely eyebrow made mute inquiry. Mrs. Murdock nodded, her eyes somewhat anxious.

"I've a job," announced Kathleen, casually, "in the chorus of 'The Sky Girl.' Rehearsals begin tomorrow." She then sat back and braced herself for the explosion.

"You've *what?*" demanded her father.

She told him again, gave him chapter and verse.

"You'll do nothing of the sort!"

"But, Dad —"

She looked imploringly at Anne. But there were steps on the small porch, the sound of voices — beneficent interruption.

"There's Laura and May!" Kathleen exclaimed, and jumped up.

"Go along with you, then," her mother excused her fondly, and with something of her girl's own relief.

Amused, Anne murmured, "Buck passer!" — and Mr. Murdock smote upon the table:

"You'll stay here!" he ordered, "and get this nonsense settled."

But he spoke to a vanishing slender back, deaf, close set ears and the twinkling

58

of high colored heels.

"Well!" he exclaimed, growing purple.

Anne said quietly:

"Let her go, Dad. If you oppose her she'll only do something foolish. It's better to have her confidence."

"But the stage —"

"Oh — !" Anne looked at him in affectionate despair, "for Pete's sake don't be such a fossil, angel! There's no harm in it. Lots of nice girls go on the stage every day in the week. Kathleen's been stage-struck since she was twelve. Let her have the experience. Maybe it will cure her. She's never cut out for business. And she has to do *something!*"

"There are other things, a damned sight more respectable!"

"Well, as to that —" Anne laughed to herself, then said soberly, "she isn't trained, Dad — not for a teacher, or a nurse, or an office, or — anything. Don't bully her into being too pigheaded."

Murdock's day had gone well. He had enjoyed his supper. He had suffered no ill effects from it. And Anne's tone and her serene rather laughing eyes had a certain weight with him. He couldn't give in gracefully, being temperamentally incapable, but deep in his heart he relied upon his older daughter's judgment.

"All right, then," he grumbled, "I'll say

nothing. I don't rate much around this house, anyway. You all do as you please. If anything bad comes out of this business you can blame yourself. Yes, and your mother too, sitting there not saying a word, letting me do it all! I wash my hands of it," said Murdock.

Much later Anne had reason to remember that placing of responsibility.

Murdock rose and went heavily upstairs into his bedroom. They could hear him growling to himself on the way up, and Mrs. Murdock exchanged a look with Anne, while the corners of her mouth twitched.

"He'll be all right now," she diagnosed comfortably. "Tell me, Anne, about that Miss Andrews?"

They talked in perfect accord and comradeship, clearing away the dishes. It didn't occur to either of them to complain because Kathleen was not at home to help. Kathleen was so rarely home that when they bethought themselves to murmur about her absence it was mechanically enough.

Later, Ted arrived. Anne had not seen him since the evening she had 'phoned his apartment and broken her engagement with him. Now he came in, inclined toward sulkiness, and Anne, looking at him, accurately gauging his temper, suggested blandly:

"It's a nice night — Shall we go for a ride?"

He nodded and spent some time with Mrs. Murdock, his ally, while Anne was getting ready, inquired for Kathleen, went upstairs to look in at Mr. Murdock, who, coat off, slippers dangling and pipe going, was stretched out on the double bed reading, and by that time Anne appeared. She'd changed her dress and shoes, pulled a perky little hat over her eyes and flung her new cape about her shoulders.

Presently he escorted her down the steps and into the new car which was his pride.

"I hear," he said, as they pulled away from the house, "that you are working for The Chief?"

"Yes." She pulled the cape tighter about her, gave a little wriggle of excitement. "I — I thought I'd be all thumbs and couldn't even hit a key straight. But I got through, thank the Lord."

"I suppose you hope to get the job permanently?" asked Ted with no sign of premature congratulation in his tone.

"Of course, if I am satisfactory and if Andrews doesn't come back — I'd be *crazy* if I didn't hope to, Ted!" she said, aroused to mild defiance by his tone.

"I suppose so." He stepped on the gas and the little car shot away. "But —"

"What, for heaven's sake?"

"Oh, hell, you don't care what I think!"

"Of course I care," she contradicted truthfully, but her heart sank. Was Ted — ? Would he ask her — again? Was he in "one of these" moods?

Ted looked around him. They had reached a street which debouched into a country sort of road. One lone flat house was in the depressing skeleton stage on the corner lot. Otherwise there was no sign of human habitation for the length of several city blocks. Ted stopped the car, and faced her, leaning forward eager and appealing.

"I love you so much, dear —" he said, huskily.

She made a little gesture with her hands, one of real unhappiness, and hopelessness. This wasn't the first time he'd told her he loved her. She'd known him since she'd entered the agency, they'd gone out together a good deal, laughed and danced and played together. And just this past summer he'd kissed her more than once — many times more than once — when the wind was soft and languid, when a silver-swimming moon rode high, when there was the scent of salt and roses out on the white Long Island roads.

But nowadays, kisses, no matter how much you liked them, didn't mean marriage.

"And you —" he was urging, "you *do* care

for me a little?"

"I — like you," she said, honestly, "so much."

"But you don't love me?"

"No, Ted," she answered, hating to hurt him.

"You haven't let me kiss you since — since August," he complained, boyish and accurate and querulous.

"Ted — you — you're so funny. I mean, the way you remember dates. No I haven't."

"Why — *why?*"

"You've just said why. Because you love me and I just like you. If," said Anne, trying to explain her code, "if you only just liked me, too — I — might. It was sweet. But, since I've known that you cared so much, it isn't fair to you, Ted, dear. Even if I like to have you kiss me, it isn't fair," she said.

"But I want you," he said, his voice roughened, "for my own. Oh, you'd love me, too, Anne if you'd only let yourself go. But you won't. You hold me off. You don't give me my chance. I — don't I know how you could love a man if you'd — forget yourself a little? I know! I want you to marry me. I can take care of you, Anne. I'm doing well. I'll be doing better. Sanders got to where he is now from the job I have. They like my work, all right. They've raised me twice this year. If you'd marry me — I swear, Anne, with you beside me I'd get to the top."

But after a moment she answered, low:

"But — I want to get to the top — myself!"

All Ted's masculinity, all his sex pride came to the surface then. He forgot that he loved her — and wanted her, remembered only for the moment that they were man and woman in business, and, in a sense, competitors.

"You'll get no further," he said. "A woman!"

"Listen to me," said Anne strongly, her quick, but usually controlled temper touched. "Nothing can stop me. I took a business course when I left school. Then, afterwards, mother was sick and had a bad operation, and I had to stay home a whole year to look after things. Then I got a typist's job, later a stenographer's. I took extension courses at night and landed, as you know, in the copy-writing department of the agency. Six months ago Mr. Sanders took me from Mr. Johnson. What's to prevent me from working permanently with The Chief if I make good and Andrews doesn't return? And you know perfectly well that with experience of a job like that I'd qualify for even better, for office executive positions. What's going to stop me?"

"Nothing," Ted told her, "if you want it. But look at Andrews. She's a woman — and

64

she's been let out, whether temporarily or permanently — because of her health. She'll never get anywhere after this, I'm warning you," O'Hara said deeply. "Anne — you were made for love — for marriage — for your own man — a home — for babies. You weren't made to waste yourself in an office, slaving for men who don't give a damn what work does to you as long as the work is satisfactory to them. Marry me — and be a woman and not a machine. I'll love you all my life; I'll carry you on my hands. I'll work for you, and you'll help me make the grade — Anne — Anne!"

But she shook her head. She was oddly, hotly angry. At perhaps the comparison between herself and Janet Andrews. She was not like Janet, she would never be like her, that sexless, monotoned woman! She was — herself, alive, vital, brimmed with the joy of life, with the instinct for adventure, with passion dimly guessed at, if only surface stirred, thus far.

Woman — or — machine?

"Nothing I've seen of marriage makes me think any too well of it," she told him finally. "Look at my mother working her life away for father, for us, cooped up in a kitchen, tied to a duster! Look at Jim's wife, in the miserable little flat with two babies and Jim away

65

all day and half the night — and — Betty Howard in the office with a man and a child to support, fretting herself sick, not getting ahead — a woman with her brain and talent! No, Ted, I think I'd rather be a machine after all — an independent one, my own master."

"If you loved me," he began doggedly, and, looking at the white blur which was his face in the starlight, and sensing how hurt and vulnerable it was, she softened:

"Oh, *if* — ! — if I loved you — I might, though I'd be an idiot! Yes — if I loved you — but perhaps — I don't!"

He said, stubborn, the gay eyes very clouded:

"But you can't stop me loving you, and trying —"

"Please," she said, "let's go on. All this — it isn't any use. We just get angry and say things and hurt each other."

He shrugged, put the car in gear.

"Where to?" he asked sullenly.

"It doesn't matter. We could dance — listen to some music —"

They drove on for several miles, danced at a little roadhouse, and had something to eat. It was one o'clock when he left her at the brick house.

There on the doorstep, the street dark and silent about them, he tried to take her into his urgent arms.

"Ah — let me — *let me!*"

"Ted," she murmured, definitely shaken by the hot breath of his desire. "Ted —" She disengaged herself gently and spoke with finality. "What's the use?" she said.

His arms dropped to his sides. Her key grated in the lock and then she was gone. He turned and went back to the little car, the brightly painted dapper little car, now so desolately empty of her.

As Anne tiptoed to the bedroom she shared with her sister, Mrs. Murdock appeared from her own room, flannelette wrapper buttoned tightly about a throat still slim and pretty. In the hall under one dim light they talked in whispers.

"Tired, dear?"

"Not very," Anne answered, and suppressed a yawn.

"Good time?"

"Not very," Anne said again and drew her troubled breath sharply and tried to smile.

Her mother moved closer to her and looked long and steadily into the girl's eyes.

"Teddy's a nice boy," she said, "and he'll go far. It's — it's a fine sort of thing, Anne, to marry young and climb the ladder with your man."

But Anne shook her bright head. Her answering whisper had a thread of laughter running through it but her eyes remained sombre.

"You can't get rid of your old maid for a while yet," she said, and caught her little mother to her and kissed her soundly.

Releasing her she admonished her severely.

"Go back to bed, Molly Murdock, and forget about me. I'm all right. You're half in love with Ted yourself and it's you he comes to see anyway! I'll tell on you if you don't behave! Shame to you, cloaking your own flirtations with your hard working daughter!"

She gave her mother a hard squeeze and then disappeared into her bedroom. Mrs. Murdock stood a moment looking after her. She was smiling reluctantly. What nonsense the girl talked! But her eyes were thoughtful. What was the world coming to when healthy pretty girls preferred typewriters to babies? she wondered.

But perhaps the right man hadn't come along yet. With this age-old solution for consolation Mrs. Murdock went back to bed.

Anne undressed in semi-darkness, hung up her frock, stepped out of her brief lingerie, found her pyjamas. Kathleen was sound asleep in the bed next to her own, one round arm above her dark head, the gardenia-texture of her cheek faintly flushed. "She's a lovely thing," Anne thought with some misgiving.

Later, lying there in the darkness, breathing the cool autumn wind which ruffled the curtains, she thought of Ted and of her mother's gallant code.

"It's a fine thing to marry young and climb the ladder with your man."

But if a girl wanted a ladder of her own, wanted to climb unhindered, to the top? And if — if she wanted her man, wouldn't it be one who had already made his way unaided, a man with strength, with tremendous driving power?

The time was passing when girls who came into contact with men, men of established position, of vision and capabilities, were willing to marry those who stood at the bottom of the ladder.

"We set high standards nowadays," thought Anne drowsily.

A day or so later she telephoned Janet Andrews and, finding she was still in town, made an engagement with her that evening.

Janet, as trimly utilitarian at home as she was in the office, went with her around the corner to one of those dimly lighted basements which provide music and a plate dinner that is pretty good, perhaps because you can't see what you're eating.

"I want to consult you," Anne told her, over very fair coffee — "oh, just office routine.

69

Every man has his own way of wanting things run. Probably Mr. Fellowes' way is different from Mr. Sanders'. I hate to make more mistakes than I can help."

She asked her questions and Janet answered, a little grudgingly at first, and then, as she looked at the small, friendly little face, more openly.

"Is — is he well?" was what Janet wished to know in her turn as they walked home.

"The Chief?" Anne looked at her astonished. "Why, I suppose so. He seems fine."

"He gets overtired," Janet explained, "and then he sometimes takes cold. When — when he works in the office at night I generally get one of the porters to go out and bring in malted milk or something. He doesn't know where it comes from half the time, but he drinks it just the same."

"I see," said Anne, and made a mental note. Surely, she thought, The Chief could take care of himself? But of course, if he were used to these extra attentions she'd certainly see to it that they were forthcoming.

Janet went on talking, warning Anne against certain importunate callers who had a way of trying to get past the desk — Masters, of the Simpson crowd; Harvey, of *Flaming Fiction* — telling Anne, a little feverishly, of her employer's likes and dislikes, of what particularly annoyed him, of the especial vexations she had been able to keep away from him.

Anne thought, amused: "I suppose he has to be coddled like all the others. I wonder if he really likes it?" Somehow, it didn't fit in with the mental picture she had of the man himself, a picture which she had carried about with her for three years, which she often looked at with admiration and by which she made, unconsciously, a good many comparisons.

Janet's flat was well furnished, but wholly lacking in charm. Anne talked when they were sitting together, and Janet was indulging in her solitary relaxation, that of incessant cigarette smoking.

"Aren't you going away?"

Janet lighted another cigarette — "Funny to see her smoke so much," thought Anne, "she doesn't seem to be the type."

"Yes, in a day or so. I've a cousin who has a farm up near Albany. I've planned to go to her," Janet answered.

Suddenly her eyes filled. She crushed out the just lighted cigarette on a standing ashtray.

"I won't be coming back — to the agency . . ." she said slowly. "He doesn't want me."

"But, Janet," argued Anne, trying to make her words and tone carry conviction —

to herself as well as to the other — "of course you'll come back. You'll get well up there and — why, The Chief can't get along without you!"

Janet tried to smile, tried to take that little sentence as balm to her sore throat.

"Yes, he can," she contradicted. "He'll forget to miss me, after a little. And you —" she looked directly at the younger girl, "you'll get the position, Anne. That's one reason why I've been trying to give you little hints about things it would take you a long time to learn, but which mean a lot to his comfort."

Anne asked, with a rather clever directness:

"If you should not return would you be angry if — if I did get the job?"

"No, not angry." Janet leaned nearer, her face flushed high on the cheekbones, and laid one unsteady hot hand on Anne's. "Take care of him," was all she said.

She returned to her original topic of the office presently and they talked until Anne rose to go. Janet went to the door with her.

"I — shan't wait for my dismissal," she said, with some gallantry, "I shall send in my resignation before my leave is up. I'll try for something else after a while. Meantime, I've something saved."

She did not tell Anne that she had already spoken to a friend of hers, the head of a large employment agency, and that Miss Mackaye had told her, if a little brutally, still in honest pity:

"You won't be easy to place, Janet. You've given too much to this last job. My advice is, to go out and learn to play before you look for a new one. Get outside interests — and if you can — fall in love."

Fall in love!

Janet turned back to the empty flat and started clearing up cigarette butts, straightening chairs and cushions. Anne — Anne would get the job.

He wouldn't look at Anne, of course, not as a person, that is. He wasn't that kind. And yet — Anne, with her ardent red lips, and her round slim body and pretty hands — he wouldn't be a man if he didn't look at her sometimes.

Would any man be content with just — looking?

She went into her bedroom and stared about it dully. She must plan her packing, must formulate mentally the phrases of her dignified resignation, every word of which would be a knife in her heart.

Over, the daily contact, the work that was all for him, the tense waiting on his word of approbation, the shrinking from his reception of an error, the lightness in her breast when he smiled — all over.

Suddenly and violently she picked up a tall glass vase and flung it against the wall. As it shattered to the floor in a hundred tinkling pieces the tension broke within her and she flung herself across her bed, sobbing.

Anne, walking to the subway, thought, with a little very decent unwillingness:

"So *that's* the reason!"

She knew her Freud and her Ellis no better than did Janet. But she needed no books to tell her, now, what was the matter with the older woman.

"Poor thing," she thought, disturbed and with an aching pity tempered with the wholesome scorn of a youngster who had not yet been deeply stirred by life. "Poor thing. Why are women such fools?"

Couldn't they keep sex out of it, save as a useful weapon? She wondered if they couldn't realize that the man was only the symbol of the earned income? Couldn't they see him as merely a means to an end?

During her following first week in Fellowes' office Anne worked hard, marked much and caught one intimate glimpse of the calibre of the man himself. She was in her outer room when Joe Brown, one of the copy-writers and a friend of O'Hara's, came into The Chief's office, papers in his hand and his usually pleasant face haggard with strain. Anne, through the half open door, heard the conversation between the two men.

"Sit down, Joe," invited Fellowes, "I want to talk to you about your copy for the Garden Silk people. Are you satisfied with it yourself?"

Brown's answer followed after a perceptible hesitation.

"No, I'm not, Mr. Fellowes," he said frankly enough.

"What do you think is the matter with it?" asked Fellowes. "To my mind it's good enough routine work — solid stuff — but it hasn't any vitality. Not an atom of punch. It hasn't the quality which lifted your work for the Dayton crowd so far above average. You've wonderful hunches, Joe. You've a good command of the written language. You know what the public wants to read, and you can sock 'em in the eye — arrest their attention. You know people. Your dealer work in the Dayton instance was great. You've a big future. You've proved it again and again. But something has been wrong for the last month. What is it? Don't you like the work — or what?"

"I do," Brown told him. "I'm crazy about it — but — I'm shot, Mr. Fellowes. My mind isn't on the job. I'm mechanical, I haven't any pep. I — oh, I know what's the matter, all right," he said, boyish and ill at ease and unhappy.

"What then?" asked Fellowes with great gentleness.

"It — it's a personal matter," Brown burst out, despairingly. "Just one of those damned intimate things that play merry hell with a man's job. I'm — I'm nearly off my head, Mr. Fellowes. I can't eat, I can't sleep, I can't work —"

He broke off short and added dully:

"But I can't tell you about it. If it means the loss of my job I can't tell you. And I deserve to be fired. I've let you down badly."

Anne's heart was beating furiously. She knew something of the canker that gnawed into young Brown's brain. Ted told her. Brown, a very decent boy, had fallen terribly in love with a woman some years his senior, and married. Of no use for his intimates to tell him he'd get over it, to point out the error of his ways. He loved her with all the depth and gravity of a boy's first passionate attachment. And he was taking it hard, as only a nice boy can take it. He hated himself, he was torn and ashamed — and he loved her — hopelessly and with an edged desperation.

After a pause Anne heard Fellowes reply, gravely:

"You needn't tell me. I understand enough to know whatever it is it's giving you a bad time. You're a good man and we don't want to lose you. We cannot see your future — and our own future depends upon the work of men like yourself — wrecked because of some emotional unbalance. I suggest that you take six months' vacation, Joe, with full pay. Go abroad, go West, go anywhere, and fight your own personal battle. Then come back to us and tell me if you think you can go on again, giving us the best that is in you — as you have so amply proved you can do."

After a little Brown's voice reached Anne dimly, choked and low:

"I — Mr. Fellowes — I can't thank you enough —"

"Don't try. We've all been up against it, sometime, one way or another. Good-by Joe, and good luck."

A moment later Brown passed through Anne's office without seeing her, so dimmed were his eyes. But his face was lighted with a new hope, with returning confidence in himself and in his star. And Anne's eyes were equally misty. She thought, "He's more than a great business man — after all; he's a *man.*"

This was his human side, the side which made him beloved, not for his business capabilities, but for himself, his understanding of his associates, and a side of him which showed a response to emotional appeal.

In his office Fellowes sat thinking of the boy who had just left him. He had heard rumors, vague but enough to give him something to go on. Sex — the primal hunger, the impetus to progress and sometimes the obstacle. Sex and a man's needs — first passion and its demands. He sighed deeply, his face suddenly lined and altered. Well, if he'd needed — excitement, the thrill of pursuit, the adventuring chase, he'd sublimated it in his work — almost — but not quite.

When some weeks had passed, Fellowes spoke to Anne:

"Miss Andrews has sent me her resignation," he told her. "Would you care to carry on with me, Miss Murdock? There'll be an advance in salary. You've done excellent work and even in this short time I've grown to depend on you. I'll speak to Mr. Sanders — if it's a bargain. Is it?"

"It certainly is!" Anne told him, and smiled, her eyes radiant and the quick color rising to her cheeks.

Then, feeling that she had been, say, a trifle informal in her acceptance of the advancement, she managed an embarrassed but perfectly adequate brief speech of gratitude and a promise to work hard and well. But Fellowes cut her short, rather reluctantly, for he enjoyed watching her expressive little face, her lovely eyes.

"It's all right then. I warn you, I'm a slave driver," he said and laughed.

As she went into her office he thought how amazingly pleasant it was to have a secretary so extremely soothing to the eyes. He had not missed beauty in Janet Andrews, but he appreciated it in Anne Murdock. He liked the way she walked, the way she carried the small shining head, he liked watching her hands, very capable, very well cared for, very prettily modelled. He liked her voice and her manner and her way of anticipating his needs, with no ostentation, before he himself was aware of them. He liked *her*. And he found himself admittedly looking forward to seeing her every day, as he had unconsciously looked forward to seeing her these past weeks.

Anne sat down at the desk — her own desk now — and tried to control the rapid pulsing of her heart. Another step up the ladder. An office of her own. Fifty a week, perhaps, in her pay envelope, and her name in gilt letters on the glass door.

But as exhilarating as office and salary and title was the thought of working permanently with Fellowes, in intimate daily contact with the man himself. She had worked so hard toward this opportunity, and was now rewarded.

She saw that her hands were shaking. She felt that her knees were unsteady, she knew an impulse toward laughter or tears. She shook herself mentally, pulled herself together. Such hysteria wasn't like her. Even a better job was no excuse, she told herself severely.

Of course, it was the thought of the job which really excited her, the job which was a sign and seal of success. The job and not the man, after all. The man was a symbol also. Yet, as she sat there and heard him moving about the inner room with his light sure step, and felt her heart thud heavily in unison, she was aware of a sudden misgiving, a creeping doubt, a frail but frightening wonder, a warning admission of his growing physical attraction for her.

She turned to her work again, setting her full lips firmly. This was dangerous nonsense, she admitted to herself. Of course she admired Mr. Fellowes, admired him greatly, but that was all.

But, as her pulses steadied, she was aware of an ironic hoot of thin laughter somewhere in the back of her brain. Had Janet Andrews once reasoned in the same manner — "but that was all?"

Poor Janet, whom once she had thought so sexless, so without color, had permitted her sex to run away with her sanity. Anne felt an unspoken challenge in that diagnosis of Janet's failure. Was it not possible for a woman to work with a man, with a dangerously attractive man, even, and still find herself more worker than woman?

She thought that it was and went back to her vigorous accurate typing and did not know that Lawrence Fellowes, listening, half subconsciously, to the rapid staccato to which business is tuned, sighed a little and smiled a little and wondered why he was suddenly so restless and yet so unwontedly content.

Chapter 3

Miss Murdock Ponders on Marriage

Lawrence Fellowes' New York home was the duplex penthouse on the roof of an upper Fifth Avenue apartment building, and among many advantages it possessed that of an expensive view of the park and the blue waters of the reservoir.

Fellowes, who had been brought up in an old red and white brick house at the lower end of the Avenue, and whose early married life had been lived in the same district in one of the Brides' Row houses, had yet to accustom himself wholly to an apartment. It wasn't lack of space that he missed, for there was space and to spare under his present lease. Nor were stairs wanting, as a flight of them led from two great living rooms, dining room and kitchen quarters, to the bedrooms, his own, Linda's and a guest room. It was, he thought, the subtle lack of house-sense, and feeling that you were too close, despite sound-proof walls and spaciousness, to other people.

But Linda liked the apartment, and, after all, it was Linda who really lived in it. He slept there, he entertained there, and there he occupied the head of the table when in town, but he did not live there in the intimate sense in which Linda did.

Shortly before Christmas Dick Jameson dined with the Fellowes. Another woman was present, Edith Lucien, an attractive widow, one of Linda's close friends. After dinner the four played bridge.

Linda Fellowes was at her best as hostess. She was an excellent housekeeper, she had less trouble with servants than any woman of her wide acquaintance. She had a genius for making people comfortable, and was by nature amiable and gay hearted. And she was handsome.

Ten years previously, upon her marriage to Fellowes, she had been a big, rather raw-boned girl, with masses of blue black hair and great brown eyes. Born Linda Schuyler, she was the fourth daughter of — as these things are counted in America — an ancient and impoverished family. Her father had been a bookish gentleman who failed to keep his visionary eyes upon investments and the property rights of Dutch and American ancestors. Her mother, left a widow in Linda's childhood, had been a brisk worried woman, eternally contemplating with affection and exasperation the mild insufficiency of her husband. She had saved and sacrificed and battled to educate her girls in good private schools, to clothe them becomingly, to take them to Europe for a final polish, to permit them to follow their particular interests — in Linda's case, golf and tennis, horses and dogs — and eventually to marry them to money.

Lawrence Fellowes had fallen in love with Linda when, at twenty-seven, he entered his uncle's advertising agency, after some newspaper experience, and a period, directly following college, of salesmanship for a large merchandising firm. And Mrs. Schuyler, seeing that Linda, in her turn, was attracted, gratefully bestowed her blessing. The other girls were safely and happily married, and Mrs. Schuyler, seeing the drive in Fellowes, the urge forward which would make him a money maker in his own right, knowing, as well, that he had inherited a small fortune from his father, the owner of a string of out-of-town newspapers, sold at his death, and, in addition, counting upon the fact that Fellowes would be his uncle's heir, encouraged the match with all that was in her, and was able some years after it had been accomplished to die in peace and luxury.

Linda, at twenty-two, had been as much in love with young Fellowes as her nature then permitted — a breezy, affectionate sort of love, which had reached the clean heights of a wholesome and normal passion. Now, at thirty-two she liked her husband enormously, admired him, was proud of him, and went her way, amiable and serene.

She was now much handsomer than in her girlhood. She had filled out, and her figure, if not molded to present standards, was, nevertheless, superb. She carried herself magnificently and was beautifully gowned. She knew how to spend money — well; she was neither parsimonious nor extravagant.

Through her, as well as by his own birthright, the Fellowes' had an established and important place in the more conservative walks of Manhattan society, and Fellowes was fond of Linda and as proud of her in his way as she of him.

Originally, he had been very much in love with her, a natural reaction from an unfortunate and tawdry episode of his youth. Her out-of-door wholesomeness, her clarity of outlook, her lack of frets and fevers, held a tremendous appeal for him. So, loving her, he had married her. This he had never regretted, although he was now perfectly aware that his affection for her was settled and unstimulating as if they had been forty years married.

There was no child. Not long after her marriage Linda had been thrown in the hunting field, and for a long period of invalidism had possessed her soul in the patience she fought to acquire. She recovered completely, her health was now flawless, but Fellowes' early inarticulate dreams of husky, splendid sons and pretty, wheedling daughters had, perforce to vanish forever.

So, they were fond of each other now, but they had outgrown each other. They had little in common, their interests lay apart. And that first sunny passion no longer existed.

Each was too busy to give much time to heart-searching. Yet each had reached a perilous period in development. The man neared forty, the woman had passed thirty. The rose blossom flush of youth was gone; they stood, as yet unconsciously, upon the threshold of their prime — their second blooming.

Now and again, Fellowes, hearing of some amazing *volte-face* of a contemporary — a violent secret love affair unearthed and given all the pitiless, sardonic publicity of the times, a headlined divorce, a complete betrayal and repudiation of old vows — would feel beneath his astonishment and contempt, hearing the whispers, "Harrington, who could believe it of him — with a wife and children?", a keen and thrusting pang of — could it be *envy?*

He had never inquired very deeply into the nature of these rare, inexplicable experiences.

Yet, he would wonder, involuntarily, what it might be like to be caught up by a devastating force which swept everything before it, which knew no law save the fulfillment of its lawlessness, which scorched and tormented, harrowed and hunted, and which contained its own punishment, and its own reward.

If he had ever heard strange gods — or more accurately, goddesses — calling, he had not followed their alluring voices very far. He had not been guiltless of minor, passing reactions, attractions and relaxations. The world is full of women willing to be comforted, amused, dined, or exhilarated. But technically, at least, Fellowes had kept to the letter of his public vow to Linda.

It was impossible that a man as vital, as physically robust and as mentally alert and psychologically alive to beauty, to the lovely consolation of living, should remain unsensitized. Sometimes he wondered at himself, at his quick, if temporary, response to the turn of a head, the fall of an eyelash, the murmur of a phrase; wondered if, had that first passionate devotion to his wife held through the years, with its initial mystery and glamour, he would have been rendered immune to — well, put it, to the visualizing of colorful and fragrant gardens lying beyond the highroad and over the high walls of his own particular matrimonial estate. And he extended his wonder to all men. Did they, too, look over the walls, those, that is, who still refrained from jumping them entirely? It was not, he reasoned, that he was purely a sensual man. It took more than the mere appeal of sex to stir him, it took mood, mystery, the vague promise, the dim warning, somewhere within his consciousness, that life is exceedingly fleet and that no man is sure of immortality.

Sometimes he wondered about Linda. How did she react to other men? What were her unfathomable thoughts? How well did he know her after ten years of intimacy? How well did any man know his wife, or for that matter, himself?

And now, over the bridge table, waiting for Mrs. Lucien to return from the telephone, Jameson asked:

"Have you decided about the Club, Larry? We've things well under way now, but I didn't want to rush you. I did drop in at the office one day you were out."

Fellowes said:

"I know, I'm sorry. Yes, I'll go in with you, Dick, but I can't promise to use the place much."

"How about wives?" Linda asked in her deep, lazy voice. "Am I permitted to invade these sacred premises?"

"As far as I am concerned you are not only permitted but urged and welcomed," Jameson told her gallantly. "Of course, having no wife myself may make all the difference in my attitude. However, if the other members' wives aren't interested in shooting and fishing I'll arrange a party just for you, Linda."

She smiled across the table at the big man. Her smile was youthful. It had spontaneity and charm. She liked Jameson. He was such a "good sort." And also, quite without vanity, she suspected Jameson liked her — more than a little. They'd been thrown together a good deal in the past two years on house-parties, at various resorts, at dinners — and he had sometimes proxied for her as escort in Fellowes' stead.

It would not have occured to Linda Fellowes to indulge in a cheap flirtation with any man of her acquaintance, that was not in her code. But as long as she did not exhibit her knowledge of Jameson's strong preference for her she reasoned that she neither encouraged him, nor imperilled herself. If this were sophistry it did neither of them any harm.

But even good women have been known to grow younger under the belief that they have a suitable, hopeless and unconfessed worshipper.

"By the way," Jameson told his host, "I

noticed at the office the other day that you have a new secretary." His eyes were amused, quite without malice, and Fellowes answered, reluctant to smile, but unable not to:

"Yes, Miss Andrews sent in her resignation some time ago. Her health —"

But Jameson's amusement was becoming a trifle too marked and Fellowes was glad when Linda interrupted with a soft little rush of words.

"Andrews gone? You didn't tell me. Poor old thing, what was wrong? She was so devoted to you, Larry!"

Now Jameson was grinning openly. He touched his trim mustache with a casual finger and said, before Fellowes could answer his wife:

"The change is for the better, old man. That's a very pretty little Cerberus you have slaving for you now."

"Larry!" Mrs. Fellowes shrugged one smooth, golden tanned shoulder, and laughed. "I'm amazed at you! I thought you couldn't stand dolls around the office — are you getting senile or something?"

"Not much," Fellowes answered rather quickly, "for Miss Murdock is far from a doll. She's pretty, as any man with eyes in his head must admit, but she has a lot of gray matter. Things have gone on as well as under Miss

Andrews' regime, or perhaps even better."

"Well, you won't keep this baby long," Jameson warned him. "She's too darned good-looking. Some smart lad will snatch her away from you. Wonder it hasn't happened before this?"

"Lord, I hope not!" exclaimed Fellowes, and was conscious of an instant inner rebellion at the thought. "She's becoming far too valuable."

Mrs. Lucien had returned in time to hear part of the conversation.

"How do you feel about it, Linda?" she wanted to know. "Beauty and the Business Beast and all?"

"Well," Linda replied, "such problems are mercifully hidden from me. I don't visit Larry's office. Only comic strip wives do that, I fancy. Look here, Larry, may I borrow this paragon some day? You used to lend me the priceless Andrews occasionally, you know."

"Oh, Linda," sighed Jameson, "I thought you were above that sort of thing."

"It's not all curiosity," she assured him. "I really need help on the Hospital Committee's business. The volunteer secretary is too dumb for utterance, and I'm swamped in lists."

"I'll ask Miss Murdock," Fellowes said, "if you'll remind me in the morning. Perhaps she'd come up some Saturday afternoon, if that's all right."

His wife smiled her thanks, nodded and picked up the cards she had dealt some time ago.

Her partner, Jameson, looked at her over his inferior hand. She was really very lovely. Her heavy dark hair, once closely shingled, was now growing out, knotted at the nape of her neck and pierced with a jewelled pin. There were diamonds in the lobes of her close-set ears, but her eyes did not suffer by that difficult comparison. The décolleté of her semi-formal evening gown was cut low enough to display the curve of her magnificent shoulders and breast. And Jameson sighed. She was his friend's wife and Jameson was a nice person, yet, he thought gloomily — "Damit, some men have all the luck. Fellowes doesn't half appreciate his."

And glancing over at Fellowes briefly, marking his strength and his attraction, Jameson's gloom increased.

"You're playing very badly," Linda said with mock severity at the end of the hand. She'd gone down the two she'd bid. But she was neither peevish nor really reproachful, and she laughed her partner's genuine apology aside.

"It doesn't matter. It's the game that

counts," she said lightly, "not the loss or the winning."

But if Fellowes did not appreciate his wife, he appreciated his secretary. And upon the following morning he found himself looking at her with increased interest and sane trepidation. She was really — exquisite. Jameson was right, devil take it, some man would probably come along and marry her and then where would he, Fellowes, be?

Men, he pondered further, choose their wives through a combination of emotional motivation, propinquity and chance, but their secretaries are selected by the intellect and with a knowledge of certain definite needs — needs which do not alter with the years.

As he had said, Anne was becoming invaluable to him. He marvelled how well and swiftly she had fitted in, how easily she had taken Miss Andrews' place. She did not "fuss" over him, as had her predecessor, yet she failed him in none of the latter's small, personal services. He had learned, too, in the short time Anne had been with him, that he could rely upon her as he had not attempted to rely on the other woman.

Little by little, he had turned over to her the duties which Miss Andrews had grown into by virtue of five years' service. Anne now attended to his personal bills, kept track of his club dues, of life insurance premiums. She was in communication with his brokers, she kept a separate engagement pad for his social activities and never failed to remind him of them.

"You are joining Mrs. Fellowes in the Upson box at the Metropolitan tonight after the Advertising Club dinner, Mr. Fellowes."

"How on earth can I break away?" he would grumble, and then smiling, "Remind me again, will you?"

Yes, she was invaluable; and might become even more so. There were other things with which, gradually, he might trust her. But, if, as Jameson had carelessly said, he could be assured that she would leave him, what was the use?

The following morning he asked her, very conscious of her warm young charm, her trim but never colorless appearance:

"Are you going to be busy Saturday afternoon, Miss Murdock?"

"No, Mr. Fellowes."

She had, as a matter of fact, a matinee engagement with Betty Howard. But Betty would understand. If she didn't, well, it couldn't be helped —

"It's not the office," he told her. "I shan't need you, but," he went on as Anne waited, aware of disappointment, "Mrs. Fellowes is in rather a jam with one of her charity affairs. She asked me last night if she might borrow you. Miss Andrews helped her out occasionally in such matters."

"I'll be glad to," said Anne.

She afterwards confessed to herself that she was a little — curious. She consciously welcomed the opportunity to meet Linda Fellowes. There was no photograph of his wife in Fellowes' office, and Anne's knowledge of her was confined to social notes in the newspapers.

On Saturday, therefore, Anne and her notebook were called for at the office by Linda's car and chauffeur, and delivered at the apartment.

Anne waited some time in the library before her employer's wife came in. Walking to the window she saw the wide sweep of the park beneath, French windows opened, terraces which in Spring would have their gay decorative utilities, lounging chairs and tea tables, ledge boxes of flowers, potted trees and plants. Turning, she looked gravely about the room in which she stood — a lovely room, restful, hospitable.

Her heart ached a little. These were the things she loved, of which she had caught a glimpse in Fellowes' office —— these beautiful material things, valuable to her not for the luxury, the expenditure they represented, but for the satisfaction they afforded her senses and spirit. These were the things she longed for and would never attain.

Yet why shouldn't she attain them in a comparative measure? she thought, looking about her, her hands deep in the pockets of her smart tweed coat with its becoming, if inexpensive, fur collar. Why not? If she could ever have a little place of her own somewhere, which would hold the things she would save up for, for which she would ransack the little shops?

Her brows drew together. Lately there had been a loud explosion in the brick house outside of town. For Kathleen, now a decorative member of "The Sky Girl" Company, had left home. She had explained patiently, and certainly Anne had seen the reasonableness of her argument, that it was too hard for her to travel back and forth from, first, rehearsals, and now matinees and evening performances. So she had gone to live with three other girls in the company, sharing a flat over a flower shop in the East Forties.

Mr. Murdock had raged; Mrs. Murdock had commanded, and then warned with rare, distressing tears, but Kathleen had been firm.

"Anne, make them see. I wouldn't get home till all hours. It's so much easier this way and not expensive, with the four of us. And Lola is providing the furniture."

So Anne, with some effort, made them see as she herself saw. For, she argued, Kathleen was sensible. Moreover she thought secretly she was more than sensible. Why shouldn't Kathleen have her good times, why shouldn't she live her own life?

But the battle had raged for weeks and she had come home late day after day, tired to death, only to engage immediately in the family discussion.

But she'd seen it through and Kathleen was forgiven, coming out often if not every day to see her mother, and turning up Sundays, flushed with her little triumphs, full of the intimate gossip of her new circle.

Anne had been to the flat. She liked two of the girls very much, pretty, hard working, healthy youngsters. Lola who had "provided the furniture," and through whom Kathleen had procured the engagement, was older, more sophisticated with that sophistication which is not surface veneer, nor yet a matter of jargon and argot and youth's easy mimicry, but more a wisdom born of personal experience — rather devious experience, thought Anne, judging by the girl's shallow eyes, light and hard as turquoises, and by the lines of her bitter, over-full mouth.

Anne was deep in her thoughts when Mrs.

Fellowes entered. Linda had been riding and had stopped at her club for lunch, without changing, as was sometimes her careless custom, and now came in booted and breeched, her derby and crop in a gauntleted hand.

"I'm so sorry," cried Linda, "to have kept you waiting."

She shook hands with the younger woman. And Anne observed, with authentic admiration, how handsome she was, and magnetic.

Somehow Anne had pictured her otherwise, more "society," harder, less cordial.

Linda said hospitably:

"Do take your things off and sit down. There are books all about. I've got to change. It won't take long — a shower and a negligee."

She disappeared, whistling in the boyish, rather engaging, way she had. Anne took off her coat, revealing a short, straight-line frock of the blue which was her particular shade, and, after a moment's reflection, discarded her tight fitting hat. She had worked hard all morning and her head was aching slightly. Without the hat it was better.

She sat down on the tub sofa near the fireplace, a book in her hands. But she did not read. She looked instead into the blue and scarlet, gold and green blazing of the driftwood fire which burned there, speaking to her with its restless, volatile voice, and, leaning back, let the serene loveliness of the room sink into every pore of her thirsty spirit. She found herself suddenly fitting Lawrence Fellowes into this, his proper *milieu* out of office hours — away from the click of keys and the shrill voice of the telephone, and all the high-pressure progress and movement of his working day.

Presently Linda came back. She wore a jade green tea gown, chiffon velvet, severely cut, with only the fall of lace at throat and sleeves to soften it. She was smoking, and she looked radiant and happy. She asked apologetically:

"Was I too long? Did you find something to read?"

Anne nodded and indicated the book of short stories she held.

"I didn't get very far into it," she confessed, and explained quickly, "I was admiring the room."

It seemed a rather school girl statement and she was angry at herself for feeling a little *gauche*, lacking her accustomed poise, in the presence of this perfectly at ease and absolutely natural woman of another world than her own.

"It is nice," agreed Linda. "I like it a lot. Do you smoke?"

"Now and then — not very often."

"Well you're better off without it; you'll save your pretty skin," commended Linda amiably, "and now —" She drew up a chair to the long library table and produced a typewritten list of names, envelopes, stamps and cards, "this is where I need your help."

She explained, with Anne, who had come around to stand just behind her, looking over her shoulder. It concerned itself with the charity drive of several hospitals, the appeals to be sent out.

"It's not hard," said Linda, "but volunteer workers are the supreme limit. Of course, I could have sent this to the office and asked you to get it out for me there, but I didn't want to take your time from your work. I thought you'd get through here more quickly and with fewer interruptions." Rising she gave Anne the material and, after further instructions, took her to a small square room off the library where there were books and flowers, and a desk with a portable typewriter.

"You can work here quietly," she said. "It is," she went on, "Mr. Fellowes' workroom. He does a good deal of work here at night, to my despair. Now, I've a woman coming to fit me to stays. I'll be back later to see how you're coming on and we'll have tea."

She smiled and departed, her cigarette in

her hand. Anne settled herself at the desk and looked after her employer's wife thoughtfully. She liked her. She had decided that at once. Yet, thought Anne oddly, for all her warmth of manner and natural good humor, you might be Linda's best friend and live beside her for fifty years and never get to know her very well. She was so — self-contained. Anne could not imagine Mrs. Fellowes staging a scene, losing her head or her temper, or in any way putting herself at a disadvantage in any given situation. She turned, sighing unconsciously, to her work.

Shortly before five, Mrs. Fellowes returned, followed by a man servant. She stood in the archway of the workroom while the tea service was being arranged near the fireplace.

"Well, how goes it?" she asked cheerfully.

"Finished — just this minute," Anne replied, and rose to stretch her cramped muscles.

"Good. You're a wonder," Linda praised sincerely. "Now, come and have a cup of tea."

Anne went with her, and, sitting beside her on the cushioned little sofa, watched the long, capable hands pour the tea into fragile cups. Linda talked on casually.

"Those committees are such a nuisance. I inherited them from my mother. Somehow I keep on with them. I don't know why!"

She was friendly. She might have been pouring tea for a woman of her own large circle. She had a rare faculty — that of setting people at their ease. No wonder, thought Anne, that she was invaluable on committees, as a link, say, between two worlds.

"By the way," Linda went on. "There's a woman on this committee whose sister is employed in the agency. Miss Ames. I've meant to ask Mr. Fellowes about her. Do you know her by any chance?"

She is trying, thought Anne, to make me comfortable by talking about things which she knows interest me, with which I'm at home.

Aloud, she answered:

"I think so. If it is Polly Ames you mean, I know her slightly."

"What does she do?" asked Linda with genuine interest. She was always interested in people. It was part of her charm.

"She's in the art department. She does — oh, borders, lettering, that sort of work. She's really quite clever," Anne explained.

"I don't understand much about advertising," admitted Mrs. Fellowes without regret. "Tell me, what does she look like?"

Anne, slightly astonished, thought the question over.

"Well," she answered after a moment, "she's pretty. She has fair curly hair and a round face. She's short, a little inclined to lots of curves."

"I see," Linda chuckled to herself. "I asked because this sister of hers is so amazing. One of these spare, lean women who wear men's straw hats and dinner jackets."

"Dinner jackets?" Anne asked, amused.

"Well, practically. Very utilitarian I should say. Rather Miss Andrews' type, only much more so. She must be forty odd, old enough to be her sister's mother from your description. She is a social service worker, and one of the more professional members of the committee."

Anne listened while Linda went on to talk of the hospital work. She was entertained by the introduction of Polly Ames into the conversation. Anne had not thought of Polly for weeks. She saw her rarely but, according to Betty Howard, Polly was intensely smitten with young O'Hara. But when Anne had once accused him of turning the girl's curly head — through sheer idle mischief, not believing it, and not caring particularly if it were true — Ted had grown stutteringly embarrassed and had flushed as red as his hair.

As a matter of record he was rather involved with little Polly, who lived in the village under the austere guardianship of her sister. It was to Polly, an excellent cook, he went for an occasional home supper, and also for soft consolation upon those evenings when Anne "stood him up" or had no time for him. Polly was restful even if she was "artistic." She had soft eyes and softer ways. She clung and had no very strong code concerning kissing. Yet she was circumspect, very discreet. She was a "home girl" — a girl who frankly admitted that earning a living was a necessity, not a pleasure. She showed Ted sketches she had made of pretty impossible country cottages, smothered in roses, with fat little chimneys from which smoke rose to a cloudless sky. She called these "my dream castles."

After tea, Anne took her departure. Linda shook hands with her, and, as she pulled on her hat, remarked absently, "You have lovely hair, it's a pity to hide it."

"Thank you again," said Linda at the door. "You've taken a load from my shoulders, Miss Murdock, and I'm really most grateful to you."

Nothing patronizing there, nothing consciously superior. Yet Anne was distinctly and rather unhappily made aware of the situation — Employer's Wife and Husband's Secretary.

Out on the street she indulged in a little defiant profanity.

"I'm too damned sensitive," she accused herself, "and it's so damned *silly!*"

She did not go home at once but went instead to her brother's flat for dinner. Linda had offered her the car, but she had refused, and went uptown, partly on foot, for the exercise, partly by subway, and arrived very tired and conscious, which was unusual, of a mental let down.

Jim Murdock, large, untidy and two years her senior, was home for a wonder, and greeted her at the door with a roar of appreciation.

"If it isn't 'The Little Business Woman!' " he exclaimed, his arm heavy about her shoulders. "What you been doing this afternoon? Putting somebody's Superior Soap on the advertising map?"

"No — I've been getting out charity appeals for Mrs. Fellowes, and feeling," Anne said, immediately restored to spirits, "something like an object of charity myself."

"How come?"

Jim pulled her into the living room and removed her hat and coat by force, and with a fraternal disregard for her hair or her comfort.

"Oh, I don't know. Just me, I guess."

"Well, sit down. Have a pipe? Have a cigarette? Have two? The Missis is out in the kitchen. She'll be along presently. Let's have a look at you. Haven't seen you for a week."

He smiled down at her, perched on the arm of her chair. He looked a good deal like his sister, his features a masculine replica of Anne's; and when he ran his hand through his thick blonde hair and smiled at her, his eyes were as darkly blue as her own.

Anne smiled back. She was very fond of Jim.

"How's tricks?" she wanted to know.

"Rotten. Hasn't been a good murder in a couple of days," he answered gloomily. "If someone doesn't shoot somebody soon, or drink poison, or dig up a scandal or unearth some graft, I'll be out of a job."

He was an alert young person, rather a favorite on his tabloid. He started in as a cub reporter and was now assigned to the more sensational cases, signing occasional articles. He made very good money and spent every cent. He gambled it, and he drank it, but most of all he gave it away. Anyone who needed a ten spot could touch Jim Murdock for it and get it.

Sara, his wife, called to Anne from the kitchen:

"Come in, will you, Anne? I've got my hands full."

Anne went in. Sara was shutting the oven door, a fretful sleepy baby in her arms. She wore a bungalow apron over her pretty dark

106

frock, and the sleeves were rolled up. On one round wrist there was an angry red burn.

She dumped the baby into Anne's arms.

"Take Pete, will you? I've the table set and just as soon as I take the pudding out I'll put him to bed. He's teething and cross as the dickens, bless him."

Anne cuddled Pete, who was fat and warm and very wet. He was a heavy baby, gay and frolicsome when normal, but heavy-eyed and feverish now. He had his mother's dark eyes and his father's blonde hair. His brother, eighteen months Pete's senior, called sleepily from his crib, in the alcove adjoining their parents' room.

"Give Junior a drink of water, do!" implored Sara, distracted.

Later, they sat down to dinner, both babies tucked away and quiet for the moment. Sara, whom Anne had not seen for some time, regarded her enviously.

"You do look cool, Anne," she said.

"Why not? It's cold as sin outside."

"I don't mean that. It's just that I'm always fussing about something." She pushed the dark hair away from her eyes, and laughed.

"I've told her to get someone in," Jim complained, tilting back his chair. "She frets herself to death and she needn't. We can afford help."

"None that I can trust with the babies," his wife said quickly. "We've had a perfect succession of incompetent colored women for cleaning and looking after the children. They're more worry than they're worth. But I have one now who takes the kids out in the afternoon."

"You work too hard," Anne told her with affectionate concern.

Sara elevated her rather charming nose, a little shiny now from the heat of the kitchen.

"*You* should know!" she said, scornfully. "It's better than being at the beck and call of some man who doesn't care whether you live or die!"

"Well, I'll take the man and an office, and no hot stoves, and my pay envelope, every day in the week," Anne told her, laughing.

Jim grinned at his wife. Sara had been a filing clerk in a big concern before their marriage.

"She's more to be pitied than scorned, isn't she?" he asked, but Anne sighed. Sara's narrow, anxious life seemed to her so tragic. Jim and his careless expenditures, his happy go lucky existence, appeared so futile, so wrong to his sister. She, the outsider, free from domestic responsibilities, looked at them both with concern, and a sense of affection. Would nothing ever make them see how handicapped they were, she thought?

"You'll think differently, some day," Sara told her as if she had read her sister-in-law's mind.

"Of course she will," Jim said. "We're pretty well fixed and pretty dashed happy, even if we bicker occasionally — just like the wealthy — aren't we, Sara?" he asked, looking across at his wife.

"We sure are," she agreed instantly, and flashed a smile at him. "Have some more potatoes, Anne? I wanted to French-fry them but I didn't have any extra time."

Later, as Anne was leaving, Sara drew her into the bedroom, lowering her voice in order not to awaken the children.

"Sorry I was upset tonight," she apologized, her hand in Anne's, "but things piled up and I was so rushed. And I don't feel awfully well. I think I'm going to have another baby," she explained gallantly enough.

"*Sara!*"

"Oh, I know it! Pete's only a year old. Well, perhaps I'm mistaken. Jim wouldn't let me do anything about it even if I'm not, and I wouldn't *want* to," she ended defiantly.

"Of course not! But — Sara — another! Don't you know any better?" asked Anne.

"Naturally I know better," answered Sara,

patiently. "But — oh, it's no use scolding and being horrified. You'd understand if you were married."

Pete woke and cried out. His mother went in to him and came back, looking prophetically haggard.

"I'm in for a night of it," she said with resignation. "And I'm so tired."

"Couldn't Jim — ?"

"Jim's going out. He has to go," said Sara.

Going home Anne pondered. Her tired mind unrolled the most shifting and kaleidoscopic pictures before her mental vision — the great library in the Fellowes' apartment, the brick terraces, the view, the books and flowers, the outward and visible signs of expensive, ordered, cultured living, and Jim's flat, that all Sara's care couldn't keep trim. Sara shouldn't have married; she'd been better off working. She'd been good at her job, minor though it had been, and she had loved it. Sara and her two babies and perhaps another to come. Jim and his drinking, his mistaken generosity. Jim who was so clever but who would never get very far because he couldn't say no.

"You'd understand if you were married."

"Married!" thought Anne, with contempt and a sort of blind terror. "Not me — not much!"

Yet she remembered that interchange of

glances between Jim and his wife — quick it had been, but warm and secret — and disturbing. She wondered if Linda Fellowes sometimes looked at her husband in that way, as if she saw him for the first romantic time, and yet had known him always. But then, Linda and Lawrence Fellowes were different, they knew nothing of this economic pressure, of the demands of babies, the selfish beloved demands.

And that set her to wondering if Lawrence Fellowes and his wife had ever wanted children, if they missed not having them.

Reaching home, she put her idle speculations aside and managed a laugh at herself, and her anxieties about her brother's little family. "Sara wouldn't thank me," she thought as she fitted her key in the lock, "but if she expects me to follow her example she's very much mistaken."

Marriage? A greater gamble than ever nowadays, thought Anne. To undertake it as the sheltered girl marrying the eligible man was one thing; to undertake it as a girl earning her living, her choice among eligibles generally limited to men on the difficult make, that was another — and too great a risk.

Chapter 4

Miss Murdock is Reassured

A day or so later, Fellowes, at his desk heard someone enter Anne's office, and found himself listening shamelessly from the first sound of the vibrant masculine voice which reached him through the half open door.

"Is the Chief available, Anne?"

"No," Anne replied, "not until after lunch. He has an appointment presently, and isn't to be disturbed until then."

"All right, it doesn't matter. I'll see Mr. Sanders." The voice lowered a little and Fellowes discovered that he was straining his excellent ears with the result that he heard: "Are you going with me to the Lindstrom party tonight?"

"No, I'm sorry, Ted, I'm going back to work."

"You always have an excuse! I never see you any more, Anne. I'm sure I don't know why I waste my breath asking you," marvelled Ted glumly, "as I'm practically certain to get the air."

"Why not take Polly?" suggested Anne, and

chuckled faintly — so faintly that Fellowes did not hear, but O'Hara did.

"Well, why not?" was Ted's defiant reply. "It's an elegant idea. She likes to go out, and she's darned good company."

"Meaning that I am not . . . ?"

"Anne, you know how I feel — as if anyone could take your —"

"Oh, run along," Anne told him, "I was only kidding. Go on, there's a good boy. Tell the Lindstroms I'm awfully sorry, but I've promised to stay here this evening."

There were sounds of departure, but presently the voice spoke again, this time, judged Fellowes, from the vicinity of the door.

"Sure you won't reconsider?"

"Perfectly. Go ahead and have a good time, Teddy."

"But Anne —" there was a distinct note of pleading in the voice, "am I *never* to see you?"

"You see me now, don't you? And I'm awfully busy." Then, apparently she relented, for she added, "Don't look so crushed, and come to supper Sunday night."

Somehow Fellowes could visualize her warm smile as she spoke and knew a curious resentment. Ted's voice reached him again, no longer overcast.

"I'll be there. Don't you dare call it off!"

A few minutes later, after listening to the steady clicking of Anne's machine, Fellowes called her from her work. When she appeared, "Someone to see me just now, Miss Murdock?" he inquired very guilelessly.

"Mr. O'Hara. I told him you were busy. He's gone in to Mr. Sanders. Something about the Parker copy, I believe."

"I see. He's a clever lad," Fellowes mused aloud. Then he looked directly at his secretary and smiled.

"I'm sorry. I couldn't help overhearing. I'm afraid I spoiled your evening."

"No," Anne assured him. "It's quite all right. I — the Lindstroms give lots of parties. I can always go."

"Well, I suppose I'm a selfish brute. I never stop to think of what your plans may be." Suddenly he asked, taking her completely by surprise, as he had intended, "You and O'Hara are pretty good friends, I take it."

Anne nodded. She was furious with herself because she could not control the hot tide of color that flushed her cheeks to scarlet. That childish trick of blushing when off her guard was the bane of her existence. And she could not possibly know how attractive it was to the man who watched her intently.

"We — I've known him ever since I came to the agency," she explained.

"I see. Next time when I ask you to stay over don't hesitate to tell me if you've an engagement," he told her, and dismissed her with a smile.

But he did not forget, and, during the afternoon, happening to be with Sanders, spoke to him.

"O'Hara's coming on well, Sandy?"

"Sure, why not? He's a good kid and a hard worker."

"He was in Miss Murdock's office this morning. They seem to know each other rather well," suggested Fellowes.

"Oh, that? He's been crazy about the girl ever since she first caught his Irish eye," Sanders answered indifferently.

"Oh? Well, one can't blame him," Fellowes answered and went out leaving Sanders to stare after him thoughtfully. Whatever he thought he did not express it, at least not aloud, and presently shrugged his lean shoulders and attacked his work again.

Back at his desk Fellowes swore definitely, if silently. It was, apparently, as Jameson had warned him. He wouldn't be able to keep Anne with him much longer. If it weren't O'Hara, it would be someone else. That was the worst of women secretaries — the good looking ones! No sooner were they trained to satisfaction than they exchanged the typewriter for the mixing spoon. Things were arranged most unfairly in the business man's world.

He had planned for some time to delegate to the efficient Miss Murdock duties more or less important — but which he considered she could admirably fulfill. Yet, why bother now? Perhaps, after all, a man secretary, or an older woman would be better in the long run. A woman whose time wouldn't be taken up by the interruptions of lovesick boys.

He knew that he was unjust. It could not be said truthfully that Anne had encouraged O'Hara to, as Fellowes put it mentally "hang around her desk." But, unjust or not, the fact remained that he had hung around this morning, and perhaps on previous mornings, not to mention the likelihood of mornings to come.

There was no harm, thought Fellowes, wondering why he was so disproportionately disturbed, in keeping an eye open, interviewing likely people, just in case —

He could return Anne to Sanders' office, on, of course, her present salary. And then it would be Sanders who would have the pleasure of wishing her God speed when she decided to change a business career for one of domesticity.

The remainder of the day went so badly

that at closing time he called Anne and told her he had decided not to work that evening, and added that he hoped she could rearrange her plans.

She said coolly that she could, conscious of an unspoken challenge in his regard. But she made no attempt to telephone O'Hara, and went home instead to spend her evening, to wonder what had happened to her employer's usually even temper.

A few days later an exceedingly well-dressed, good-looking, brisk young man marched into her office.

"Richmond is my name," he announced, wasting no words, "I have an appointment with Mr. Fellowes at ten-thirty."

Anne looked at her pad. The hour had been left blank. Personally she was aware of no such appointment. She rose, however, and went in to Fellowes.

"A Mr. Richmond to see you, Mr. Fellowes. He says he has an appointment."

"Quite so," Fellowes answered, "send him in."

And Miss Murdock, returning, ushered the mysterious stranger into the office.

"Miss Mackaye sent me," began Richmond at once.

"Sit down," Fellowes interrupted hastily and Anne turned back to her office, carefully closing the door between, and proceeded to ponder.

It appeared that the plot thickened. Miss Mackaye? Of the Secretarial Employment Agency?

A little later, as Richmond passed through on his way out, she heard Fellowes' parting words:

"Nothing yet, you understand. Miss Mackaye told me that you were comparatively satisfied with things at present. However, I'll let you know."

It occurred to Anne that her employer sounded a trifle relieved as if Mr. Richmond had been somewhat too brisk and self assured.

During the course of the next week various other strangers wandered through Anne's office, more alert young men, a middle-aged gentleman, and one quite elderly woman.

It therefore became apparent to Anne by the visit that Fellowes was interviewing possible private secretaries.

She was angry, and, she judged, with cause. And she was amazingly hurt as well. If he was not satisfied with her why didn't he tell her? Why resort to this underhand — yes, it *was* underhand! — method of replacing her? What sins of omission or commission had she committed? It wasn't fair, she thought, going home evenings, her mind aching with speculations, her heart heavy with fear and a sense of betrayal.

Perhaps she thought wearily, it had been too easy — the years of congenial, coming forward work, the eventual, apparently logical reaching of the goal ambition had set her.

She was abstracted at home, cool to Ted when he came, and inclined to be unwontedly sharp with Kathleen, who had taken to borrowing money from her. "I must dress, Anne. I can't get ahead unless I have proper clothes. I have to be seen about town with Lola and her crowd — I can't look shabby."

On this last occasion Anne gave her money for the third time in as many weeks but was not sympathetic.

"I'm awfully sorry to keep touching you," Kathleen told her with a fleeting compunction, "but it isn't as if you hadn't something put away."

"I know I have. But I'd like to keep it," Anne informed her, "there's nothing to this business of living up to every cent you earn. I've managed to save my raise and buy clothes and incidentals and give Mother what's due her."

"But she doesn't demand it," Kathleen said discontentedly. "She and Dad can get along beautifully. It isn't as if you *had* to help."

"It's just because she doesn't demand it that

I want to," Anne replied, "I like her to have something extra. I wish she'd spend it on herself. If I weren't living home, Kathleen, I'd be paying rent somewhere."

She drew a deep breath. She, oh, she didn't want to desert her own people, of course; but to have a place of her own, a small place with a little beauty in it, a quiet place, seemed more than ever as time went on a dream of next door to heaven.

But now, faced with the fear of losing her position with Fellowes, she was unhappier than she had ever been in all her life. If she had gained the promotion merely to lose it again, she might as well never have left Sanders! He'd liked her work and said so, and as far as he was concerned it appeared she might have stayed with him forever.

Apparently, for a little added prestige, more exciting surroundings and a ten dollar raise she had imperilled her present and future safety.

But the thing that cut was Fellowes' attitude.

"He might have told me," she kept repeating to herself. "It isn't like him. He might have told me."

Whenever she was free to think of her own affairs she found herself reviewing, mentally, all the details of her association with him, trying to see where she'd failed, where her judgment had erred, where she'd hindered instead of helped. Of course, she'd made mistakes, a lot, but they'd been minor, and were to be expected in taking over a routine it had taken Miss Andrews five years to perfect. And for any and all the mistakes Fellowes had had no word of anger or impatience for her.

The morning of Christmas Eve Anne found a box of Sherry's on her desk with Fellowes' card slipped into the great purple bow. She looked at it, dully, her eyes filling with unusual tears.

A box of Sherry's! It represented so many pounds of cold poison to her if he had given it to her knowing that in the course of time — tomorrow — next week — a month away — he intended letting her go.

Just before the lunch hour he called her to him, and she found him frowning at a scribbled slip of paper which lay before him on the desk.

"Miss Murdock," he said, and flicked a finger at the slip, "I wonder if you could help me out here?"

She leaned nearer and looked. She saw a list, a rather scrambled affair. Names and addresses written in a firm hand and pencilled notes after each, rather wavering, and question-marked.

"Christmas gifts," explained Fellowes with a groan. "Mrs. Fellowes attends to our mutual friends and the servants, but these are acquaintances, business associates and the like to whom I give personally. I've made some suggestions but you needn't follow them. Here's a list of the shops in which I have accounts. Could you take this afternoon and go down and buy the things, and see that they're sent special delivery?"

"I'd be glad to," she said, but her tone was a little cool and he looked up at her ruefully.

"I'm sorry I always do things like this — at the last minute," he said, and then asked with the first note of personal interest in his voice that she had heard for sometime, "Get your own shopping done all right Saturday?"

"Yes, thank you," Anne answered, thinking of the crowds and press and weariness of that afternoon. To really wrap your gifts in the authentic Christmas spirit, she had thought exasperatedly, you have to have leisure and peace of mind. Luckily she'd not had much to get, having picked up gifts for the family at odd times during the autumn. As for the tree and the stockings, her mother attended to them. It was one of Molly's great joys, to which she looked forward all year.

Anne picked up the lists — candy, flowers, books and hosiery for the few women upon it. Ties and socks, cigarettes and cigars for the men. Simple, manlike, a little monotonous.

"I'll go," she told him, "right from lunch. It needn't take long."

"I don't know what I'd do without you," he commented abstractedly, forgetting that he had been vaguely planning to do without her for all time. "Mrs. Fellowes has so much to do for Christmas herself. I can't burden her with this, and I can't get away myself. Miss Andrews has attended to it for some years."

He looked at her and smiled and drew a breath as if a load had dropped from his shoulders.

"I don't know *how* I'd get along," he said again.

Anne, with this for encouragement, took her business life in her hands. It might not be ethics, but her future was too important for her not to take the risk. She asked, quietly:

"Mr. Fellowes, has my work been satisfactory?"

"Perfectly," he replied and looked at her in, first astonishment, and then misgiving.

"Then — I suppose I shouldn't say anything," Anne cried out and twisted her hands together with sudden nervousness, "but I couldn't help knowing you — have interviewed secretaries lately. One, a woman — asked me things. And, I thought, if my work was not satisfactory perhaps you'd tell me now before you —"

He was as embarrassed as she was, and interrupted quickly:

"I didn't go about it very well, did I?"

Somehow, there was something so boyish and absurdly crestfallen in this question that she had to smile, and Fellowes smiled back and went on:

"Your work has been splendid, Miss Murdock. I couldn't ask for better. But, frankly, I understood that you were thinking of making a change yourself, and so, I thought —"

He broke off. He couldn't say, "It was gossip, perhaps, but forewarned is forearmed." Nor could he tell her honestly, "You're much too pretty to waste your youth in an office."

"I? A *change?*" asked Anne in astonishment.

"Thinking," he explained, "of getting married. Of course," he went on, "it was to be expected. You're young and —" before he was aware of the indiscretion, the truth had slipped out, "so very pretty," he ended and halted, a little annoyed at himself as he waited between fear and hope for her answer.

"But I haven't the least idea of getting married!" repudiated Anne firmly, wanting somehow to laugh, feeling her heart lighten to a featherweight, wanting somehow to get away and remember secretly what he had said — "and so very pretty," he'd said.

"You're not — engaged or anything?"

"Of course not. I — I shan't get married ever!" announced Anne extravagantly.

Now, Fellowes, drawing a tremendous breath of relief, found himself able to laugh at her a little, to tell her:

"Come, you don't mean that!"

"Yes, I do. Why — I like my work, Mr. Fellowes," Anne told him breathless with earnestness, "I'm an idiot over it, I like it so much, and I wouldn't exchange it and my independence for any man living!" she cried. "I can't imagine why you'd think such a thing!"

"Oh," said Fellowes, "that's an old challenge! Still, if you assure me that marriage isn't in the immediate future for you I'll have to let the challenge go unargued."

"Well," Anne told him, "if I ever went crazy and changed my mind I'd tell you first, 'way ahead of time."

"Good!" he said, heartily.

It was their first purely personal conversation. Each was aware of it, Anne rather tremulously, Fellowes with a sense of mounting excitement, or was it just — business interest?

After a moment:

"I am selfishly glad, of course," he told her. "Please forgive my leaping at conclusions, won't you? And in turn I can safely promise there won't be any more interviews. I couldn't stand any of 'em anyway," he confided, youthfully, experiencing a purely personal sense of happiness which transcended his natural relief at not losing a good secretary.

Anne went back to her work. It had been office gossip. A foolish mistake — a *canard.* He liked her work, he wasn't going to let her out — and somehow Christmas was really Christmas and not just another holiday.

At lunch time she put on her things and sallied forth to snatch a sandwich and a glass of milk, and to do The Chief's shopping. She accomplished this accurately and swiftly, and was amused to admit to herself that it gave her a definite kick, to sail into the shops, place her order, demand special service and "charge it, please."

But she didn't forget the more or less innocent source of her worry and misgiving, and she reminded herself that she must speak to Ted. He came for Christmas dinner, but, beyond a slight battle of words when he caught her under the mistletoe, she had no opportunity to speak to him alone. But an evening or so later, when they were at the theatre, that opportunity arrived.

"Ted, you'll have to stop coming to my office except for honest-to-heaven business reasons."

"Now why that edict?" he demanded.

"People are talking. I won't have talk. I hate it. And besides, you interrupt my work."

"Anne, you're damned hard on a fellow!"

"No, I'm not — and if I am," she said inconsistently, "I can't help it. I won't have people gossiping about us, Ted. Now don't set your jaw and start a discussion. The curtain's going up."

And she settled back, her eyes on the stage, her color coming and going, forgetting Ted, forgetting everything but the glamour of the lights and the magic with which a good cast can invest good lines and romantic situations.

Said Fellowes to Jameson, at the club on an occasion of a holiday dinner and raffle:

"You were all wrong about Miss Murdock!"

"Whom? And why especially? I'm always wrong."

"My secretary. I had a talk with her recently and she told me she wouldn't marry the last man on earth."

"Well, who would," inquired Jameson reasonably, "or rather, who *could?* The competition would be something fierce in that case."

"Oh, be sensible, you incomparable ass. I mean, the girl's modern. Her job means more to her than love in a walk-up."

"Are there any?" Jameson mused.

"Any what, for Lord's sake?"

"Modern girls. Here," said Jameson in mild astonishment looking at the dark, pink burden he was carrying, "what the hades can I do with a suckling pig? Take it home to Linda!" and he thrust the beskirted deceased animal in Fellowes' arms.

Fellowes proceeded to check it, quite gravely, at the hat-stand. Then he slipped an arm through his friend's.

"Come on and have a drink, and let's find some one for bridge. You'll have to eat the pig with us some night soon."

He was more light hearted than his subsequent, moderate consumption of Scotch warranted. He needn't worry about losing the best secretary a man ever had. He believed her. She had a quality of sincerity which impressed him enormously. She hadn't fluttered and Oh — Mr. Fellowes'd! when he'd taxed her with his fortunately erroneous impression. She had just come out with the flat denial, as frank as a boy.

Since then, they'd been a little closer in the personal sense in some intangible way. And as the winter progressed he entrusted her with more and more of his private affairs, giving her his power of attorney for use, if necessary, when he was away on one of his frequent trips.

Late that Springtime, Anne was with Fellowes in the conference room at an informal meeting with important clients, The Hatton Woolen Mills people.

Half a dozen men sat around the long table. The room was furnished as a library, with bookcases set between long windows, open to the warm, golden sunlight. In one corner a grandfather's clock swung its heavy pendulum backward and forward, the symbol of inexorable time.

The Hatton concern had recently purchased a smaller competitive company, and a new advertising campaign had been discussed and tentatively agreed upon.

Anne, her notebook in hand, was listening to Lawrence Fellowes who, leaning across the table, spoke quietly to Hatton, the President, and Mayne, the General Manager.

"If I might make a suggestion," he said, smiling.

"Of course —" Hatton, an elderly, long-upper-lipped man, responded with his habitual, refrigerated geniality. "Always glad to listen to any suggestions from you, Fellowes."

"It's this, then. I know it is the custom, in taking over another concern, to replace a number of their men with men of your own. There is, I suppose, much to be said for this.

You, for instance, have your own policies, your routine, your particular way of going about things. And it is doubtless more difficult to convert your new company to your ways than to put your own men in and carry on without, practically, a break. But I'd like to make a plea for the men in the Smithson Company who have given twenty and thirty years of their lives to the building up of the business. It is no light thing for them, at their age, to be thrown out of work. All the kind regretful words in the world, coupled with bonuses or two months' salary, won't help them. They've lost much more than a job, Mr. Hatton. They've lost — if they are good men, and I presume they are or their company would never have reached competitive proportions — they've lost the very mainspring of their existence. It's like," he paused and laughed a little, but his eyes never swerved from Hatton's, "bringing up a son, seeing him through all the perils of infancy, watching him grow strong and healthy and mature, and then handing him over for adoption. Not only have you lost your life work and the rewards thereof, but something you care for deeply has been taken from you. Wouldn't it be possible, Mr. Hatton, to try and utilize such men as are still active factors in the Smithson Company, taking the trouble to train them to your methods, interesting them in the larger scope of the new concern? It seems to me that it would be very worth while. They can't have held their jobs as long as they did without having their own ideas. And those ideas may be — probably are — helpful and constructive."

Hatton emitted a sound between a bronchial cough and a grunt.

"There's something in what you say," he admitted, with his maybe-yes-maybe-no manner.

He turned to Mayne.

"Day, the old Superintendent, has a very good record," he remarked, casually.

Mayne nodded. He was a younger man than his Chief and a little less cut and dried.

"He's responsible, I believe, for most of the improvement during the last ten years," he said, noncommittally.

"It certainly won't harm your prestige," suggested Fellowes, "to be known as one of the few companies which, upon buying a competitor, refuse to follow the ancient and honorable — although the latter term is open to argument — custom of firing all the lesser executives of the purchased concern."

"I'll think it over," said Hatton, which was, with him, tantamount to an agreement.

Later, Fellowes back in his office, grinning

like a youngster asked Anne:

"Do you think I put it over?"

"I certainly do!"

"I hope so," he went on. "I've sat in on dozens of such conferences, always with the gloomy mental picture of men given the gate after years of service. It's been a dream of mine to persuade some more open-minded concern to do the generous thing, even at the expense of a more difficult task of reorganization. Hatton's a pretty tough nut to crack. When we first got that account I was up against it. He rarely committed himself. Their advertising methods were old-fashioned in the extreme, their copy wore crinolines. It took everything I had to persuade him to a tremendous increase in appropriation and the modern slant. He was under the impression that he had hired a couple of bright boys to write pretty copy and draw pretty pictures for him. It took a long time to prove to him that we did more than that. He wanted his work done in six months. I said, 'No.' That interested him. He wasn't used to being crossed. I made him give us a year — which wasn't time enough, really — and we sent a man into the field to make a complete survey; we sent others to the dealers; we worked like nailers. That was my first big job on succeeding my uncle. And Hatton has grudgingly admitted to me that their returns from their half million yearly expenditure — an expenditure which took the skin off his New England bones — have been enormous. Lord, during that campaign I ate, drank and slept wool — from the sheep to the blanket. We gave 'em a new trade mark, we concentrated on advertising quality — the generations of tradition and integrity back of them. And now, I hope, I've won him over to my pet theory — that it's a waste of good material to throw your competitor's old employees out when you take them over — material which you could, with a little trouble, utilize to your own ultimate benefit."

He paused and laughed.

"I appear to be in the lecture room," he said, apologetically.

"I was terribly interested," Anne told him. It was true. But if it hadn't been she would have said so anyway. She was a good secretary.

"I know it. I watched you during the first rather heated moments of the conference. Do you know, you have a most expressive face? You should never play poker. I can always tell when things are going well or badly by your eyes. And, because I rely upon your judgment, you've become a sort of barometer."

Anne laughed. She felt very near her employer in the rather garrulous, boyish moods which always followed a victory or the promise of one. She thought, going home that night, how well she had grown to know him. She had learned to tell in the instant of their meeting if he was tired or out of sorts, if the day was going well or badly, if he looked forward to a battle or simply wearily girded himself for it without much enthusiasm.

She saw him practically every day. She saw the quick temper which he had so well controlled, the vitality, the occasional pettiness, the worry over delays, the rare evasions. But she saw, too, the manner in which he handled the big issues, the sureness of his important judgments and decisions, and the never sleeping vision — the dreamer's vision — which was not locked in his desk at closing time, but which went everywhere with him, far-seeing, daring, broad of scope, working, planning, seeing ahead, all his waking moments.

It was this vision coupled with the practical mind, the grasp of a situation, and the dogged attention to detail which made him a big man.

So big a man in fact, that Anne found herself consciously judging all other men by this high and difficult standard.

She was seeing him, also, in his home. For lately she had been called often to work there with him at night. At first they had worked in the office, but the office was never quite silent; there was always someone there — a belated copy-writer or Higgins, the layout man, or Sanders. The telephone never slept. And now when Fellowes had a piece of work to do which required the maximum of concentration, he found it practical to work in his small study at the apartment. On these occasions Linda would be out, returning late to drag her husband and his secretary from their work and insist that they rest — have something to eat and drink — before Anne started on the long, lonely trip home.

Upon one such occasion —

"Upon my word," said Linda, appearing in the study sometime after midnight, "you two are gluttons for punishment!"

The night was unseasonably warm. Fellowes, his hair damp and lank on his forehead, one cheek branded with the mark of a blue pencil, a green shade over his eyes, looked up from the paper-strewn desk a little blindly, as if Linda's deep, cool voice had called him back from another world and he could not quite adjust himself. Anne, pale with fatigue, the boyish stiff collar of her blue serge dress wilted and soiled, looked up, too, from the smaller typewriting desk which Fellowes had had put in the room for her. She smiled at

135

her employer's wife with frank admiration.

Linda had dined out and been to a play. She was wearing a charming gown, sea green chiffon, from which her shoulders rose superbly. Not a hair was ruffled upon her high-held head, and her slight make-up, leading cleverly up to the carnation red of her smooth lips, was as fresh as when she had evolved it before her mirror hours earlier.

"Gosh, but she's lovely!" thought Anne with a miserable feeling of depression which certainly wasn't envy.

"I've ordered food," Linda told them briskly, "and you two will kindly rise up and follow me. Miss Murdock looks ready to drop, Larry. Simon Legree was an angel of mercy compared to you. Don't you know the girl has to sleep long enough to be able to conduct your nefarious business tomorrow without dying at the post?"

"Ten minutes?" begged Fellowes, but he observed Anne with sudden sharp anxiety. She did look white, the dark blue eyes were heavy and circled with fatigue.

"No, not five! Come along this instant! Roberts has sandwiches, coffee and fruit cup and things. I dodged the Garretts' supper party just in order to break up this little tête-à-tête!"

Fellowes rose, filled with compunction, yet casting a reluctant glance at the desk. It had been pleasant to work there in the quiet room at top speed, with the sound of the ashes falling in the fireplace in the next room, with the curtains drawn and with Anne beside him, silent and quick and — and near.

"Nice reputation you're giving me!" he told Linda.

"My dear, you deserve it. You forget that Miss Murdock is not of your superior sex, does not stand five feet ten or so, does not weigh one hundred and sixty pounds or whatever it is."

"I'm sorry," Fellowes told Anne. "Why on earth didn't you stop me?"

Anne rose, tired in every muscle.

"Why should I?" she asked him. "I'm not tired. I was glad to get the work done — I — enjoyed it," she said with a faint suggestion of defiance, and looking directly at Linda.

But Linda only smiled and led the way to the supper table.

A day or so later Mrs. Fellowes, motoring to a polo game at Fort Hamilton with Jameson, remarked, resignedly, as they took the curve and sweep of Manhattan Bridge:

"I tried to persuade Larry to come but he's working today, and then catching a train to Washington. He likes polo — he used to play on a scratch team, but he hasn't lately."

Jameson answered, his hands steady on the

wheel of the high geared roadster:

"He'll be busy with golf soon."

"Oh he plays so sporadically — too hard when he does — too rarely to do him any real good. If it weren't for that trainer who comes in and puts him through the mill every morning he wouldn't keep fit."

After a moment she said, absently, her eyes on the busy life of the river, silver blue under the sunlight:

"Look at those gulls. They'll never build a plane to rival them in effortless grace. Dick, I think Larry's little secretary is falling in love with him!"

They had shot over the Brooklyn approach and were negotiating traffic before Jameson answered, very carefully:

"That's a — pity. Does he know it?"

"Not yet. Perhaps she doesn't either. Poor Andrews was mad about him, and he never guessed until, I think, the time she left. She went off at the deep end, hysterical and all that. No, he didn't tell me. It came to me in a roundabout way from the sister of one of the girls in the art department. And all she said was, 'I understand Miss Andrews has had a nervous breakdown.' That was enough for me. But Larry was deaf, dumb and blind while she was with him. I was sorry for her — and I'm sorry for this girl. She's very pretty and quite young, and life surely holds more for her than sitting around taking orders from a man who doesn't know she exists, except for his business convenience."

Jameson was not so sure that Fellowes didn't know Anne existed. But he said, merely:

"It happens very often. Office wives."

"Is that what you call them?" asked Linda, delighted.

"Not original with me. I assure you. It's as current a term as T.B.M.," Jameson told her.

"Perhaps, but I've never happened to hear it before. Office wives. It's odd," mused Linda, "the complete separation of personality."

"How do you mean?"

"Office and home. In a way that little Murdock girl knows far more about Larry than I —"

Jameson was Lawrence Fellowes' friend. He liked him. He admired him. But Jameson was in love with Fellowes' wife. He was an honorable man. He was careful never to overstep the limits he had imposed upon himself. He was grateful for what she gave him, a close understanding friendship. He might, easily, have said something — given her a hint. He knew himself much in her confidence. But he bit on the curb and said nothing, for his emotions were authentically involved. Still and all, he was no more than human and could not help permitting himself a warning, not, be it to his credit, set down in malice.

"The little Murdock is a very different type from Miss Andrews, Linda. It would be one thing to awaken to the devotion of an unattractive woman of forty and another to awaken to —"

"Anne's?" Linda was thoughtful. "I suppose so. But, I'm not alarmed. Larry has had his moments. I suppose all of you do. I've known and said nothing. There was nothing to say. Besides, we understand one another. He knows that I could not tolerate anything of the sort you suggest — any more than he would tolerate its counterpart in me."

After a moment they spoke of other things and presently, reaching the Fort, parked the car and took their seats. The beautiful ponies raced down the long green stretch; the crack of the mallet sounded loud as a pistol shot on the clear air. It was the end of the first chukker. Overhead a plane was stunting lazily; not far off were the blue waters of the Narrows. The band struck up — some commonplace ballad of the day, but oddly stirring in that setting. The captain of one of the teams galloped past, a heavy man and a perfect performer. Linda said, settling back, drawing her sables about her full throat:

"What a game — *what* a game!"

She had forgotten about Anne and Fellowes. But Jameson had not.

If Anne were really in love with her employer? If, as was certainly on the cards, Fellowes came to a realization of that fact?

Not that there was any comparison between the two women thought Jameson, loving Linda, and loyal to her, but he and Larry Fellowes were two very different men. Fellowes was pretty well immersed in the business he'd built up, and Linda had, frankly, no interest whatever in his work save to deplore that he gave too much time to it. But Anne's interest was probably keen, doubtless unfeigned. There was a meeting place, and one made to order. And between Linda and Larry there was no mutual ground at all, unless, pondered Jameson uncomfortably, being a decent man, and respecting reticences, as well as being in love, unless it were the common or garden ground of physical passion. But, that, after ten years of slow drifting apart, Jameson very much doubted; or preferred to doubt.

"Goal for the Whites!" exclaimed Linda. He turned and smiled into the brown eyes. If Larry, in his turn, should fall in love with Anne, what of Linda then?

Linda was a sportswoman; more than that, she was a good sport, thought Jameson, and permitted himself to dream a little under the arching blue sky.

In the office that quiet Sunday afternoon Fellowes and Anne were working together. A long distance call came through for him and Anne listened to his terse answers:

"No, I can't, possibly."

"No, I'm leaving for Washington tonight to be gone three days."

"Mr. Sanders is out of the question. He has to carry on here."

Later, he hung up and turned to Anne:

"How," he asked her with normal bewilderment, "can I go to Chicago and be in Washington at the same time?"

He shook his head, regarded Anne, frowning, and went on:

"Air mail won't do. There's a hitch in the tentative plans I sent out to the Lawson Lock people. Somebody has to explain it to them. Lawson is convalescing with the flu. He can't come here. He doesn't think anyone in his outfit understands English, apparently, so he won't send a substitute. Sanders would do but he can't leave —"

He ran his hand through his thick hair and stared at Anne a moment. She'd been with him the better part of a year; he had come to trust her as he had never trusted a living person. She was absolutely reliable. She knew how to think for herself, and for him. She'd been over the Lawson Lock plan a dozen times with him.

Anne waited.

Suddenly he smote the desk and asked, startling her:

"Look here, Miss Murdock, could *you* go?"

She had been thinking — If he asks me to go? wondering if he considered her capable. Yet his question came as a shock of surprise with an increased sense of power, and brought with it a thrill of pure delight. She nodded, grave eyes intent on his own:

"Of course I'll go," she said.

And Fellowes thought, still watching her, "Of course I'll go." Just like that. "Of course." No why and wherefores. "Of course, she would, the *darling!*" said Fellowes to himself.

Chapter 5

Miss Murdock Spends Her Vacation

In the little silence which followed Lawrence Fellowes' gray eyes encountered his secretary's. The look which endured between them for a second or so of time was curiously, searchingly deep. On his part, it was a look of trust, of gratitude and of something more, something unreadable, and veiled. Upon hers, in her answering eyes, there was loyalty and an unspoken reassurance.

"Fine!" said Fellowes, following that appreciable pause. "We'll go over the ground again together. Get Lawson back on the wire for me, will you?"

She did so and a little later Fellowes was saying to an impatient man in Chicago:

"I'm sending my secretary to you — Miss Murdock — yes, she knows what it's all about. She's leaving on the Broadway Limited, two-fifty-five tomorrow afternoon. See that she's met."

A moment's listening, and then Fellowes turned to Anne:

"He wants to know what you look like!"

he reported, aggrievedly.

Anne chuckled. He was staring at her over the telephone as if he had never seen her before. No, not quite that, but as if he were labelling her in his mind . . . small . . . fair . . . blue eyes. . . . She proposed, hastily:

"If you'd tell him not to bother meeting me, I could take a taxi to his house."

Fellowes with a sigh of relief, transmitted the message and hung up.

"I didn't suggest that you go tonight," he said, "because it might make it difficult for you to arrange your plans. And there's today's work to get through with tomorrow morning. So, if you're willing, tomorrow afternoon's time enough. You'll reach there shortly after nine on Tuesday, and can probably get an afternoon train back."

When the Lawson plans had been gone over again and Anne had had her instructions, Fellowes looked at his watch.

"I've an hour or so before train time," he said, "and my bag's at the station. Suppose we go out and have some dinner?"

She assented quietly enough, but her heart was racing. The moment seemed to mark a new milestone in her secretarial progress. She had often heard comments, a little caustic, on girls who went dining with their bosses. Well, why shouldn't they?

They went to the Pennsylvania and there was good food, and pleasant lights, and the melody of music flooding across the tables to veil the clatter of service, and the sound of voices with a dreaming sound. Anne looked at Fellowes over the little separating width between them. He was talking animatedly, not of business but of a book he'd had time to read which she, too, had read; of a play they'd both seen. He listened to her observations and said, as if casually, "We'll have to do a show together sometime, Miss Murdock. If you get as excited as this over a mere discussion of a play you've seen what would you be like in the audience watching one? I think you'd be a stimulating companion. Most of us have grown pretty — blasé."

Anne laughed.

"I'm a fool, of course," she admitted frankly. "I once knew a girl rather well who played small parts. I used to go back and see her between acts — and, well, I suppose it was disillusioning, back stage, and yet when I got out in front again, I was as convinced that the things I saw happening were perfectly real as if I'd never seen the wheels go round on the other side of the curtain." She mentioned a horror-mystery play of the previous season. "I acted like an imbecile when I saw that," she confessed further, "screamed in a whisper and clutched Ted — the man with me," she ended hurriedly, flushing.

Fellowes remarked, watching her, smiling:

"Don't apologize! He was a lucky man, whoever he was," he added, with a smiling challenge.

She went home that night in Fellowes' car, after leaving him at the lobby doors — he'd walk across, he said. Leaning back against the upholstery she found that she was tired, that she was wide awake, that she was excited — more excited than she'd ever been at any play. She'd dined with — Lawrence Fellowes. They hadn't talked business. They might have been friends — a — a very little more than friends.

She told her family of her mission to Chicago and asked, as casually as possible:

"Haven't we a small bag I could take?"

Mrs. Murdock beamed.

"He does trust you!" she commented and went to look for the bag.

But Murdock was wontedly gloomy.

"I don't like it," he protested, "Shipping you all over the map! A young, unprotected girl! Anything might happen! Look at the papers!"

"I do look at them," Anne said gaily, "but it's only papers like Jimmy's which manage to see the dark side of everything."

Jim, his wife and babies, had been having

Sunday supper with his parents. They were still there, the babies rolled up asleep, one on an armchair with a straight chair in front of him, the other on a couch. They'd all waited for Anne.

Now Jim came forward, as usual, to champion his sister.

"She's safe enough, Pop. She'll find her way home. What's the big idea, Sis? Anything for The-Daily-What-Have-You? You might give me the break. What's it all about? Treaty between Mayor Thompson and Great Britain?"

"Don't be silly! It's business!"

"Not in my line. Sara, Junior's awake. We'd better go home. He has had the cow jumping over the moon one hundred times since, by the grace of God and the BMT, we arrived here. He'll never be president, according to recent standards — he talks too much."

"So do you," said Jim's mother, returning, with the bag. "Here Junior, come to Grandma!"

"Never thought you'd go back on me, Molly," her son reproached her, "Anne, are you getting out your armour plated lingerie?"

"Her *what?* Whatever for?" asked Mrs. Murdock amazed.

"Chicago!" Jim laughed and then said soothingly, "Don't worry, Ma; it hasn't the monopoly on gunmen."

Anne's tickets were secured for her by the office. She had a drawing room, owing to the orders Fellowes had left. She travelled comfortably, slept fitfully and presented herself at Mr. Lawson's enormous house without mishap or misgiving.

Lawson, a middle-aged gentleman in a brocaded bathrobe, received her in his study. He had the frail look of the convalescent after a bad attack of flu. A nurse, ushering Anne in to him, disappeared discreetly, after warning her,

"Mr. Lawson must not be agitated."

Anne somehow, judging that he had been born that way, did not worry. She opened her brief case, laid certain papers on the library table while Lawson stared at her.

"But you're a woman!" he exploded, "a young woman!"

Anne decided not to reply to this obvious statement.

"I thought, of course, you were a man!"

Anne answered, demurely:

"Mr. Fellowes said 'Miss,' and 'she.' "

"Well, that could sound like 'Mr.' and 'he' couldn't it? Well, you're here now," said Lawson in an it-can't-be-helped tone, "let's see what you know about the muddle."

Anne explained. She then re-explained for the better part of an hour. After which Lawson remarked, grudgingly:

"You've a good head. Tell Mr. Fellowes it's O. K. with me."

He asked her to stay for luncheon but she refused.

"It's my first trip to Chicago," she said, "and I'd like to see something of it before I return."

The library door opened before he could reply, and Mr. Lawson, Jr., a gay and personable young man, came in.

"Hey, Dad —"

He stopped and stared.

His father made the presentations and explanations. But although Allan Lawson was not interested in Lawrence Fellowes or his works he, in common with other gentlemen, preferred them blond — or brunette — or red-headed, as long as they were young and pretty. So, half an hour later, Anne found herself committed to the daytime sights of Chicago, and environs, luncheon and a safe convoy to her train.

She wired Fellowes the successful conclusion of her business and wondered how he would like the way she'd elected to cool her heels till train time, if he knew it. Not, of course, that he'd care — nor was it any of his business, after all — but still —

Lawson Junior was entertaining; Anne was

amused; the time passed pleasantly to the tune of a little light-hearted flirtation, and eventually he put her on the train with candy, magazines and flowers enough to take her to San Francisco.

"May I look you up when I come to New York?"

"Why not?" asked Anne.

When Fellowes returned from Washington she had a verbal report for him. She then said, a little defiantly because she felt curiously awkward:

"After the business was over Mr. Lawson's son took me to lunch and we drove about the city."

"Young Allan? He's a nice boy," Fellowes said carelessly, and added, "Glad you had a good time." And Anne found herself relieved and a little absurdly disappointed.

"I didn't know if you — he and his father engineered it. It wasn't strictly business," she explained, unnecessarily.

"You deserved," Fellowes told her, "some reward for the trip."

But later he happened to remember, and with no perceptible pleasure, that Allan Lawson was an attractive youngster, and a very eligible one.

Therefore, when two or three weeks later Allan walked blithely into the office of Miss

Murdock, her employer again had occasion to recall his attraction and eligibility.

Fellowes, who was talking to Anne at her own desk, greeted the caller, and listened to Allan remark coolly:

"I'm taking Miss Murdock to lunch."

Anne shook her bright head.

"I haven't time — I'm sorry."

"Dinner then. Where'll I meet you?"

He quite ignored Fellowes whom he'd met once or twice. So the older man stood back, trying to feel amused, but only succeeding in experiencing irritation. Anne, sensing that irritation and the inappropriateness of the conversation, answered quickly:

"At — Oh you'd never find your way there! At my sister's, then." She gave him Kathleen's address and named an hour. She'd taken to leaving a dinner frock and a change of clothes at Kathleen's. It was easier than going home when she worked late at the office before an engagement in town.

When Allan had gone as casually as he came:

"A fast worker," commented Fellowes.

"No." Anne smiled up at him. "It's just that he's one of these young men with nothing to do, and lots of money to do it with," she answered, a little scornfully.

"You don't admire the masculine lily of the field then, I take it?" Fellowes asked her, feeling a little better.

"Not me!" said Anne with plenty of emphasis if little grammar. And it was true enough. Yet she emphasized it deliberately.

That night she dined and saw a play, and went to a night club with Allan Lawson. He was as amusing as he had been on their first meeting, and she liked him well enough, but confessed to herself that she was soon bored. He was a little younger than herself, not long home from a trip around the world after leaving college.

"My old man wants me to go into the business," he told Anne over the dolls, balloons and trick fans on the narrow table against the wall. The club was crowded. There was a scent of powder and heavy perfume, of food and liquor, of the bare flesh of women in the low-ceilinged room. A Frenchwoman was singing on the small stage, and the sweating orchestra wailed out the accompaniment. It was all very noisy. "I suppose," thought Anne, "you can only enjoy it if you're in the right mood. I generally am. But not tonight."

Cigarette smoke hung blue and thick on the still, heated air. Her eyelids drooped. But she groped out of the drowsiness that threatened her to ask Lawson, indifferently:

"You will, of course?"

"Not if I can help it! Lawson Locks! Isn't

that ridic? I spend my time breaking, not making, them. Love laughs at them, or at their manufacturers, and I," said Allan, "have a sense of humor, too."

Anne laughed with him. And he went on: "I've a few shekels of my own thanks to a dear dead grandma. Work is the only thing I can't see. I'm not sure how long I'll live —"

"What!"

"Who is, nowadays, what with wars and machine guns, airplanes, bad booze and banana peels?" he asked cheerfully. "Anyway, I'm rather sure I'll be dead a long time. So, while I've the use of life and limb I intend to suit myself."

He took her back to Kathleen's, and following his usual routine tried to kiss her as they stood together in the dim hallway.

"No? Well, no hard feelings, then," he told her gaily. "I'm no Shylock. That isn't intended as a pun, darling. Some of you kiss and some — fewer — of you don't. When I meet a pretty girl of the don't-class that's my hard luck and her poor judgment. Lunch with me tomorrow?"

Anne laughed. She marvelled, silently, "a year ago I might have let him kiss me — just — oh, just because. Why not now, I wonder?"

"No," she told him, "I can't. Remember

I'm a business woman."

"Gawd, how I pity 'em. Listen here, if I go into business after all, will you come and be my little secretary?"

"I certainly will not!" said Anne.

"That settles it. I won't go. I sail tomorrow at midnight anyway. So this is Paris, said our hero. Good-night. Look here, girl, take my tip and don't sew yourself to a typewriter. It doesn't pay. Life's too short, and you're too damned pretty."

It is on record that she never saw him again, but she remembered — the slim boy with his top hat tilted on his fair sleek head, his arm flung carelessly about her shoulder, his gay voice whispering, advising, warning.

The next day Fellowes, a little against his own judgment, asked her how the evening had gone.

"It was fun," Anne told him, "but did you know," she asked, "that he doesn't mean to work — *ever?*"

Fellowes laughed at the gravity of her accusing tone.

"Why should he?" he answered. "He inherited several millions on his coming of age. There'll be more, later. The business is safe enough. Safer without the boy than with him, I imagine. There's an older brother, a sound sort, not very clever but a plugger. This one's a wild kid, but harmless. By the way, he's the catch of the season in his home town," he added, watching her, keenly.

Anne tilted her little chin. A gesture which not quite unconsciously drew the attention to the soft red curves of her mouth.

"I can't imagine," she said, "wanting a man who didn't work either with his hands, or his head. Think," she said, "of a husband always under foot. One who went about throwing ten dollar bills around."

Fellowes chuckled.

"I don't think Allan would be much under anyone's foot. Did he really? I mean, throw the bills around?"

"More or less."

"So you can't imagine wanting Lawson," mused Fellowes. "Well, what sort of a man could you imagine wanting?"

He leaned back in his chair and watched her, turning fountain pen between his fingers, his gray eyes amused and intent.

"No kind at all! But, if any," Anne contradicted herself, "one who'd fought his way up. He needn't have a lot of money, but he'd be the sort to want to make it. Not for the money itself, but for the success it stands for. A big man with vision — a man who'd be willing to take risks and be a sport if he lost out — a — well, a man!" Anne wound up in a burst of oratory.

After a moment's silence Fellowes said, looking at her directly:

"Do you know, I think a man such as you describe would want, when it came to that, a girl very like yourself?"

Then Sanders came into the office and Anne slipped out without answering. At her desk, she thought, a trifle uncertain.

"I wonder if I've been an idiot? Of course, I was describing him. I meant it, all right — but I meant him to *know* it, too. And he got back at me, rather — I left the opening. Men," thought Anne further, "hate to be too consciously flattered. Still, he might have thought I spoke of a type, a type all business women meet and if he also thought it applied to him, well, there's no harm done."

It was not the first time she had said such things to him. As it happened she had meant them.

And once, not long since, she had remarked, in speaking of another man, whom Fellowes knew in a business way and upon whose attraction for women he had commented, that "such men" were always married.

"But not always happily married," he had answered quickly and had ended the discussion with a sudden switch of the conversation as if he trod on dangerous ground.

157

Since then, she had been thinking —

From the little she had seen of Linda and Fellowes together she had reached the conclusion that while they were excellent friends, they were not much emotionally involved one with the other. And because she now admitted to herself that Fellowes attracted her, strongly, in a physical sense, she marvelled at the dullness — or coldness — of the other woman's reactions. She thought shrewdly enough that the time would come when Larry Fellowes would tire of — friendship and turn elsewhere for a warmer comfort.

But it was impossible not to follow that to its logical conclusion. She knew now that Fellowes was not indifferent to her presence, to her nearness. She had seen him flush when, occasionally and accidentally, their hands had encountered. She had looked up to find him staring at her, ceasing in his dictation, his eyes lost upon her bowed head.

If she were right, if he cared very little for his wife and Linda for him, if he should seek elsewhere, and in seeking, chance upon the nearest person — herself — what would she do?

She told herself, defiantly, that she would be hurting no one save herself, that none need ever know. She could keep, she thought, a clear mind even in a disturbed body. For she did not love Lawrence Fellowes, she argued, it was merely that he attracted her as no other man had ever attracted her, and that he was moreover englamoured in her eyes by the situation in which she saw him and herself, the respective positions of employer and employed. Love, she thought, must be something different, something sweet and sane and tender.

No, she did not love Lawrence Fellowes, but she wanted him. She wanted too, quite honestly, the business protection and surety that a love affair with him would afford her. She was not ready to admit that such protection and surety is built upon shifting sand.

And both consciously and unconsciously she began deliberately to trouble Fellowes; the accidental contacts became more frequent and less accidental, and, because she was aware of her body, he became aware of it too. But he made no sign and she began to believe that she was a fool, to dream of risking so much, to dream of entering, hot blooded but cool headed, into a more intimate relationship with her employer — a relationship of excitement and danger, of half measures and half loaves, which could lead but to one of two conclusions — complete rupture or complete surrender.

She began to go out a good deal again with O'Hara. She was not consciously cruel in thus encouraging that hopeful young man. She was simply seeking distractions, protective coloration. But Ted, when they were alone together became more and more urgent, and when they were with others, the crowd — his — did not interest her. It consisted mostly of rather "arty" young people who did a great deal of talking in loud voices and who did not, to Anne's mind, accomplish much. The Lindstroms were, of course, the exceptions, delightful, successful people in their middle thirties.

Nils Lindstrom was a painter of some note, and his wife a sculptor, her speciality being the charming vital figures one sees in so many lovely gardens. Her children — there were three — sat to her for fat urchins and slender ten year olds who were depicted playing ball or embracing marble dolphins, flowering up in static beauty of line and limb from the restless beauty of moving water.

Anne liked the Lindstroms and went often to their studio where entertaining evenings were always to be had. And she went often to see Sara, and the new baby, a girl, who brought her welcome with her.

Toward midsummer Fellowes took his secretary to Southampton with him. Linda was giving a rather big house party, and had persuaded him to, at least, show himself, although his work pressed. She had captured some visiting lions, Russian and English; and Dempster, the polo player, a member of the American team in the Internationals, was there. Jameson was included and several pretty smart women.

So Fellowes worked with Anne during the mornings of the "long" week-end. But Linda arranged for Anne to go to the beach for swim and relaxation, and tried to make her comfortable and at ease.

It was out of the question that Anne would fit into the party, having neither the clothes nor the desire. Her meals were served her in the small sitting room of her own suite through the windows of which she had a glorious view of green velvet lawns, gardens and a wide expanse of ocean beyond. Linda had provided a bathing suit for her, a becoming one, and saw that she had plenty to read and to amuse her, and a car was put at her disposal to drive her about the Shinnecock Hills or the other Hamptons if she wished it. An odd position, reflected Anne without bitterness — neither servant nor guest.

But a little later that summer, she went down again when there was no one there save Mrs. Lucien and Jameson, and was, at that occasion, a guest as the others were.

"Be sure and take Miss Murdock swimming," Linda told her husband one morning.

"Dick and I are golfing. You'd better knock off work by eleven."

On the fairway:

"Are you wise? Aren't you throwing them too much together?" asked Jameson, reluctant that he must, yet feeling it only fair.

"My dear Dick!" said Linda, amazed and a little offended.

"But in view of what you told me — that the girl might be interested?" he reminded her, uncomfortably.

"What of that? He can't bring her down here and work her to death without my taking a hand. She has to have some recreation."

"Linda," Jameson exploded, "you are either a saint or a fool."

She turned her alert brown eyes to his:

"Neither," she observed, quietly.

Oh, she knew — she knew now — how much Jameson cared, without a word spoken, and she was turning to him for the companionship, the response to her complicated yet basically simple needs, which her husband did not give — had never given her.

So, dismissing Anne and Fellowes from her troubled mind she wondered instead: "Am I seeing too much of Dick?"

And a little after eleven Fellowes and Anne together on the hot white sands were sunning themselves before their swim. Anne's suit,

Linda's gift, had short trunks of deep Madonna blue, and a heavy white shirt, with a modernistic design of blue upon it. She had tanned, very slightly; a faint golden glow lay like a veil on the white skln of her beautifully molded arms and legs. Her hair was bound back with a blue gypsy handkerchief, and she sat with him under Linda's gay umbrella and watched the sea with eyes as blue as the water under sunlight. The curves of her young body were very lovely — her small breasts rose, firm and rounded, cupped by the tight contoured lines of the suit. And Fellowes, looking at her, letting the sand trickle idly through his fingers, the sun warm on his bare powerful shoulders, thought, even as he smiled lazily at her:

"Am I being wise?"

And, he knew that he was not, yet, did not care, not wishing to look beyond this blue and gold moment of sun and sand and sky — and — Anne.

Anne's two weeks' vacation fell in September. She had thought to welcome it, and Mrs. Murdock made great plans for her. Breakfast in bed every morning, and lazy hours on the sun porch lounge. She must not have a hand in the housework — it must be a peaceful restorative period.

"You look peaked," little Molly scolded severely. "You've been overdoing. No, not a word. Don't talk back to me! If you go on like this I'll speak to Mr. Fellowes, that I shall!"

"Mother, I'm all right, please don't worry."

"A mother knows," remarked Mrs. Murdock, darkly.

And Anne, after the first day or so found herself very bored. When the week-end came with Labor Day to lengthen it, and the Lindstroms asked herself and Ted to their cottage in a Catskills art colony, Anne was glad to accept.

"There you go!" reproached Molly, "running off again the instant minute I get you home."

"You got to expect that," remarked Mr. Murdock sardonically. "Children don't want to stay home nowadays with their folks. They have to be having excitement somewhere else."

Challenged, Mrs. Murdock flew at once to the defense of her daughter.

"Sure and why shouldn't she go? It's little enough vacation the child gets, as it is; and it's no fun for her staying around the house with just me for company. It will do her a world of good," she argued, with a complete change of attitude.

Murdock eyed his wife, shook his head and

returned to his paper with a grunt. But a reluctant smile twitched the corners of his thin, straight-lipped mouth. It always amused him, less secretly than he knew, to see his Molly run to the defense of her young.

The Lindstroms' rented cottage was attractive, the Lindstroms themselves, hospitable people in the true sense of the word. They permitted Ted and Anne to amuse themselves. Mealtime was a happy go lucky, but hearty affair, and Anne, playing with the attractive, intelligent, well brought up children, or sitting mouse-still near Nils while he worked, or helping Mrs. Lindstrom do her apparently effortless housekeeping, felt rested and envious.

For unconsciously, the Lindstroms were showing her the other side of the matrimonial picture. From Friday to Tuesday she was with them, observing their unostentatious, deep regard for one another, sensing the close-knit, beautifully patterned fabric of a completely happy and adjusted family life. She said as much to Joan Lindstrom, with wistfulness.

"It's wonderful to be with you here. There's something so restful and happy about the way you and Nils and the children live."

Joan, a big raw boned woman with fine features and beautiful coloring, looked at the girl, quickly.

"I'm glad you feel that way," was all she said.

Sitting there on the veranda Anne looked over the rolling hills that towered up into the dark green-blue of the Catskills.

"Most people seem so — feverish. There's so much bickering and quarreling."

"Everyone goes through a period of adjustment," Joan told her, practically. "Nils and I have had ours. It's in back of us. It wasn't easy when we were poor and struggling, and so ambitious, and the children came along to complicate matters. But if people love each other enough they'll win through."

Anne said, more to herself than the listening woman:

"There's Jim and Sara — they do love one another and yet — Oh, I don't know — they have so many worries, the children are under foot and Sara gets overworked and nervous, and Jim — Jim's like most men, pretty impatient when things aren't going smoothly. It does seem to me that nothing I've seen of marriage — except yours — would make me feel I wanted to risk it."

"You're wrong," said Joan, definitely. "There are many happy marriages. I think you see the others because you are looking for them. Aren't you trying to find excuses for yourself, Anne?"

"I wonder?" Anne told her and smiled, a little tremulously. "Perhaps I'm a coward. Mother and Father, now — they're happy, I suppose. Father sort of goes his own way and Mother's wrapped up in us. It seems to me," Anne said, very youthfully, "that their way of marriage is so — dull."

"You're too close to your own people," Joan pointed out. "Happiness right under the eyes is hard to see."

But Anne was turning over another problem in her troubled mind.

"How many people who marry really love one another?" she asked.

"As to that, it depends on what you mean by love," Joan answered, smiling faintly. "There's — just the youth urge, of course, the mating instinct, the purely physical attraction. That passes, unless it has a foundation of trust and respect, and comradeship upon which one — or rather, two — may build safely and enduringly."

"But how is one to know?" Anne persisted, feeling Joan had touched very closely on her own case.

Joan shook her tawny, cropped head.

"There's no rule. But if ever you meet a man whom you'd follow barefoot and hungry and thirsty to the world's end and back, a man you'd work for and work with, you can be pretty certain. It's not the man you can be happy with — for women in their curious way can be happy, after a fashion, with a dozen different men — it's the man you'd be desperately, achingly *unhappy without* who is the man for you. But no one can tell you, Anne. You have to find out for yourself."

To herself, she observed, a little sorry but not astonished. "She's not in love with Teddy, then." And when Nils, a little later, asked his wife with genuine interest, "Think Anne and Ted'll make a match of it, Joan?" she shrugged and was noncommittal. She was that rare person — a woman who did not pry into other people's minds and emotions, or discuss them with her friends or her husband, close as she was to him.

Because the Lindstroms were happy, because they showed her a side of intimate life which she had hitherto known only from books or glimpsed fleetingly, Anne was particularly sweet to Ted O'Hara during that visit. She was still curiously tired, mentally, and Ted was very dear and considerate — and there was something hauntingly like Spring in the quiet September days. The trees yet flung their green, courageous banners, and there were late roses blooming in the cottage garden, and a moon blossomed whitely in the garden of the sky.

If Ted had asked her then she might have said — yes — partly because of the influence which briefly caught and held her, and partly because she was aware that in her ceaseless preoccupation with Fellowes she was rapidly drifting into a desired danger, a danger which blinded her to standards of both ethics and morality. The last night at the Lindstroms', when lying in the cool little room and thinking somehow of her last visit to Southampton, wondering, as a natural result of her talk with Joan, how close to each other Fellowes and his wife really were, she felt a dull depression and at the same time, picturing involuntarily, and without effort, the laughing face Fellowes had turned to her at the beach that day, the slant of sunlight over his shoulders, the idle strong hand groping in the white sands, she experienced a deep, dreadful troubling of the blood, a clouding and flaming of the senses, no longer new to her.

Yes, if Ted had asked her — because she was aware of the danger. But he did not ask her. And this was due to Joan Lindstrom to whom he also went for advice.

"I love her. I've asked her to marry me about a hundred times. Sometimes," Ted told his hostess, "she seems to care — a little. Other days, well I'm less than the dust, that's all."

"I don't," said Joan, "usually give advice. Still — go slow, Ted. She's just at that restless, uncertain sort of stage. I think that girls in business — well, that's neither here nor there — women are kittle-cattle. Don't try and rush your little Anne into a decision."

So he withheld his hand; he did not speak but tried to content himself with being a good playmate, and Anne returned home as dissatisfied as ever.

There was only one thing to which she could definitely look forward; with pleasure, with even excitement, with, as the days went on, a sharp and desperate longing; and that was her return to the office. To the man in the office.

Chapter 6

Revelations at Hot Springs

When ten days of Anne's vacation had passed Fellowes telephoned her from Southampton. When her answering voice reached him over the thin tension of the wires the sudden relief and pleasure that flooded him was distinctly at variance with his apologetic tone.

"I'm so ashamed," he said, "to ask you to cut your vacation short, but I've been ordered to Hot Springs by my doctor. Could you possibly come along with Mrs. Fellowes and me? We leave day after tomorrow. I have work that must be done and the medical despot permits me to do it — provided I'm away from the office."

"I'll go, of course, Mr. Fellowes," she answered instantly.

"That's fine!" The deep vibrant voice, relieved and friendly, and grateful, reached her, as intimate as a hand clasp. "That's fine," he repeated.

He went on to make the arrangements and when Anne turned from the receiver she was flushed, and her eyes were bright with the fever of excitement. She went to look for her mother, running almost, her cheeks hot and her hands cold.

"Mr. Fellowes has been sick," she reported to Molly, "he's been ordered South. I'm going with him!"

"And that you are not!" exclaimed Mrs. Murdock, scandalized. "A young girl traipsing all over the land with a married man! Whatever's come over you, Anne Murdock?"

"Oh, Mother —" Anne laughed, and it was the first time for ten days that her mother had heard that light-hearted sound, "Mrs. Fellowes is going too, of course."

Molly had the grace to be slightly ashamed. "That's different," she admitted.

Hot Springs meant clothes. A girl couldn't go in rags. Anne went to town within half an hour and withdrew some of her savings. Luckily she was a stock size and it wasn't hard to find sports things and a dinner frock or two. Her mother had been considerably agitated over what the well dressed woman wore in the south in September.

"Don't worry," Anne told her. "Nowadays what with magazines and helpful authors even the humble secretary may dress decently, no matter where she's sent."

To herself she added: "I'll look well if it breaks me!"

The trip down was pleasant. She and Fellowes — their meeting had been in the press of a railroad station, yet they might have been alone, somehow, for the definite excitement which possessed them both — worked together in a compartment, and Linda yawned over the novel she pretended to read in the adjoining cubicle, and wondered if Dick Jameson would be at Hot Springs as he had said — and hoped he would — and feared it.

"I certainly am a brute dragging you away," Fellowes told Anne, smiling at her over the set-up card table. "There's nothing wrong with me, really — headaches, a touch of neuritis — my doctor was visiting us, so I couldn't stall advice. He felt that if I went off for a couple of weeks and took the cure I'd be all right for winter. We've a busy season ahead," he advised, thoughtfully.

"I — I was thrilled to come," Anne told him, frankly, "I've never been anywhere much. It's just a longer, much nicer vacation for me, that's all."

"It won't all be work," he promised. "We'll try to give you a good time."

He thought, as her responsive smile reached him, how glad he would be to let all the work go, necessary as it was, and devote himself to that good time. She had earned it if anyone had.

Anne was, she told herself, perfectly happy. To work with The Chief in such surroundings, to be treated by Linda, not as secretary, or pseudo-guest, but as "family"; to wake mornings and see from her wide windows the green, green mountains shading to that inimitable misty blue, to breathe the peculiarly clear air and to feel, woman-like, satisfied that her gay little sweaters and short pleated skirts were "right" and that she really differed very little from the dozens of pretty, smart women — that, thought Anne, was happiness — or very near it, near enough for confusion.

Jameson arrived in a day or two. And things settled to a routine. He and Linda played golf in the morning while Fellowes worked with Anne in the living room of the suite. They all lunched together in the grill and had coffee on the terrace. In the afternoon Jameson and Linda usually rode while Fellowes took Anne driving in a comic little carriage, through winding roads with their glimpses of silver-running streams, and with great trees arching overhead.

On these drives they talked little of business. Anne grew to know Fellowes, the boy and the young man he'd been, rather well; and he, in his turn, learned something of her life beyond the office. She had a trick of describing people. "Mother? Oh, she's little and red-headed, and Irish and sweet; scolds you, chatters like a squirrel at it — then if someone else does, turns into a little tigress, all claws to defend you —" And Kathleen — "I wish you could see her. She's so awfully pretty, and so — pathetically young. She thinks she's having an awfully good time now, but I wonder, and I believe she does."

At about five they would return and Fellowes, with reluctance and laughter, would march Jameson off for their not very arduous cures. Linda was not taking the cure that season and she would usually walk with Anne or sit and talk to her lazily, or they would go to their rooms to rest. Then came dinner and the motion pictures in the Japanese room, and afterwards, dancing. Jameson danced very well and he and Linda were a graceful, striking looking couple. He danced with Anne too and Fellowes, who swore he despised dancing, would stand in the doorway and watch, until the night he announced that, after all, it was only walking to music and took Anne in his arms and made the circuit of the floor with her.

She grew breathless at the proximity, the unexpected awareness sense of being close to him in the permitted embrace of the dance.

"Why do you say you dislike it? You dance so well?" she asked, her lashes lifting with some difficulty. Close in his arms she felt curiously drowsy, drugged — yet dangerously wide awake.

"Do I? But I'm told I don't. It must be you," he murmured, feeling her so light and warm and supple in his clasp, sensing the flow of her limbs against his own, the pressure of her little breasts, the nearness of the bright hair beneath his bent head.

Linda, when they stopped, applauded.

"Larry, you're coming on! Now, you'll have to dance with me once. You can't get off again. Have you been taking lessons or something?"

And after that he danced every night with Linda, and with Anne. And Anne thought, half panicky: "I — I oughtn't to dance with him."

She knew that she shook, she knew that her knees were weak, that her heart was light, and yet terribly burdened. She was afraid lest she stumble, lest she betray to the onlookers this encroaching disturbance. But there was no way out — every evening they danced and every evening she was shaken, pulse and body.

She tried to argue that it was absurd. She had danced with so many men, hundreds of miles, she calculated, trying to laugh at herself. And, yes, she admitted, by some she had been attracted; by others, not at all. But this emotion had the wine of violence in it.

Anne grew round and rosy and tanned. The air, the appetite she brought to her meals, the night of deep sleep, the exercise worked wonders. Fellowes told her jokingly, yet with a deeper note in his voice:

"If you keep on getting younger you'll lose your job."

"How? Why?"

"I can't have a child in my office, can I?"

Happy? Oh, she was happy, and so was Fellowes. He'd not had a real vacation for so long and this was most pleasant — just enough work to keep his mind unrusted and work under such playtime circumstances. Work, he admitted, with so delightful a companion.

For she was that. The finest playmate and co-worker a man could imagine. She brought an amazing enthusiasm to everything she did, whether it was taking a letter, following around on the links, whipping his notes into shape, walking, driving or dancing. She radiated vitality and he had never been as at home with anyone. When he thought of the inevitable ending of this playtime he was instantly rebellious and depressed.

So the two weeks lengthened into three. Linda and Jameson, riding over the beautiful paths, deep into the woods pulled their horses into a walk. Linda, hatless, her linen shirt open at the throat, struck idly at her boot with her crop.

"I've never seen it so beautiful all the time I've been down," she told her companion.

"Nor I." Jameson pulled nervously at his mustache. His big, rather handsome face was pale under the bronze. The horses walked slowly under the roofing trees. Sunlight slanted through, green and gold, and near by a bird sang.

"Linda —"

He'd come closer. Their horses brushed flanks. His hand was on her gloved hand. It had to happen. He could not longer prevent it. But — *"Linda!"* — was all he said.

She was pale now, paler than he. She whispered in confession, with pleading, "Ah, Dick — don't — please."

"All right," he told her heavily, "just as you say — but — you *know?*"

"I know." She looked full at him, the rare tears clouding the brown eyes, "I know — but — there's Larry, Dick — there's always Larry and — and — we can't hurt him, can we?"

There was a wilderness of question in her tone — as if she longed to hear Jameson say, "But we *must.*"

After a long pause he answered as she had known he would answer:

"No," he said, "no, we can't."

They rode on, neither speaking, and Jameson thought, miserably, "God, I've got to get away."

He was wretched. And yet he was triumphant. After all, she knew and she cared.

He could give her everything in her world — the out-of-doors life she loved, the close companionship with it. They could travel, they could journey with luxury or rough it for adventure's sake. They would be so happy — but there's Larry, Dick, we can't do anything to hurt Larry.

How much did Fellowes care for this lovely wife of his? How much?

So Jameson, pleading urgent telegrams from New York, left on the following day. And Linda knew the terrible, dull, let down, the rebellious ache which follows on sacrifice and virtue. Easy to commit yourself to do the right thing, easy to make up your mind — but, once deep in the doing of it, how damnably hard.

She amused herself as best she could — golfed, played bridge, rode — there were plenty of people to take Jameson's place. But none could.

Why had he gone? She would argue womanlike with herself — couldn't they keep the relationship as it was — on the brim of disaster? Couldn't they hold the delicate balance?

But she knew, being clear sighted, that they could not. Life wasn't like that. You go forward — or you cease utterly to move altogether.

She was a very unhappy woman.

Anne had not been unobservant. She had watched quietly, without permitting herself much speculation, the frank intimacy between her employer's wife and Richard Jameson. And it had angered her loyalty to Fellowes but it had excited her. It was a weapon in her hands.

She was up in arms for her Chief, her loyalty was as much his in this situation as in any other.

What on earth could Linda see in this man? Linda, who was married to Lawrence Fellowes?

True, Jameson was attractive in his big way, rather witty, and a friendly person. True, he had a great deal of money which he spent well and lazily. But he was not a worker. He was simply a pleasant, idle man of large means. He had, thought Anne, scornfully, and thereby wronged him, no depth, no real force of intellect. All he thought of was horses and golf and games. Besides, he was old.

He was, as a matter of fact, only forty-five, and did not look that. But in comparison with Fellowes, from Anne's standpoint, he was ancient.

Nor was he as good looking as Fellowes, as brilliant, and to her reasoning he was nobody — a man who'd set no mark upon the world. She said something of the sort to Fellowes himself.

"You've got Dick all wrong," Fellowes contradicted her. "He was originally a very clever engineer. He inherited a whale of a lot of money when he was thirty, and gave up his profession. A pity. But he turned his hand to inventing and has been very successful at it. He has invented two gadgets that have been adopted by the railroads and which bring him royalties he doesn't need. I understand he's established a research laboratory lately, turns his royalties into it, and keeps a number of clever young men busy."

"But he doesn't really work."

"No, not in the every day sense."

He thought, later, how different Anne's attitude was from Linda's. For Linda, when Fellowes had come into his uncle's money, had urged him to retire.

"We've enough now to live well, and you'd retain your interest in the agency," she had said. "But what's the use of slaving your life away for a little more income? It's not worth it. We could have a marvellous time, live abroad part of the year, take a place in England, perhaps, for the hunting. The only time to enjoy life is while you're young and most people don't have the opportunity. We have, Larry, why need you wait till you're too old to enjoy things before you give up work?"

"It isn't the money," he told her, "I swear it, Linda. It's the work itself, the building. I can't give it up. I'd go mad with nothing to do."

Five years ago. Lately she'd made no complaint, had not mentioned the issue again. She had adjusted herself to it, he supposed. Yet, he supposed further, she couldn't understand his entire lack of sympathy with her proposition. Perhaps a woman had to be in business to like being in business, before she could, he thought; and that brought Anne back to his mind again. She was never very far from it.

The day before they left, at tea in the Casino, Fellowes and Linda fell into one of those half serious, half joking arguments so common among married people. It was almost the first time, Anne realized, as she sat there listening, that she had heard anything approaching intimacy between them. It was thus forced upon her as never before that these two were — *man and wife.*

She lowered her eyes and set down her cup, very carefully. Her throat ached suddenly, she was terribly aware of embarrassment, and of something else, something hot and painful and angrily insistent.

Fellowes and Linda had connecting rooms, and from Fellowes' the living room opened. Anne's room and bath were off Linda's. That night, after Anne had gone to bed, while she was drowsily plumping up her pillows, she heard a door open, heard plainly Fellowes come into his wife's room, and the low sound of their voices.

Her mind turned blank, her heart shook within her. She pulled at the blankets childishly, huddled down into them, crammed even her fingers in her ears. But long afterward when the room next door was very quiet, when only the night spoke with a thousand small voices, it seemed to her feverish imagination that she could still hear that muted incessant murmuring — the deep note that was Fellowes speaking, the lighter, mingled tone that was — his — wife's.

She had to face it then. She was compelled to face it because of the jealousy which tore and wracked her. She admitted finally, and for all time, that the thing she had known so many months, which she had labelled purely physical attraction and which she had actually planned to use, by degrees, to safeguard her business future, was something much deeper, was something irrevocable, something which had the power to destroy her. It was made intolerably plain to her by the sudden, searing, inexpressible agony. She knew that she loved Lawrence Fellowes with all her heart and soul, and quivering body, knew that she loved him so much that, barefoot and hungry and thirsty, she would follow him to the world's end and back; so much that she would go desperately unhappy all her life without him; so much that she would be willing to lie under his feet if, in some undreamed of future, he would lift her to his embrace, hold her against his heart.

All that night she lay awake arguing, thinking, feeling, fearing and crying frantically into the muffling of the pillows, wishing she were dead, wishing she might die before dawn.

The return journey was a nightmare to her. In retrospect, thinking of the trip down, of the happiness and excitement which had been her secret travelling companions, it seemed to her that a leaden century had passed, and that a different human being sat for long hours at a stretch, looking blindly from the windows, listening to the wheels beat out their inescapable, miserable refrain, love — *him* — love — *him* — love — *him* —

"Well, what of it?" she found spirit enough to ask herself. And her chin went up in the small militant gesture, peculiarly her own. The dark blue of her eyes deepened to night-black — the black of moonless and storm-threatened skies. "Anyone who knew him as I do would have to love him," she told herself.

But there was small consolation in that. And as soon as she was home again she had to go through the concealed torture of exhibiting a cheerful face, of talking about the trip, of watching Molly's eyes grow round at her description of the big rambling hotel — "clean as a pin, Mother — someone always scrubbing, polishing brass, mopping —" And — "just think, the golf links, right at the door — all so much prettier than the postals I sent!"

Her father tuned in here. He had recently purchased three clubs and some repainted balls, and was to be traced to the public course almost any Saturday or Sunday, or on late long summer afternoons. He demanded a complete plan of the links. And then:

"Did they treat you well?" he wished to know.

"Of course!" She was a little indignant. . . . "They were wonderful to me — as if —

as if I *belonged.*"

Murdock shook his dark graying head.

"I didn't mean, nor want that," he said. "That's not sensible — to make friends out of your class. They employ you. You give them your services for a wage. Stick to your right. But keep it at that," he warned.

"Well," flared Molly, "as if the child wasn't good enough to walk out with the Prince of Wales himself! Not that I think too highly of the English gentry," she added, hastily recalling her traditional prejudices.

Anne managed to laugh. But she wanted to get away, to lock herself in her little room, to think things out.

"I must resign," she told herself repeatedly, as her predecessor before her had done. "I should —"

But she couldn't. The job — and above the job, the man — these were the very breath of her existence, her whole intimate life.

"I musn't let it hurt me," she warned herself. "Not — too much. It musn't spoil everything. It's too big and real."

For there was pride in loving him now that the first shock of full revelation had blunted a little. For no woman had ever loved a man so entirely lovable. Except Linda. Linda was his wife. Ergo, Linda must have loved him — once. But not now, thought Anne. She couldn't — so cool with him — taking him so for granted — and besides — there was Jameson.

She returned to the office, schooling herself to meet his needs, and to encounter his friendliness — a friendliness now warmed and colored by the remembrance of their three weeks of close companionship in such different, relaxing surroundings.

It wouldn't have been so hard had not her senses betrayed her by a leaping of the pulses, by a shaken knowledge of all his purely physical presence meant to her.

During the weeks which followed, she became clear with herself. She had known for a very long time that Fellowes attracted her; she had thought that she attracted him in return. And because she was ambitious, because she had believed in the modern — yet not so modern — code of living your own life, taking the dangers and the perils and the consequences in your stride she had planned — actually planned — to use this mutual attraction, to foster it, and by its means perhaps, in some dim but not far distant future, to gain over Fellowes the one infallible hold — a hold which may not be enduring but which, nevertheless, serves its purpose. She had thought it would be easy because, attracted as she was, she would have no more shrinking than she would have scruples. She had imagined that Linda did not care passionately for her husband, nor Fellowes for Linda. That speculation had increased to certainty when she had seen Jameson and Linda together. She had argued that she would be harming no one but herself if she entrenched herself firmly, made herself necessary to Fellowes' emotions as well as to his business. She had thought that she could manage him, rather cleverly — the old, rare, Napoleonic combination of the cool mind in the warm flesh —

But it was all changed now. She loved him, she had been compelled to admit it to herself. It had taken the basest and strongest force in the emotions — physical jealousy — to reveal that love to her. And loving him, she knew she could no longer play the game, for there was no longer any game to play.

She told herself, quite honestly, that she had vaguely fancied that if he came to care for her, in the devastating way of men, if she played her cards rightly, it might be possible that, giving a little and withholding a great deal, she could tempt him to the solution of disrupting his marriage — for her.

But that was all over now. She loved him. And she loved him too much. She knew now that she couldn't hold out against him — for marriage. She knew that, if she wouldn't be harming herself by accepting the unlegalized position, she would be harming him, exposing him to rumor, to gossip, and hurting him through his business, through his friends. She could imagine the raw, scornful comments . . . "another Big Business Man gone goofy over his steno — !" "Hear Fellowes is having an affair with that pretty little what's-her-name in his office — what a damned fool he is —!"

She shuddered. She had heard such comments often enough.

She wondered frantically if she should seek another situation. She realized that she was in much the same position as Janet Andrews had been — Janet whom she had regarded with both pity and contempt, Janet who had loved Fellowes, with all the passion of frustration.

Well, Anne thought, dully, she'd been a fool — more of a fool than poor Andrews. Probably she'd been in love, really in love, with the man all along and in concealing it from herself, concealing everything but her purely bodily desire for him, she had built up this little fiction, this legend of wanting him to become aware of her, wanting him to care for her in order to further her own ambitions. Now that the legend was thin air, now that she knew the truth, she knew also that not only could she not harm him in any sense, but she would not be content with what she had formerly desired he should give her. She would agonize, she would suffer, she would be devastated by anything less than love itself, body and mind and spirit. The game remained only a game as long as two played at it. When one of the players was in earnest, when one of the players staked everything that mattered upon the turn of a card, it was no longer a game.

She could not set herself to win the easy, light response from Fellowes upon which she had counted. She must have everything or nothing. And as it was out of the question that she would have everything, she must take nothing in its stead.

She therefore set herself the task of undoing all the subtle, scarcely perceptible damage she had already done.

She was very cool with Mr. Fellowes. She was most remote. What it cost her, who shook at his nearness, God alone knew. And Fellowes at first wondered, then speculated, then grew angry. What had he done, he marvelled, to change a warm, glowing, ardent personality into something composed of tinted ice and flexible steel? Their hands no longer met in fleeting contact. When she stood at his desk she stood as far away from him as possible, a withdrawal not alone of body but, he dimly felt, of spirit. He was no longer able to catch her gaze and hold it and watch it deepen. No longer able with a carefully careless, calculated word to make her flush, instantly, entrancingly.

He went over their entire association in his mind. He lived again their comradely, happy weeks at Hot Springs; he thought of her in his arms there on the dance floor, so light, so yielding, so perilously, marvellously close. But it was a very different young woman who now took his dictation serenely and coolly, and who never addressed a word more than was necessary to him.

The alteration in her and his subsequent anger and astonishment brought about an inevitable tension, and then a snapping of control. They might have gone on indefinitely — or at least for some time — in that other anomalous situation, waiting for the spark that would set the waiting tinder aflame. But after weeks of slow, almost imperceptible, approach on her part, this withdrawal accomplished for her what she would have hailed with unastonished satisfaction not so very long ago.

"Look here," he demanded one evening, when they had been working late and were about to leave the office to have some dinner before going, each, his respective way, "what's the matter with you lately, Anne?"

Her heart missed a beat. It was the first time he had ever called her Anne. She controlled her voice and asked in return:

"What do you mean?"

"You know what I mean as well as I do — Have you taken a dislike to me, or something?" he asked her, half laughing.

"Of course not —"

She walked toward the door of his office. But he reached out a long arm and caught her by the slender shoulder. And as he did so, feeling the close satin texture of her skin under the thin frock, desire flared up in him, desire and anger, the deadly combination.

She tried to pull away, but he held her firmly and turned her until, still holding her, he had her face to face with him. But he was forced to bend his head to look into her eyes.

"I thought we were such good friends," he reproached her.

"Of course we are — please let me go, Mr. Fellowes —"

"Why do you — ?" But he never finished the question. He looked at the red mouth, quivering a little, there beneath his own. He drew nearer and kissed it, realizing as he did so what a fool he was — how much in jeopardy, how failing all his resolutions, how betraying all his beliefs — but he kissed her nevertheless, carelessly, lightly, and then again with a scarcely controlled savagery.

Anne wrenched herself back. She had thought she would die under that terrible pressure of his mouth upon her own. She had wanted it so, and so it had come to her, as once she had planned it would, with desire, with lightness, with carelessness, with passion. And she hated it and loved it and wished she might die where she stood. Once it would have been enough for her, sufficient to ease — and intensify — her body's ache, and sufficient to create in him a longing for repetition — and with every repetition she would have woven a cord to bind him. But now she loved him and it was not enough. It was worse than nothing. It was dreadful and degrading, because she loved it. It was unendurable because it was so sweet and so empty.

She stared at him, the back of her hand caught against her mouth. She said, muffled — "you — *you* —" and the slow tears rose to her eyes and fell.

He looked at her, fascinated by the spectacle of the slow dropping tears, and the small, abased figure and the convulsed face that tried so hard to steady itself.

"I'm sorry," said Fellowes in a shaken voice, a tone very unlike anything she had ever heard from him before. "It was unpardonable of me. I'm sorry," he said again, almost stupidly, so wretched was he at the sight of her tears and the silence. "I — I was angry, I guess. We'd been such darned good friends; you've meant so much to me, and it seemed lately that you — Oh, I don't know — shrank from me, disliked me or something. Can you ever forgive me? Can't we go on as we did before and forget my idiocy?"

Now was her opportunity. One of two things she could do. She could throw herself into his arms and cry out to him that she loved him and she wanted him and was his to do with as he pleased, for as long as he pleased! Or she could tell him, quite steadily, that everything was now altered between them, and she would send in an immediate resignation.

She did neither.

For his own sake as well as for the sake of her love she could not surrender to her love and to him. Neither could she leave him. So she said, very low:

"All right —"

"That's — wonderful of you —"

He held out his hand eagerly, smiling like a boy caught in mischief and yet forgiven. "Please —" he begged, "to show that you have pardoned me?"

She put her hand in his, with what reluctance only she knew, but which, disappointed, he felt, and then said, slowly:

"Please never mention it again — and, if you don't mind," said Anne, "I'll go home now."

"But —" he was crestfallen — "but we were to have dinner?" he said.

"No, not tonight —"

And before he could answer, before he could urge her to keep to their original plan as a further proof of her forgiveness, she had managed a smile and had slipped away to her own office to get her things. He heard her go presently, and made no move to detain her. He stood where she had left him, frowning, ill at ease, angrier with himself than he had ever been with her. What a fool he had been — what a stupid, tawdry thing to have done because his sex pride had been wounded. He'd acted like the sort of man he'd always condemned. Taken advantage of their respective positions, taken advantage of an intimate evening alone together in a quiet room — to — to make love to his secretary. Well, not make love, exactly. But to express upon unwilling lips his anger and his sudden desire and his male urge for supremacy. To imperil himself like that, to risk losing the best secretary a man ever had!

"Damn it to hell!" said Fellowes.

But he was disturbed to realize that all that evening, after his solitary dinner, the memory of the soft, warm lips beneath his own persisted, the memory of the pliant body in his arms. He swore his way through a tasteless meal and went to his club to find a poker game in progress. He played idiotically, he lost a hundred and eighty-seven dollars; he drank himself into a bad head and a general wretchedness, and went home in the early hours of morning — still remembering.

Oh, he'd known for months how much she attracted him, but as long as he kept way from her it hadn't been dangerous. But now —

He liked her too much to hurt her. Yet it had been a good many years since he had been so stirred, so plainly disturbed.

Their meeting on the following morning was formal in the extreme. If she hadn't been so upset — if she hadn't spent so hideous a night — if he hadn't been so aware of his danger now, if he hadn't had three times as many Scotch and sodas as he'd wanted — both Anne and Fellowes might have seen the humorous side of their careful greeting, their cautious attitude all through that next everlasting day. But they were beyond humor now.

After that it was easier for Anne to keep

to her resolutions, for Fellowes, unconscious of them as he was, was ready to help her. Instead of one person being on her guard and the other speculating about it, two were on guard now.

And then something happened that pushed Lawrence Fellowes temporarily into the background of Anne's thoughts, for when she reached home one evening, her mother met her and drew her aside with a troubled expression.

"I'm worried about Kathleen," said Mrs. Murdock.

"Why?" Anne threw off her hat and regarded her mother a little wearily.

"Nothing and everything. She'd not been out for over a week. And so I ran into town today. Jim had asked me to go and see Sara — Sara's miserable," explained Mrs. Murdock. "And so I went down to the flat. That Lola was there. I don't like her — she's good for nothing. She shouldn't be influencing Kathleen. She was nice enough," said Mrs. Murdock, grudgingly, "but while I was there someone rang up on the phone — someone named Dolly — and they had a talk. I couldn't get much from it, but it was about Kathleen they were talking — and some fellow, someone named Georgie. I wish you'd find out what it's all about — I don't like it, at all," said Mrs. Murdock.

"Oh, it's probably nothing," said Anne easily. "What difference does it make? Kathleen's bound to meet men, Mother."

"Don't I know that? But what *kind* of men?" asked Mrs. Murdock, dramatically. "I heard that Lola say, 'Well, I can't tell her to stay away from him, can I? If he's your property, why don't you manage it?' she asked. I didn't like the sound of that. Perhaps it's a *married* man!" offered Mrs. Murdock, in a sepulchral whisper.

Anne thought a moment. Then she said, evenly:

"I'm going to the theatre with Betty tomorrow evening. I'll spend the night at Kathleen's. I've a key, you know. Don't worry, Mother, Kathleen can take care of herself."

She patted the little woman on the back and went up to her own room. Could Kathleen take care of herself? Could any woman — in love? She, Anne, had once thought herself so much wiser and cooler and more self-contained than her younger sister. But she thought so no longer.

After she and Betty had sat through a current success which Anne hardly heard or saw, so preoccupied she was, Anne went on to the flat, and was there alone in the gaudy little apartment until the first of the stragglers, Lola, came in. Although the two had nothing in common, they were on good terms. Anne had seen to that.

"Well, if it isn't Anne!"

"In person. That's a pretty frock, Lola."

"Like it? Want it?" asked Lola, always generous when on the crest. "Take it if you do — too tight for me, anyway."

"Thanks a lot — it's not my color. Too much red in my hair. Home early, aren't you? Kathleen's out; she gave me a key."

"I'm dead," said Lola, flopping on a couch and lighting a cigarette. "I haven't been in before three for weeks. You don't honor us often, Anne. Why not?"

"Busy. And tired at night. I saw 'Hurry Up' tonight. Good music. And as good a chorus as 'The Sky Girl.' That's a pretty girl, by the way, over there in the leather frame. New isn't it?"

"Doll? She's forty if she's a day," said Lola carelessly. "But she photographs like seventeen — she even gets movie jobs!"

"What does she do?" asked Anne. She had looked at the picture before Lola came in, idly enough and then attentively when she saw the name written across it in violet ink — "To Lola with Dolly's love."

"How do you mean, what does she do? She's

199

out of the chorus nowadays, but she walks on in good-looking, giddy Mama parts in the musical shows. She's playing now in 'Her Husband's Wife,' at the Gaiety."

Anne said, with apparent indifference:

"It sounds good. I must see it — and she looks attractive."

"She's a fool," commented Lola, without malice.

"Why?" Anne wanted to know.

"Oh, you're too young!"

Anne expostulated indignantly, and Lola went on, one handsome arm behind her head and the other lax hand flicking ashes on the floor. "It's just one of those things. She's got a twenty-five-year-old sweetie in tow — and he keeps her broke most of the time."

Anne's face was expressionless at the information and she asked, with studied naïveté:

"Are they engaged?"

"Child, don't make me laugh!"

"Is he an actor?" persisted Anne.

"No visible means of support except the races," Lola answered. "By the way, he's met Kathleen a couple of times, and is quite keen about her. Doll's ready to scratch her eyes out."

Anne thought, in despair, "Then Molly was right!" and she remembered her father's warning: "If any harm comes of this —"

Aloud she said, idly:

"Is that so? I'd like to meet him."

"Well, you could give Kathleen a run for her money," commented Lola, eyeing her critically. "There's a Sunday night party up at Doll's. Why not come along — you can stay here over night?"

And that was that. When Kathleen came home much later she found her sister asleep on the couch, her hands beneath her cheek, and guileless expression on her dreaming features.

Sunday night Anne went to the party at Dolly Davis'. It was quite incredible and very different from any party she had yet attended. There was considerable drunkenness, and a good deal of loose conversation, and a great many cigarette butts, and wet rings on end tables, and much noise and laughter.

Kathleen remarked, as they were starting out:

"Why on earth *you* want to come — ?"

"Curiosity. And just bored."

"Oh, very well. . . . But if you fall down and go boom, don't say I didn't warn you. It's apt to be lively."

Anne made herself agreeable to the hostess. Dolly Davis was a cosmetic beauty, looking amazingly young. She still had her fair hair and her Southern accent, and she was characterized among her close friends as a good-hearted, damn' fool. The twenty-five-year-old "sweetie" was much in evidence, playing the host — a narrow chested, rather handsome boy, with sleek dark hair and lines under his eyes, and a vicious, over-red mouth. His name, Anne discovered, was Georgie.

During a rather rabid encounter between Georgie and Dolly over, it appeared, the matter of too many dances with Kathleen, Anne was able to interfere satisfactorily.

"I like you," remarked Dolly, with maudlin affection. "I like you a *lot*. You're worth a thousand of that high-hat, hell-cat sister of yours. I like you, Anne, I want to do something for you. Have lunch with me — tomorrow — next day — every day. Come up to the flat and have tea. You're a good kid, and I *like* you," she repeated, inanely.

Anne said, quietly:

"I'll come — tomorrow."

The relationship between Dolly and her sleek-haired Georgie was perfectly obvious to Anne. But was it to Kathleen? Anne knew that opposition was fatal to a young person of Kathleen's nature. She knew, too, how futile it would be to try and force an admission from Kathleen as to her apparent interest in Dolly's "property," or to plead with her to see the inevitable error of her ways. There was only one thing to do, Anne thought, and that was to become intimate enough with Dolly herself to get the story first hand from her. And, once having obtained it, to go to Kathleen with it. Then, doubtless, Dolly would be an invaluable ally, disliking Kathleen as she did, afraid of her as she was. She asked Fellowes, for the first time in their association, if she might get away a little early from work. He consented, regarding her curiously. A few weeks ago he would have asked her why. A few weeks ago she would have told him. But not now. And when she had gone he observed the empty office with dissatisfaction and displeasure.

So Anne went to Dolly's for tea, several times, and found her ready for confidences, for the easy, terribly intimate confidences of the woman of her type. She talked, almost exclusively, of "Georgie," and told Anne that it was hard for a sensitive boy like him to get ahead in an unkind world.

"He's been unlucky with the horses," she said.

"Doesn't he work?" Anne wanted to know.

"Well, he's a swell hoofer," Dolly said proudly, "and used to dance in a night club, but his heart isn't strong. He can't stand the gaff."

Anne thought silently that if Georgie's

mother had drowned him at birth the world would have been a brighter and cleaner place.

But all her careful cultivation of Miss Dolly did not result in any plain statement of fact. Dolly liked Anne in her careless, warm-hearted fashion. But Anne was Kathleen's sister, and Dolly knew how to be wary. She would wait until she knew Anne's game before she gave herself away with naked entirety. That last afternoon, however, she delivered a warning.

The flat in which she resided was smothered in the lace and taffeta and satin of pillows; and there were heavy, dusty Oriental rugs on the floor, and rose-shaded lamps scattered all over, and dozens of long-legged, perverse looking dolls with bright red curls and metal cigarettes stuck in their painted mouths. There was overstuffed furniture and there were many heavily scented flowers crowded into garish, "modern" vases; and the whole place was permeated with a strong odor of French perfume, Scotch whiskey, and stale cigarette smoke.

Dolly was carefully coiffured, manicured and enameled, but her elaborate negligee was frankly dirty and her hands none to clean at the knuckles. And, while Anne drank weak tea and refused highballs, Dolly made a sudden demand for coöperation.

"You tell that sister of yours to keep away from Georgie!" she ordered, viciously.

Anne made wide eyes and her face retained its serenity.

"I didn't know she knew him — that is, well —"

"What you don't know would fill books," said Dolly. "Now I'm not insinuating anything, you see, but just tell her to keep away — that's all."

"Are you engaged?" Anne asked, so naïvely that she overdid it, and Dolly looked at her with sudden suspicion. But naïveté was a game two could play at.

"Well," drawled Dolly, "it isn't announced yet, of course —"

This encounter left Anne no better off than before. She knew Kathleen well enough to realize that an "unannounced engagement" would never stand in her way if she were really infatuated with Dolly's young man. In the *milieu* in which Kathleen had settled herself, property rights were very lightly regarded. But she had enough faith in the younger girl's basic decency to believe that if ever Kathleen could be brought proof of Dolly's actual relation to that same young man, she would sicken and run away. But so far her efforts to establish that proof had been wasted.

She determined not to lose sight of Dolly,

and because of that determination she joined, one night a little later, a party at a night club. Dolly was the titular hostess, although a certain breezy gentleman from the great open spaces paid, under protest, the bill. "My God, it's the war debt!" he was heard to exclaim when it was handed to him. The entire tone of the party was tuned to the "Hello, sucker," motif, but Anne found it rather amusing. She welcomed in those days anything that helped to numb her acute and constant realization of Lawrence Fellowes. The work in his office was becoming a nightmare to her. She couldn't stay — and she couldn't leave. And she was growing haggard with it and with staying out late at night so that she might be able to get home and sleep heavily and dreamlessly, worn with fatigue.

There were a dozen others in the noisy party, and Kathleen had, quite pointedly, not been included in Dolly's invitation. The fact that Georgie did not appear either was significant to several at the table, and Dolly grew morosely drunk as the night went on. Anne, dancing with the Westerner, became suddenly aware that a man, standing in the low doorway, was watching her intently. She looked up and into her employer's eyes.

A moment later he cut in.

"I didn't know you went in for this sort

of thing," he said, and held her closely, as, mechanically, she followed the mazes of the music about the small crowded room.

"I don't — often."

"I'm alone," he said, "my party hasn't shown up yet. May I come to your table?"

He did so and was presented to Lola and Dolly and the rest. He stayed with them for perhaps half an hour, until several uproarious gentlemen arrived and claimed him, after which pretty girls were produced from nowhere in particular and the two parties merged.

Anne offered no explanation of her presence. Why should she? It was hardly possible to inform Mr. Fellowes that in order to keep a watchful eye upon Kathleen — who wasn't even present — she had cultivated Dolly and her little playmates! Besides, she told herself defiantly, she had been having a good time until he came in.

As for Fellowes, when Anne decided it was time to go home, he excused himself from his friends and took her the short distance to Kathleen's flat.

"Sorry not to have met your sister," he said, sitting in the far corner of the car.

"We expected her," Anne said, sleepily.

She was wishing she hadn't gone on the party. She was wishing Fellowes hadn't chosen that particular night club for his own evening's entertainment. She was wishing she wasn't shut up with him in the dark intimacy of the automobile —

And Fellowes, driving home alone thereafter, found himself wondering why he hadn't taken her in his arms and kissed her — again.

After all, he knew very little about her, outside of his office. After all, the crowd she ran with was pretty swift. He knew Dolly Davis by reputation; and Dolly, while playing the Westerner skillfully enough, had intimated that he, Fellowes, might call if he cared to.

His senses were a little unsteady, not entirely from the usual concomitants of the evening. When he'd taken her in his arms it was with the sense that she belonged there. Could he ignore any longer, he asked himself, the urgent turning of his whole being toward her?

"Oh, hell," he thought, gloomily, "it doesn't mean anything serious, it can't, it's just the unexpectedness of finding her there, just the drinks and the music and everything —"

But when he entered the office the next morning and found her sitting there, small and supple and quiet, he had not forgotten. He remembered only too well. And he admitted to himself, with a sick feeling of uncertainty in the future and danger in the present, "I'm crazy about her."

Dictating, talking to her, watching her move about the office, he told himself again and again, "I'm crazy about her," and then asked himself the inevitable and unanswerable question:

"What am I going to do?"

Chapter 7

Dolly Speaks Her Mind

This was the realization that Fellowes took home with him that evening, with which he must face Linda, which would accompany him through the dinner table conversation, sit at his elbow, a companion unseen by Linda, but one of whom Fellowes would be perfectly aware. This was the realization, that he had fallen in love with his secretary, that she had become necessary to him as a woman, that his blood ran hot at the dream of her, that he wanted her — *wanted* her — and could not have her. Or — could he?

It had been so long since this surge and sweep of emotion had caught him — even in his boyish love for Linda there had not been this mature necessity — that he was bewildered and staggered and was entirely incapable of searching the situation back to its inception. He tried, after a miserable evening and a sleepless night, to tell himself that it would pass, that it was a temporary, if strong, attraction, based upon propinquity, upon Anne's own charm and appeal, and brought to an ephemeral flowering by their close companionship at Hot Springs, by the moment in which, recklessly, he had her in his arms. It could not last — for her sake, for Linda's and for his own. The situation would become intolerable. It was something that he must stamp out, root and branch — something that Anne must never guess, even dimly. He must go on as if this devastating thing had never happened. Any other solution was — impossible.

He tried to keep himself from speculating upon the probable nature of her regard for him but to do so was humanly impossible. He was forced to the lover's inevitable wonder: Does she care? Can she care? If so, how much? And, if she cared, if he knew that definitely, in how far would it change his attitude?

Had it been anybody but Anne — a woman working under his business protection, a woman he saw every day, in the now artificial environment of his office — had it been someone whom he had met outside, he wondered if his deliberated attitude would hold. Might he not, then, under such different circumstances, try to find out if she cared for him and, if she did, forget Linda, forget the world, take upon himself the secret responsibility for a woman's happiness? And, if he did so and found that the attraction held, was as strong throughout as it now was, would he not do the honest thing — and ask Linda to divorce him?

But Linda was innocent, Linda had been, still was his loyal wife. Could he endure to sacrifice her because he'd fallen in love with another woman?

The age old problem ate at him — to sacrifice himself and another, for Linda's sake? or take happiness for himself and that other at Linda's expense?

But Anne was — Anne. Aside from the fact that she was his secretary — he'd always been somewhat contemptuous of men who went blindly into affairs with their employees — she was Anne, herself, not the sort of woman to whom one offered an illegal connection, not the sort of woman to accept that offer. Yet, if she cared for him — ? And she was a sophisticated young woman, not a child.

But no, the thought was impossible. He pushed it into the background of his mind that was now like a squirrel cage. All the arguments, all the speculations, all the wondering and wretchedness went on, round and round, unceasingly. He contradicted himself a thousand times, he set himself a hundred problems — as every man in the same situation before him has done.

And reached no other conclusion save the

first, which was that he must never let her know, never burden her slender shoulders with the knowledge, never try to find out if she regarded him other than a friend, an employer — never try to win her to another regard — for what would that avail them?

It couldn't last, he told himself stubbornly.

He dreaded seeing her again, and longed for it, intolerably.

In the office his attitude toward her was schooled enough. But the memory of their embrace remained, and so the atmosphere had changed. That, he could not prevent. He became markedly formal toward her, more so than he had ever been. Yet an undercurrent remained. Each knew it.

The good resolutions remained, but seeing her every day, aware, and so deeply, of her physical presence, he was able eventually to delude himself with a masculine disregard for danger. As long as he didn't speak, as long as he gave no further sign, he harmed no one, and he would have the oblique happiness of seeing her, knowing her near him. Otherwise he'd have to let her go, and for that sacrifice he had neither strength nor heart.

In the late autumn of that year came Indian summer. Anne took this precious warmth into her blood, and the cool, wine-heady wind into her veins. She worked, and played — wholeheartedly — and loved, and was happy as never before in her life. For, once having faced her love and admitted the impossibility of its fulfillment, she adjusted herself to living in the moment, much as men do, but as women rarely can.

Occasionally she went to Kathleen's. She continued her casual acquaintance with Dolly Davis, biding her time. Dolly and the sloe-eyed Georgie rarely came to Kathleen's, because of the older woman's violent jealousy; but when, now and then, Anne met her somewhere or other, she was as brimmed with intimacies as ever, as confident that some day Georgie would marry her.

"He's all for this companionate marriage stuff," she told Anne one night quite seriously. "But I say what's the use of going into a thing and saying beforehand it won't be successful? I was married once. Did I tell you, darling? He was a trick bicycle rider on the Big Time Circuit — but he had more wheels in his head than on his machine. I was going to divorce him, but what with one thing and another I forgot it, and he killed himself a couple of years ago doing a brand new stunt. So I'm an honest-to-God widow. But, as I was saying to Georgie, the Lord knows marriage is a big risk nowadays, and there's no sense in admitting it when you stand up before the judge. That's bound to make it happen."

Anne controlled her features with an effort. Companionate marriage and Georgie!

Ted O'Hara was present at this particular party. It was a festal occasion — one of Lola's admirers entertaining her and sundry of her friends at a Sunday dinner at Arrowhead — and Ted was unpleasantly impressed. Anne had asked him to take her, as it seemed wiser to bring her own escort.

When they had left, earlier than the others, and were driving home by the river with the curving, lighted shore line on their right and a full moon rising:

"I wish you'd keep out of that crowd," he complained.

"It's Kathleen's —"

"What of it? It hasn't improved her."

"I'd rather you didn't criticize her, Ted."

"Well, she's pretty independent. She won't thank you for chaperonage. The way she plays up to that sickening little fool — what's his name, George something — is —"

"Please Ted!"

"Don't get miffed. It doesn't matter to me what *she* does. But I didn't like you talking so much to that Davis woman. She's obviously this cad, George's, property. I thought she'd take a lobster fork to Kathleen once during the dinner."

"I'll talk to whom I like!" announced Anne in no uncertain tones.

"But she isn't your sort; she's a million miles off; looks like a wilting cabbage rose turning mauve. She was half lit before the party started and slopped all over you as if you were the two orphans separated at birth and just reunioning."

"Ted, what I do and with whom I talk is not your affair."

"Marry me," implored Ted, suddenly, "and let me make it my affair. I tell you, Anne, I'm worried about you."

Anne chuckled. She couldn't help it.

"Of all your proposals, this one is the most ridiculous."

"I'm glad you think so. Never mind how it strikes you; it isn't being pulled before a camera. We're not Gilbert and Garbo," Ted pointed out truthfully. "The fact is — you're working too hard. Fellowes has a hell of a nerve, keeping you overtime, taking your Sundays and your evenings —"

"It's part of a job which I intend to keep," Anne told him, fighting a very spirited little temper of her own.

"Well, there's talk in the office. I'm only telling you for your own good," Ted broke out suddenly; and then cursed himself silently and heartily for sixteen different kinds of a damn fool. He hadn't meant to say anything.

Anne flung around at him, her little face whiter than the moonlight could make it.

"Talk? About me and Mr. Fellowes?" she asked incredulously, not evading the implication.

"Yes — if you will have it. *I* know there's nothing in it, but it does look funny; you're with him so much —"

Betty Howard had tried to warn her, a few days previously. But she had been tactful to the point of incoherence. Now, Anne twisted her hands in her lap and said, steadily:

"Miss Andrews held the same position, did much the same work. I never heard any gossip about her."

That, she thought, was not strictly true. A number of people had, in Anne's hearing, commented on the other woman's obvious devotion to her Chief.

"Oh, be yourself!" advised Ted. "Andrews was Andrews. You're twenty-five to her forty. And you're so pretty; you're *beautiful,* to me," he added with a rather touching sincerity. After a moment he went on:

"It makes all the difference, you see — the sort of girl you are, the sort of dried-up old maid Andrews was. Can't you see?"

"I suppose so. It's absurd, of course," Anne replied, and wondered if she was going to cry.

"I mustn't cry," she thought, frantically. Her eyes stung and her throat ached, and she dug her even white teeth into her underlip to still its quivering.

"Oh, Teddy," she turned on him, exasperated, "I don't want to be taken out of it; I want to stay. I don't want to be taken out of it; I don't want to marry anyone; I don't want to marry you."

"Then there's some truth in it, after all," muttered Ted, sullenly.

"In what?"

"That the Chief's in love with you," he accused her.

"Ted — that's idiotic! He doesn't know I exist except as his secretary. He — he has the loveliest wife — he's crazy about her," Anne answered with no real conviction; but the ache, like a bruise, rose in her throat again.

"Well, you're off your head over him, then!" commented Ted.

"*I — am — not!*" She managed to lie, defiantly.

But terror seized her, flooded her, the blood rose in a warm tide flooding her whiteness to scarlet.

"You must be. No woman," said Ted, doggedly, "gives herself like you do — spends herself, sacrifices herself for — a *job*. The only reason a woman drives herself all day and half the night — is for a *man*."

"You're a generation back," Anne told him. But the brutality of his conclusion had not escaped her. Was it true? Was it only her love for Fellowes which made her difficult work so easy for her?

"Drive quickly — and get me home. I'm tired. And if you say another word to me about this — this nonsense, I'll never come out with you again!" she threatened, childishly.

Home finally, and in bed, she tried not to think of what Ted had said — "not for a job, but for a man."

She tried to picture another man in Fellowes' place, another Chief — as big a man, as clever — like, for instance, Fellowes' close friend, the head of a rival agency, Burroughs.

To her horror and her bewilderment, she found she could no longer visualize the job without the man she loved.

She was illogically, femininely angry at Ted for having told her the truth. So she saw nothing of him for a time, but went to Jim's instead, helped Sara to entertain the friends who dropped in at all hours, and saw Kathleen, who was rehearsing for another piece.

But Kathleen was no longer as open with her as formerly; and Anne, remembering Ted's caustic comments began to worry. She saw that the younger girl's interest in Dolly

Davis' sleek-haired shadow was growing, and becoming obvious. And it alarmed her. She spoke of it to Fellowes one day when, casually, he asked about Kathleen; simply because the need was in her; she had to tell somebody.

"I'm worried about her," she told him.

"Why? The stage nowadays," said Fellowes, "is as safe a profession as any."

"I know it. That's what I argued when she made up her mind to take it up; and the family — Mother and Father — were so set against it. But she knows the wrong people."

"What kind of people?" Fellowes asked, instantly seizing on any pretext to keep her talking to him as openly and in as friendly a fashion as now. He acquitted himself of any effort to regain the old confidence. Manlike, he thought: "She started it!" And so welcomed the opportunity to drop, like a mask, the guard he had set upon himself of late.

"Oh — not the girls she lives with, really, though there's one I don't like much. But — you met Dolly Davis the other night, at the club. Do you remember her? There's a man — he wasn't there that night — he and Dolly —" Anne shrugged, left the implication open. "He's a wretched little beast, sleek as a seal." She went on, "he's been paying attention to Kathleen. I've warned her, but she laughs at me. She announced recently that she was planning to leave the chorus and dance with this creature at some night club."

"Perhaps she'll change her mind."

"I don't know, but it does bother me," said Anne, and suddenly, realizing their regained intimacy, she dropped the subject to speak of office matters. But Fellowes, his veiled hungry eyes on her exquisite troubled face, experienced a selfless pity and tenderness remote from passion. She gave so much to her job, and he had never done anything for her. Now, he wanted to, desperately. He would, he told himself. He'd allow himself to show a more personal interest. He owed it to her and to his love for her — a love which, if unacknowledged, gave him some right to help her.

Shortly afterwards, one night, very late, the telephone in Anne's home shrilled alarmingly. Murdock answered, expecting there'd been trouble at the shop. It was for Anne and he called her. Mrs. Murdock, coming to her door, demanded anxiously. "What's wrong? Is it Kathleen? — or Jim? Is it one of the babies?"

Anne slipped on a kimono and went downstairs to the instrument.

"It's Dolly," a voice reached her, far away and husky.

"What is it?"

"I must see you at once."

Anne said, patiently:

"It's very late. Is anything the matter?"

"If you care anything about that kid sister of yours," Dolly told her, "you'd better step on the gas."

"I'll come," said Anne, and hung up the receiver. She was trembling and she twisted one hand tightly within the other, and tried, walking slowly upstairs again, to rearrange her features to some sort of composure.

Mrs. Murdock was asking, in despair:

"Will she not answer me, my own daughter? What is the matter, Anne? Tell me at once!"

"It's all right," Anne told her. She thought frantically, then lied easily: "It's Betty Howard. She's been taken quite ill and is alone, so I'm going to town at once. Don't worry — I'll stay the rest of the night with her."

"Poor child," Mrs. Murdock commiserated, all sympathy and relief. She liked Betty — but, thank God, one of her own was not threatened! "But it's after midnight! Sure, and can't someone else be with her until morning? Tell Anne to stay home!" she ordered her husband.

But Murdock was in bed again and on the verge of slumber.

"When have I been able to tell any of them anything?" he wanted to know.

Anne dressed and Mrs. Murdock, fluttering competently about her, nearly drove her mad.

"Here are your shoes. Aren't you going to brush your hair? I've chicken broth in the ice-box; take a jar; tell the girl I'll come and look after her tomorrow in case she has no one."

Anne refused the broth and evaded all her mother's questions. Shortly afterwards she stepped out into the still, eerie night and shivered at the first touch of a chilly blowing wind.

It was after one o'clock when she knocked at Dolly Davis' door, and Dolly, fully dressed, a cigarette in a holder half a yard long in her hand, opened to her.

Dolly was haggard, but her eyes were over bright.

"So you're here," she said, with some hostility. "You've had time to go to St. Louis and back."

"I came immediately," Anne said. "What has happened?"

"Nothing yet. Only your precious Kathleen is planning to run away with Georgie — that's all. I found a note from her in some clothes I was sending to the cleaners," Dolly said, bitterly. Then she laughed as she saw Anne's expression. "Don't look so upset. He lives here, most of the time — and on me," she announced.

Anne sat down. She rarely smoked, but now if ever she needed something to steady her nerves. She reached out for a cigarette and lit it, her fingers shaking.

Dolly flung herself in a deep chair. Her high-heeled, snakeskin slipper beat a tattoo on the polished floor.

"If she doesn't stop, I'll scream," Anne thought.

After a moment Dolly began to talk, incoherently.

"After all I've done for him, the little rat!" she said, and proceeded for three minutes to inform Anne what she thought of Georgie, and his family before him. Anne listened, fascinated. Dolly's mouth was painted in likeness of a curved red bow, and from that bow the black curses, poison tipped, were released like little arrows.

When that was over, she said sullenly:

"I love him — I've fed and clothed him — and I despise him — and I love him so much that I'd kill myself for him tomorrow. I *will* kill myself, damn him — I'll haunt him all the days of his worthless life!"

She began to cry, with no warning, making no effort to stem the drenching tears and the hoarse, tearing sobs.

Anne rose and passed through the untidy living room into the bedroom and bathroom. She hunted in the medicine closet, stained and dusty, and found a bottle containing spirits of ammonia. She washed a glass, measured the

224

dose and returned to Dolly, who was still crying, her arms flung over the back of the chair, her face buried upon them.

"Turn around. Drink this!" Anne ordered, quietly.

How to find Kathleen? How to stop her? How to make this pitiful, hysterical woman talk — sense?

Dolly swung around, her face ravaged. She pushed the glass aside.

"Take that stuff away! Get me a drink — out of the cellarette!"

Anne removed the medicine and poured a straight dose of whisky. Dolly drank it, wiping her mouth with the back of her hand. The rouge came away in a long crimson streak. She stared at it as if it were blood.

Anne said, still with forced repression:

"Let's talk quietly. When are they going? Where? Tell me everything you've found out at once!"

"I don't know," Dolly said, sullenly. She jumped to her feet, rummaged in a desk drawer and returned with a three-cornered note which she flung in Anne's lap.

"Read that."

Anne read, eagerly yet reluctantly:

"Darling," Kathleen had written, "I know you love me. We'll go away and be happy somewhere together, and that woman will

225

never bother you again —"

Anne read no more. She dropped the note and commented:

"But she mentions no definite plan here."

"What of it? I haven't seen him all day. He didn't come this evening. I was to meet him for dinner. I waited in front of Ching Lee's for an hour, then I had to go to the theatre. I 'phoned you as soon as I got home."

Suddenly she leaned forward, her eyes and lips hard.

"You'd better take care of your sister. The little bitch," she warned, and clenched her fists with their sunken, over-reddened nails. "Take care!"

Anne was conscious of sickness — a sickness of fear. She began remembering certain sordid headlines in the tabloids. But anger took her — anger that anyone as beloved and basically sound and sweet as Kathleen should be threatened with people like Dolly, like Georgie — clean hot anger, flaming in her eyes and cheeks.

"I'll take care of her all right!" she told the older woman. "Do you think for one moment I'll let her have anything to do with that slimy beast if I can help it?"

"Keep your tongue off him!" Dolly warned her, "I'm the only one that can run him down. He never raised his hand to her. She chased him — silly little fool — making eyes and cooing and — pitying him on my account. What's she got that I haven't? Youth, perhaps and better looks," Dolly answered her own question grudgingly. "Well, if I ever get my hands on her she won't look as pretty, and she'll feel a damned sight older!"

"Don't be an idiot," Anne ordered, sharply. "Look here — have you anything to prove your — your relationship?"

"Relationship?" Dolly stared and then with her sudden changes of mood laughed heartily. "Proof? He's got a latch key, if that's proof. And here" — she rolled up her sleeve and exhibited a bruise, faintly, darkly visible under the liquid powder of the make-up she had not removed — "here's a finger print!"

"I can't take those to Kathleen," Anne told her, disgusted.

Dolly's eyes were enormous.

"Do you mean to tell me that she needs — proof? She must be more of a fool than I thought. Why doesn't she bring her rattle to rehearsals?" Dolly commented.

"I know Kathleen," said Anne. "She's young and gullible. I don't know what your precious Georgie has told her — but whatever it was it wasn't the truth. When she knows that she'll have no more to do with him."

"Look here," Dolly interrupted with ominous calm, "are you trying to tell me that Georgie isn't good enough for your sister?"

"Well, is he?"

"He's a dam' sight too good for her," Dolly exclaimed passionately. She stopped and looked at Anne. Anne was leaning back in her chair, her red golden hair against the garish upholstery. Her face was very white and her eyes, no longer disgusted or angry, were darkly pitying. Nearby a long-legged doll was flopped half on, half off a table, its purple hair all wild ends, and its white Pierrette costume stained and soiled. Dolly got out of her chair, like an old woman. She came over to Anne and knelt down beside her, her arms flung across her lap.

"Help me," she whimpered, "to get him back again. He's all I've got in the world — and I'm getting old —"

Her raddled face worked nervously. Anne touched her hair, and hated herself for the physical repulsion which accompanied the gesture. In this moment of victory over the hostility and rancour she had encountered on her entrance, she felt no triumph, only a dull sort of relief.

"You don't know what it is to lose something you care for," Dolly murmured, "nor what it is to be jealous. My God, sometimes

I think I'm half crazy! He's no good, Anne, but he's *mine*. I'm not much good, either, but I want him back. He'll forget her; he's been like this before, though never as bad —"

"Get up, Dolly," Anne told her. "I'm going to see Kathleen now. It's after two, but that doesn't matter. I'll straighten things out."

Dolly got to her feet, swaying on her ridiculous heels.

"I'll do anything," she promised. "I'll go away. I've a chance to get work in Chicago if I care for it; we're closing here. He'll go too." Dolly's face hardened. "He'll *have* to go."

Anne put on her things and started wearily for the door.

"You're a good kid," Dolly told her, following her. She stood close to the girl in the narrow hallway, and Anne was enveloped in a scent of Black Orchid, stale cigarette smoke, cosmetics and liquor — "a good kid — I'm sorry I cut up rough."

She held out her soft, hot hand.

"Good-by," she said.

Anne took the hand, held it a moment.

"Good-by and good luck," she told the older woman.

Dolly answered, gripping the firm, slender fingers:

"Say, isn't life comic? Listen, did I ever tell

you I was married once? Yeah — to a trick bicycle rider. He's dead now — and dying was the only decent thing he ever did in his life. But he uster say 'Kid,' he uster say to me, 'you take a lot funnier falls in life than you do on the boards.' And, damn him, he was right."

The door closed behind Anne. She leaned against it a moment, sick with fatigue, and from the apartment she had left she heard the shrill sound of Dolly's lonely and ironic laughter.

On her way to Kathleen's she thought of the other woman. It was impossible to condemn her, that tawdry, generous, passionate creature. Anne thought: "If things had worked out as I once planned?" She shuddered back from the mental pictures, but forced herself to follow them to their conclusion. If she had not really fallen in love with Lawrence Fellowes, if she had kept her head clear and her heart free over and beyond his physical appeal for her, if she had encouraged that one dangerous kiss to lead to other embraces, if she had surrendered herself for a little fleeting security, for a little easy satisfaction; if he had tired, if — if — *if* she had become, eventually, one of the regiment of women in which Dolly marched?

She cried out loud, and quickened her steps.

She must forget Fellowes, she must forget everything now but Kathleen and her immediate need. If she could tell Kathleen that she too knew, that she had been tempted. And she faced the realization that in loving Fellowes she was no less tempted than when she had fancied she did not deeply care for him.

It was uncanny walking through the silent, dark streets. She met no one save a solitary policeman who looked at her a little curiously as she hurried by, and then went on, walking heavily, ringing his nightstick on an iron railing. But cars slid by, some illuminated from within. She saw one couple locked in a mindless embrace in the little moving room of the limousine, the single light glaring down on them with a sardonic eye, lighting their passion and the dark dreams behind their closed lids. She saw one woman, a uniformed chauffeur steering the costly toy she rode in, sitting erect, her face a tragic mask under the paint, jewels glittering briefly on her clenched hands. She saw a girl and man lingering in a dark doorway opposite.

Presently she reached Kathleen's.

"You don't know what it is to be jealous," Dolly had told her.

Ah, did she not? She thought, climbing the stair, of that hideously revealing moment in the bedroom at Hot Springs — then shut her mind to it.

Lola let her in, yawning but wide awake.

"Holy Cat." she exclaimed. "What's up?"

"I want to talk to Kathleen. Is she asleep?"

"I guess so. I just got my clothes off," Lola indicated her pretty shameless nightgown. "What's wrong with you?"

"Nothing."

"If you've heard about Georgie," Lola advised her, "go easy. We've all tried to head her off — that kid's a mule. I hate to see her get mixed up with a rotter like that," Lola went on, and Anne saw the warning and sympathy under the patina of the years.

She went into the bedroom which Kathleen shared with one of the other girls, now out of town. Kathleen was sleeping as she had so often seen her sleep in their room at home, one arm flung up, the lovely face flushed and childlike.

She sat down on the bed and touched her gently.

"Kathleen?"

The girl turned, woke, blinked at Anne a moment incredulously, and then sat up. There was a dim light from the living room, but Kathleen snapped on the bulb above the bed and it fell upon her, rose-shaded. She was thinner, thought Anne, a little harried looking.

232

"For heaven's sake!"

Anne got up and closed the door and, returning, sat down on the edge of the bed.

"I've been with Dolly Davis," she said.

Kathleen colored.

"What has she been saying about me?" she began, furiously.

"Never mind that. We've no time. Is it true that you are planning to go away with George — ?" She stopped, realizing absurdly that she did not know the man's surname.

"If I am, what of it?" Kathleen challenged. "I can do as I like, can't I?"

"I suppose so. Where are you going?"

"To the Coast. He has a chance in a night club there — we are going to work up an act."

"Kathleen, listen to me. Do you expect him to marry you?"

"George doesn't believe in marriage," Kathleen told her defiantly. "He — he says it ruins personalities. He believes in a union bound only by love and respect," she went on glibly. Then she met Anne's eyes and her own fell. "But — I think he'll marry me — *after* —" she whispered.

Anne's heart leaped — *"after"!* The implication was that it was not too late, that whatever hold this fatuous wretch had upon the girl was not the last, the strongest hold of all — not yet.

She said, rather casually:

"Dolly's expected for some time that he'd marry her."

Kathleen rose to the bait.

"He doesn't give a snap of his fingers for her; he's just sorry for her."

"So sorry for her that he allows her to buy his clothes, to share her apartment — to keep him, in fact?" Anne suggested.

"That's a lie!" Kathleen's eyes were furious — and frightened. "I heard all that talk — most of it from her. He told me he was ill and broke once and she looked after him. He was grateful to her — as — as a son might have been," Kathleen explained ridiculously, "and she spoiled their friendship by falling in love with him — a woman old enough to be his mother!" the girl concluded, scornfully.

"He told you that? And you believed him? Kathleen look at me!"

The girl did so, unwillingly, her lovely mouth sullen.

"Have I ever lied to you?"

"No. . . . "

"I am not lying now. I have heard what you have heard, but I have seen what you are not willing to see — his clothes in the apartment to which he has a latch key, his finger marks on her arm. He misuses her," Anne said, "he would go to any lengths for money."

Kathleen said, breathlessly:

"I don't believe it!"

"Yes, you do. You just won't face it. You must. God knows I wouldn't ordinarily interfere in your love affairs. As you've said, your life is your own. But you can't throw yourself away on this worthless creature — this kept boy — this man who abuses women. *Man!*" repeated Anne, in disgust, "bird of prey would be better! I don't know why he wants to take you away with him," Anne went on.

"He — loves me," Kathleen told her in a small voice.

"He doesn't. He can't know the meaning of the word," Anne answered. She put her hands over her eyes and shuddered. "If I thought — if I thought that he planned to exploit you —"

There was a silence, and then Kathleen shrieked, suddenly.

"What is it? Oh, do be quiet," Anne implored her, frantic with fear and foreboding. "Tell me, Kathleen — it doesn't matter what you've done — only tell me —"

"I haven't done anything," Kathleen told her unhappily, the back of her hand caught across her mouth, "only — I just remembered —"

"What? What have you remembered?"

"A man — Georgie said — he wanted me to meet him. I was to be nice to him — he was an old man with lots of money, a Polack — he owns a string of night clubs on the coast —"

She stared at Anne. Anne said, quietly, sick to her very soul:

"You see?"

"I don't want to see. No, I'll not believe it. He's been — so dear — such fun. It's all Dolly's lies, Anne, jealous lies!"

"No. Listen, I'll get into bed with you; it isn't long till morning. Promise me that you won't see him or write until we've talked it over again quietly. I'll come tomorrow after work. Now, I'm so tired, Kathleen."

She pulled off her clothes, found a nightgown of her sister's, and a few moments afterward lay beside her in the narrow bed, the graying dark pressing down on them. Her arms went about the younger girl's smooth, warm body; she pressed her cheek to the round shoulder.

"You're — crying — Anne?"

Kathleen's voice was awed. She hadn't seen Anne cry in years.

"It's all right. Don't mind. I'm tired and miserable —"

"On my account," Kathleen thought. She turned and took Anne in her arms.

"I'll do as you say," she promised. "Perhaps you're right — I don't know. I'll be good, Anne, I swear it. I'll wait. If he really loves me he'll — he'll prove that these things aren't true."

But fear is the beginning of wisdom. She knew in her young, easily pierced — as easily healed — heart that these things were true.

"I was — I *am*," she corrected herself, "so crazy about him; and it was so — exciting."

There was the keynote. Anne realized it, but was too tired to think it out. She said, drowsily:

"Hush, try and sleep. We'll talk tomorrow."

"I know. But if you ever cared about anyone, you'd understand."

"I do care about someone," Anne told her, "with all my heart. Someone fine and wonderful and so terribly worth while —"

Kathleen held her closer, forgetting her own problem in her youthful amazement.

"Anne! Who is it? Are you going to be married?"

"He doesn't know I exist," Anne told her wearily. "And he isn't free to marry me even if he did know, and if he wanted me I'd go to him tomorrow, if it wouldn't harm him. But it would, so I can't, and even if it didn't hurt him I want more than just makeshift. I'm telling you because you're the dearest thing in the world to me — except — that one other person, and I want you to know that I understand what love can do to people. Only, forgive me, darling, I don't think you have loved anyone — not yet."

She was asleep before she had time to regret her confession. But Kathleen lay awake. Anne in love! Ted? But Ted was crazy about her, and Ted was free. Who else?

Suddenly she knew. It wouldn't, of course, take much effort.

Oh, poor Anne, thought Kathleen, and presently slept, one arm flung, as if protectingly, over the other girl.

She was still sleeping when Anne rose next morning and tiptoed to the kitchenette and made herself coffee. Lola slept too, and Sally, her roommate. Anne scribbled a note on a pad to Kathleen:

"Remember your promise. I'll be in this evening."

She left it on the pillow, took one last look at the sleeping girl, and went to work.

Things went very wrong that day. She made half a dozen foolish mistakes; she was irritable; she had to retype several letters. Toward the close of the afternoon, Fellowes spoke with concern:

"Miss Murdock, what's the matter? You're so unlike yourself. Are you ill?" he asked, unable to conceal his alarm.

"No," she forced herself to smile. "No — I was up almost all night."

"Someone throw a late party?" he asked, much disliking this very probable explanation.

She shook her head.

"Illness in the family?" he probed further, wondering what he could do to help — flowers, baskets, hospitals, doctors — Good Lord, everything he had was at her disposal — yet he dared not tell her so.

"No," she answered, thinking, that after all, it was illness. For Kathleen was sick of a malignant fever, a poison in the blood.

"Can't you tell me?" Fellowes begged and laid his hand on the desk, palm up in the oddest little gesture of appeal. "You — you've been pretty generous with me. I'd like you to feel," he said, and his voice deepened, "that I'm your friend."

His heart cried out there — "and your lover, Anne, always your lover."

She had no one to whom to turn. Her parents were out of the question. Ted — ? She knew what Ted would say, and even Betty Howard, good comrade that she was, could not help her here. She felt terribly incompetent. She could handle Fellowes' affairs, keep

239

her head in his emergencies. She could even muddle through her own problems alone. But when her own flesh and blood was darkly threatened, when she knew that the smallest psychological mistake would be irretrievable, she felt that she could not fight the battle single-handed; and this man was strong and sane; she could trust him — and she loved him.

"Can't you tell me?" he repeated, very gently.

So, stumbling a little, trying to keep back the nervous tears, she gave him chapter and verse, ending with her visit to Dolly and her talk — part of it — with Kathleen.

"She promised — I think she was frightened. But if she sees him again — or thinks it over and believes that I've lied — I don't know what she'll do — she's headstrong, Mr. Fellowes."

Fellowes had listened, frowning.

"You'll have to get her away from that crowd," he suggested. "Couldn't you — live with her — take an apartment for the two of you?"

Anne said, thoughtfully:

"I never thought of that."

"Would she consent?"

"I think so. We're very fond of each other and," Anne laughed shakily, "Kathleen's fastidious, in some ways. She hates disorder, but she won't remedy it. It was the same at home. And the place she lives in now is generally in such a mess — four girls, their clothes and belongings strewn all around. She doesn't like it — she's said so. If I could get a place and keep it the way she likes —" Anne suggested, hopefully.

"If you do," Fellowes advised seriously, "don't put too many restrictions on her — beyond this man. She's been used to liberty for a little while. You can't take the hen and one chick attitude."

"I know. But — oh, if he'd only leave town," said Anne, wretchedly, "I know things would come out all right."

"We'll see. Find out his name. I have powerful friends at Headquarters. You say he plays the races and has no other visible means of support. They keep *dossiers*, even in this country. They'll give a man rope enough and when he's ready to hang himself they have the goods on him," Fellowes told her. "I think that I can arrange to have him receive an official warning that he'd better clear out of New York *alone*. There's the Mann Act, you know," Fellowes reminded her.

"If you would — ? If he goes," Anne said, relief in her heart and eyes and voice, "Dolly will join him, I'm sure of that."

241

"So much the better. Find out his name to-night, and call me at the house."

"I hate to trouble you. I'm so grateful."

"You don't. And please don't be grateful. I don't do half a quarter enough for you. I never can," he told her.

His heart was so warm toward her. This softer, frightened side of her was one he had not seen before. It endeared her to him even more, brought her closer. But when she had left him he looked down on the fist he had clenched, unconsciously, on the desk and wondered how he had kept from taking her in his arms and comforting her — and — himself.

With Kathleen that night, Anne found her restless, inclined to regret her promise, on the defensive, abusive of Dolly, of gossip, sure that it couldn't be so. But Anne managed to make her give her word that she would not see the man for a few days at least. Meantime, Anne discovered the name he went by — the very elaborate one of D'Argent — and tele-phoned, from an outside booth, the name and address to Fellowes.

Two days later Mr. George D'Argent left town hurriedly — and without a word to Kathleen. But Anne had a hasty scrawl from Dolly:

"Kid, I don't know how you did it, but

Georgie and me are on our way on separate trains. He's promised to be a good boy — I'll send you a slice of the cake — while he's in this humor he'll marry me and be glad of it — I've got the promise of a job," she ended, "and everything looks rosy."

It was signed, in purple ink, "Fondly yours, Doll."

Anne showed the note to Kathleen. The girl read it, threw it on the floor, burst into angry tears.

"She's — *a cat!*" sobbed Kathleen.

"He couldn't have cared for you so much," commented Anne, with studied brutality.

But Kathleen fled and locked herself in the bedroom.

Anne left her alone for a time after that. In the interim she had a talk with her parents, and she told them, despite Murdock's growls and Molly's tears, that she was moving to town.

"Kathleen isn't happy with her friends," she explained, "and she can't come home — it's much better for her in the city. She doesn't want to be alone, and it seems wise and practical for us to take a place together. Don't cry, Mother. I'll come home often. I ought to live in New York anyway. I have to go away so much — I work so often nights."

Later, Molly asked shrewdly, the mother heart touched with foreboding:

"Kathleen? The child's been misbehaving?"

"No, dear," Anne told her. "Only she's very young and I don't like the people she travels with. She'll never come home to live — she's way past that. It will be better if we are together."

Mrs. Murdock nodded her gallant red head.

"I don't know what you're keeping back," she said, slowly. "I suppose Kathleen's been headstrong and foolish. If she were in real trouble, now, sure and she'd come to her mother with it," argued Molly, under the old, the tragic delusion, "but you've a good head and a clear eye — and — it's all right with me, Anne," her mother told her, "and I'll make it all right with himself."

Anne moved to two rooms and bath, and a real kitchen on West Eighth Street, and Kathleen, subdued although not admitting herself convinced, moved with her.

Chapter 8

Linda Speaks Hers

"You're a Quixotic idiot!" Sanders told Lawrence Fellowes with affectionate exasperation.

"Quixotic — I doubt; idiot — certainly; but neither, in this case. No, Sanders, I can't see it."

"It's one of the biggest accounts that's been offered us," Sanders commented with deceptive mildness.

Anne, from her own office, listened shamelessly. The door was half open. For two days this bloodless battle had raged, ever since the Warner account had been under discussion.

"We don't," asked Fellowes, "take dubious medicines, we don't take cure-alls, do we?"

"Nope."

"We employ a reputable physician, at a retainer fee, to investigate any medical statement made in our advertising, do we not?"

"We do," agreed Sanders, somewhat bewildered.

"Doctor Mathews has made a report on this infant food," Fellowes proceeded, "and while it appears harmless — in other words, it isn't canned Herod, guaranteed to kill innumerable babies — it simply does not measure up to the claims made for it. The concern insists upon making these claims. Therefore, if I have anything to say about it, we will not handle the account."

"But," argued Sanders, "if, as you say, the product can do no harm, couldn't you stretch a point? It's a hell of a lot of money, Larry."

"We can struggle along without this particular 15," said Fellowes, grinning. "The business was built up upon a foundation of integrity. We believe in our clients and what they offer the public. That belief stands back of every piece of copy which goes out of this office. It's more than honesty — it's honor. No, I can't see it, Sandy. The Warner people will have to take their problem elsewhere. As far as that is concerned, they want the campaign launched in three months. We could give them showy, superficial copy — but nothing else. Mark my words, if we took this job we'd find ourselves up against fierce opposition if we tried to send men into their factories —"

"Well," Sanders told him, resignedly, "it's O. K. with me. You're the big boss — only, of course, I hate like thunder to see that much jack get away from us."

"So do I — I'm only human," Fellowes admitted. "But in this particular case I cannot be convinced. For every cent we'd gain, we'd lose two cents — later on. Lowering the standard even once is bound, eventually, to affect the business. Sorry to disagree with you, old man. I don't — often."

"Forget it," Sanders said gruffly, a little embarrassed. "I'll tell the Warner outfit to run along and sell their papers at another stand."

"I thought you'd see it," Fellowes told him quietly. "By the way, I've got Merle Dawson, the music critic, to take over the superintending of the musical end of our broadcasting."

"That's good," Sanders told him. "Well, I'll get back to work. See you later."

He went out through Anne's office, stopping at her desk to speak to her with his air of detached friendliness. Anne, a little later, went in to see Fellowes.

"I'm afraid I've lost face with Sanders," Fellowes told her, smiling ruefully, yet boyishly wanting her approbation.

Anne knew all about the Warner proposition. She said, trying to keep back the idolatrous warmth from eyes and voice:

"You were right."

"Well, that doesn't always make one popular," Fellowes laughed. "It isn't the first time such a question has arisen, but it's never meant as much money before." He looked at her and, against the better judgment of his mind, followed his heart.

"Look here," he said, "I think I rate a reward for virtue. Couldn't we have dinner and go to a show? It's been so long —"

"I'd love it," said Anne, instantly forgetting all her resolutions.

She had tried to school herself to an unnatural calm in his presence, but sometimes, as now, the mask slipped, and he saw, and his heart missed a beat, and he dared to wonder —

Anne, back at her desk, knew that things were increasing in difficulty with her. She wished he hadn't asked her to go out — and she was radiant with happiness because he had. She had told herself that loving him would make no difference in her work for him. Now she knew the falsity of that. She worked — no better. It was harder. She wanted to be near him. She wanted with a terrifying longing to touch him. She was as panicky over his slightest indisposition as Janet Andrews had been.

It seemed to her that in some inexplicable way he belonged to her. Sheer fantasy, of course. He belonged to himself and — a conclusion which wounded her deeply — to Linda. Or at least legally, to Linda. She had no share, no part nor parcel in him. Yet the belief persisted, as, unknown to her, it did in him, that love and a working comradeship gave her — some rights.

That night they dined uptown in a small, expensive, very good place on a side street, and went to the most discussed play of the season. They talked across the table of a thousand superficial things. Anne experienced, each of them, the necessity for concealment, the excitement of this unofficial nearness. So the play, good as it was, was wasted on them both.

"I mustn't do this again," thought Anne, when he was leaving her at her door, holding her hand for an appreciable moment in farewell and she was thanking him — for — "a pleasant evening."

"I'll have to cut this out," he thought, getting into his car, "before I've more than begun. It's too damned pleasant — and unsatisfying — and dangerous!"

During the winter Fellowes went to the hunting club in Virginia for a time. He had to get away, away from Anne, to face the admission that the attraction persisted, grew no less. And during his absence her daily routine seemed endless and uninteresting. That frightened her. If she was losing her interest in the job for the job's sake she might as well give up.

At this time Linda asked her help again and she went to the apartment, hating herself for being so unwilling. Yet they had been very friendly since their closer contact at Hot Springs. Linda had even enlisted Anne's aid in small plots against Fellowes: "See if you can't persuade him to put off that St. Louis trip for a day, I do so want him to go to the Marshes' with me." Such conspiracies were not very serious, and when they did not really interfere with Fellowes' business Anne allied herself with Linda, generally with success. Fellowes told her once, secretly delighted:

"It's amazing how you manage me! Oh, don't shake your head. I'm on — I'm not wholly blind!"

"If," she stammered, "If I've seemed officious — ?"

"Come, don't be foolish. I am content. All good secretaries manage their bosses. I've no objection — rather like it, in fact."

He mentioned it to Linda; he couldn't help it, Anne's face had been so — dear and embarrassed. He felt an absurd necessity for partial confidence.

"She blushed like a kid," he said, "and I was sorry I'd said any thing."

"Office wives," Linda murmured.

"What's that?"

"Nothing — only — think it over," Linda

250

advised, unmalicious, "some one has to manage every man. When the wife at home can't or won't the proxy wife in the office must."

"I don't think I quite like that," Fellowes told her.

"Larry, you're a nice person," his wife told him, "but on certain occasions you lack humor."

"Now, do I?" he mused, and asked Anne the next day.

Anne looked at him. He'd never invited her to analyze him before, and she couldn't, really, he was too near — and too remote — and too beloved.

"Tell me the fatal truth," he urged, "humorless people are intolerable."

"If," Anne said slowly, "you mean a kind of custard-pie sense of humor, I don't think you have it."

"What other kinds are there?" he asked, enjoying her gravity and confusion.

"Oh," Anne told him seriously, "an ability to see the comic side of serious things. Sort of the difference between wise cracking and wit," she explained.

"And I've not that sort?" he questioned.

"Oh, yes — if you hadn't you wouldn't think you hadn't."

"That's rather Irish."

"I come by it naturally," she told him.

251

He picked up a letter on his desk, smiled at her, thanked her gravely, but with laughing eyes, and they got to work. He thought afterwards Linda had been right, in part; perhaps, where Anne was concerned, he did lack humor. But — that office wife remark had carried a certain sting with it. Linda didn't know, couldn't guess; still, the sting had been there.

One Sunday evening Kathleen was out and Anne was at home alone. She sat before the fire in the small hearth and thought of Fellowes — of his slow smile, his eyes, kindled with enthusiasm or narrowed to speculation or warm with friendliness, his sure, fine hands, his voice — the voice she heard all through her working day, and which she loved. The novel she had set herself to read lay unopened, and she sat back in her big chair and looked contentedly about the small apartment.

There was not much furniture in it. She wanted the best; and that cost money. If ever her ship came in, she would buy things . . . a small, comfortable couch, and tables, another deep chalr.

In the bedroom she had the two narrow beds from home and the dressers and vanity table. These she had painted a cool, misty green. She had bought her pretty curtain material at a remnant sale and Mrs. Murdock had made the curtains for her. There were pictures on the walls — good prints which she had had for some time — and two fine ladder-back chairs which she had found in a junk shop, paying three dollars for them and restoring them herself, lovingly and carefully.

Her mother had given her enough to furnish the kitchen, and Anne had amused herself painting the old-fashioned plastered bathroom a curious sea-blue.

Some day, the living room in which she sat would be — just right. Now it looked bare, but one could live in it, and there was a pot of ferns on the gate-legged table, another good old piece, which Molly had resurrected from the dusty home cellar for her children's use.

Tbe doorbell rang, and Anne, aroused from her dreamings, rose and let Ted in.

"Hello!"

She looked so astonished that he accused her, crestfallen:

"You didn't expect me."

"No," she admitted.

"But I told you I'd come by and we'd go to a movie or something!"

"So you did! I'm getting absent-minded. I'm sorry, Ted."

"Well, it's not a flattering reception. Get your things. Where's Kathleen?"

"Out with Frank Young — he's on the

Times — a friend of Jim's."

"Does your highness approve?"

"Oh, quite; he's a very nice person," Anne said, abstractedly. "Ted, come in and look at the bathroom wall. It does look speckled."

He'd helped her to paint it. He followed her in and stood gazing with a critical eye.

"So it does. Tell your girl friends it's distempered — the latest thing," he advised her.

On the way back to the living room he suddenly caught her in his long arms and drew her golden-red head back against his breast.

"Ah, Anne, are you never going to have me, then?" he asked. "We'd have such fun, dear, fixing up a little place of our own —"

She struggled and after a moment he let her go.

"No, Ted — I don't want a place of my own — at least I do want it and I have it, but —"

"But what?" he demanded.

"I want it — alone."

"Kathleen?"

"She's my sister. You know what I mean," Anne told him.

He digested this a moment in silence. Then he said, unhappily, "I suppose I do know what you mean. Well, get your coat and hat and we'll go out."

She said, after a moment, gently:

"You look tired. Would you rather stay here?"

He swung around at that, his pleasant, boyish face dark with emotion.

"Good God, no! To be alone with you — like this — and not be able to touch you!"

After a moment, she said, comprehending fully, out of her own love's bitter wisdom:

"I'm sorry, Ted."

"So am I." His mouth twisted in a wry smile. "But — it can't be helped — and I don't expect you to understand. You're a girl — and — so cold —"

Cold? She said nothing, but wondered. Cold? Not she, whose blood burned to her very finger tips when she was near Lawrence Fellowes! Cold — and not understanding! She knew that she understood only too well.

They sat through part of a cambric tea film, and then walked through the little park, and by ten o'clock presented themselves at Polly's.

The austere sister was not present, but Polly had filled the small flat to overflowing with young people. Ted knew most of them, but Anne did not. They were of the arty type, but the sort of art that flourishes on greeting cards. The apartment was attractive, but, as Anne told Kathleen afterwards, "terribly over-sexed"; at which Kathleen asked with a gurgle of amazement, "Whatever do you mean?" and Anne answered vaguely, "Oh, cushions and bows on everything — not really bows, perhaps, but you get that impression. Only the sister's bedroom is different — and that looks like a monastery."

There was no conscious attempt at — say seduction, in the appearance of the place. It was not like Dolly's impossible rooms, for instance. It was simply clinging and wide-eyed, if a room can be that, and had, as Anne recounted faithfully to Kathleen, "an inferiority complex."

Someone played the piano; someone sang. They rolled up a rug and danced to a victrola. Ted, with Polly in his arms, his eyes roving about the room in search of the flaming gold that was Anne's hair, whistled the current piece under his breath: "There's one little girl who loves me, there's one little girl who don't."

"Ungrammatical," thought Ted, "but pretty darned near true."

For Polly was cooing at him:

"You haven't been here in ages. I've missed you so much. Have I done anything too offend you?"

"Don't be ridic!" Ted told her, mechanically.

"Anne," Polly remarked, "isn't looking

well. She works too hard, doesn't she?"

Now there was nothing in the friendly concern of that question to anger Mr. O'Hara. Nevertheless, he replied, with some frigidity:

"I don't think so. She has an important job, you know, and it doesn't stop with office hours."

"Now why, for heaven's sake," he wondered, "am I defending Anne's damned job?"

"Yes, one hears that," Polly answered, silken.

"Hears what?"

"That she works — out of office hours."

"Now what do you mean by that, exactly?" Ted demanded, very warm under the collar.

"Teddy —" Polly looked grieved — "I don't mean anything. Why do you always take that tone when Anne Murdock is mentioned? Of course everyone knows you're crazy about her," Polly went on, drooping, "but you needn't go about with the attitude that if a person mentions her she's being insulted."

There appeared to be something wrong with the syntax of this sentence, but Ted ignored it.

"Of course I'm not crazy about her — what a silly idea!" Ted denied, hotly, and had something the feeling of a Peter who repudiates his most sacred emotion.

Later, there was "something in a chafing dish" and very good coffee and chocolate cake which Polly had made herself. After which Ted took Anne home.

"I'm afraid you were bored."

"No — Polly would make most anyone a good wife," Anne remarked thoughtfully.

"Look here, are you trying to — ?"

"Of course not. Thanks a lot for tonight," she told him, and left him, to get ready for bed and read drowsily, waiting for Kathleen.

How dull it had been. She thought back to her evening with Fellowes. But that mustn't happen again. Well, tonight had been stupid — stupid — but Sundays passed and Monday came again.

During that winter Fellowes was so busy that he saw very little of his wife. Linda was always away, somewhere, and it was borne upon him during the first week in March, when she was again at Hot Springs on her way home from Palm Beach, how very little he missed her.

Dining one night with old friends, an especially happy couple, he found himself unconsciously comparing his marriage with their own. What had been lacking for so long between him and Linda?

They were friends. They respected each other. For a time their only deep tenderness had been physical, a holdover of their original attraction. They'd been too fond of each other, too innately decent, not to bring to that intimate relationship gentleness and affection. but that relationship had ceased so gradually, even as a matter of human habit, that during the last year, it might never have existed, an unconscious, and unobvious sort of cessation until — until Fellowes had fallen in love with Anne. Since then, quite consciously, he had been unable to touch his wife — even for the small fleeting comfort and release his right to do so might have given him.

They had drifted further and further apart. Not as so many did, in bitterness, with scenes and hostilities, but quietly, naturally, as if, one by one, the threads composing their bonds had frayed and snapped without sound.

If he and Linda both realized this fact — and surely she must realize it — might it not be possible to go to her and say: "Linda, I've fallen in love with someone else?"

But how did he know she felt as he did? How did he know that she wasn't perfectly content in her cool way? Had he the right to break up her house about her ears, demand a fuller freedom than that which she gave him?

But on the same evening, after dinner was over, his hostess, who had known Linda since their mutual girlhood, took him aside and spoke to him seriously, jarring him out of his self-absorption.

"Larry," she said, "forgive me in advance if I overstep the bounds of a long and happy friendship — to — warn you."

"Just what do you mean?" he wondered.

"Linda. I'm devoted to Linda — and to you. We both are, John and I. And I am so sorry to see —" she stumbled and then raised her honest eyes to his — "to see things going wrong between you."

"But they are not," he denied mechanically. "We're happy. Of course, I haven't been able to give Linda the sort of companionship she wants. I'm a busy man, Frances, and I love my work too well to relinquish it —"

"If you don't give it to her, someone else will."

It was entirely in keeping that he took that quietly — did not flare up, grow melodramatic. It wasn't in him — nor in the quality of his affection for his wife. Besides, he knew Linda, and trusted her.

"She cares for someone else?" he asked, going straight to the point.

"I don't know," Frances Marsh's charming face was dark with trouble, "but I think so."

Larry Fellowes was silent a moment, thinking. The answer came to him quite naturally. After all, it had been there all the time, under his eyes, yet so unobvious in a tawdry sense.

"Dick Jameson?" he asked, very controlled.

"I think so," Mrs. Marsh said, unhappily. "They like the same sort of things — they've been thrown together so much. They were with us at Placid this winter — you wouldn't come, Larry, you never do, more's the pity — and I couldn't help seeing. Oh, it was nothing that you could put a finger on. Only I've known Dick so long — he's John's second cousin, you know — and for the last few years — well, he's given up everything, even that very old, almost matrimonial entanglement — you remember? And he's always to be found where Linda is. I — I'm not a trouble-maker, Larry, I just want to tell you — it isn't too late," she ended, haltingly.

"Thank you, Frances. Oh, I mean that. I'm not being sarcastic. I've been, I think, a good deal of a fool."

He sat up late that night, alone in his bedroom, his teeth hard on a cold pipe, thinking, wondering, speculating.

Twice he got up to write to his wife, a frank, honest sort of letter: "We've made a sort of mess of it, haven't we, dear? Isn't there any way out?"

But he could not.

Did he in stark honesty want to — begin over again?

He knew that he did not. He knew that he had for Linda no single flame of passionate longing, no spark bright enough to flare up into the ancient fires. And he knew that this quality of emotion, lost to him as far as Linda was concerned, still burned within him, a compelling flame — and for another woman.

The question was: what did Linda want? He must put himself and his own desires apart. How far had she really left him? Was she unhappy? And did she care, with the passion of full maturity, for the man who was his friend and hers?

If she did — ? If she wanted her freedom — ?

At this stage of his thinking his heart shook with the natural implication it led to. If she wanted her freedom, and he, after a decent interval, could go to Anne?

But he couldn't speculate further, not until he knew what Linda wanted. It might be a *canard,* bred of Frances Marsh's genuine affection and concern for them both.

He did not write Linda. He decided to wait until her return, and during that period Anne had an attack of influenza.

Fellowes did as he had done during any illness of Miss Andrews', he got along as best he could. But everything went wrong. People reached him, personally and by telephone, who had no business reaching him; the one young salesman whom, contrary to his usual custom, he had wished to see — because Anne had told him, frankly, "He's different; I wish you'd see him next time he comes in, Mr. Fellowes; he doesn't look or talk differently from the others, but he's so tremendously sincere —" that young man was not admitted to him, and went away empty handed. And letters were lost and 'phone calls forgotten, and nothing was right.

To say that he missed her is an inadequate term. He lacked her, achingly, in his personal life. He had not fully realized how much her nearness had meant, how he had delighted in watching the changing light on her lovely hair, her altering expressions. He had not comprehended how much he'd loved her low, pretty laughter — so few women laugh well — and her clipped, clear speech; how much he liked to argue and discuss things with her as unselfconsciously as if he'd thought aloud.

In their months of close association he'd come to depend on her judgment and reticence. His business mind relied on her to smooth the daily path for him. But what he had not completely realized until she'd gone was that his eyes relied on her too, and his ears — a dependence of the senses.

This sense of loss, of a lack irreplaceable

until she should return, was the very roots of love; roots which, planted and nourished by propinquity, by the daily response of his blood to her flesh and blood reality, would flower — *had* flowered, he thought — in its own time, into the full and perfect blossom.

This he knew. Knew too that the days were long and tiresome and that he came to his work fagged, with little enthusiasm. He made daily inquiries through the office about Anne; sent novels and flowers, glad of the excuse to do so, and, when she'd been absent for ten days, he went to see her.

Perhaps, he told himself, he shouldn't. Yet, if a valued employee falls ill, her employer calls upon her. What was out of the way in that? But he wasn't calling as an employer; he knew that perfectly well, and so, perhaps, he'd better not.

But he went, one night after a lonely savorless dinner; and Molly, who had been staying at the apartment to nurse her daughter competently, admitted him; and they liked each other on sight. Molly saw nothing odd in his visit. Why shouldn't he come to see the poor child?

Anne, convalescent, was sitting in her big chair, a blanket over her knees, a soft satin negligee molded to her lovely figure, and one of Kathleen's frivolous pillows behind her head. Fellowes recognized instantly and with sharp anxiety how frail she looked, how white and thin. But her old smile flashed to him, lighting a face almost transparent in its pallor.

Molly disappeared presently into the bedroom and Anne said, as Fellowes drew a chair close:

"Please smoke. No, I don't mind. How's the office? Have you had a bad time?"

Very bad, he thought, but said, aloud:

"I get along. Now, don't worry. Who's looking after you?"

"Mother. She put up a cot in here. Kathleen's away evenings and mother has no confidence in anyone's nursing save her own."

She laughed a little. She was remembering the night Dolly Davis had sent for her and she'd been forced to tell Mrs. Murdock that Betty Howard was ill. What a time she'd had next day, over the telephone, telling her not to come to town. But she'd explained, in part, to Betty; and Betty had helped.

She said, as he watched her, so content to be near her, and yet not content:

"Monday, I'll be back. The doctor won't promise but I think I can persuade him."

"Don't think of it until you're quite strong. Hadn't you better take your mother and go somewhere to recuperate? South perhaps? The office will take care of your expenses,"

Fellowes told her, reluctant to delay her return, but aching with tenderness, pity and the desire to protect which is the very heart of love.

Yet he wanted to say: "Please come back Monday — I can't do without you."

Anne was saying hurriedly, gratefully:

"It's awfully good of you — but I'd rather come back as soon as I can. I'm not used to this elegant idleness. It nearly drives me crazy."

She asked him some questions relative to business, and they talked for a time, rather as business partners do; almost, but never quite forgetting that they were man and woman.

Molly returned with hot milk and thin toast for Anne and a cup of marvellous coffee and a plate of light, sugared doughnuts for Anne's boss.

"I thought you'd like a bite," she told him, cheerfully, "and then you must go — the child's tired."

"Mother!" expostulated Anne and now her white skin was tinged with scarlet.

"And are you not? Do you deny it, with your hand shaking so you can scarcely hold the glass?" asked her mother severely. "You've been up long enough."

"Of course she has," Fellowes agreed. He

drank the coffee, ate a doughnut or two with appreciation and then rose to depart. The flowers he'd brought in were in a vase Mrs. Murdock had set near Anne.

Anne indicated them:

"I haven't thanked you properly — or for the lovely ones last week — and the books."

"Don't try." He stood beside her so close she could feel his male vitality emanate from him to wrap her in a glorious warmth. "Don't do anything but get well. We — miss you so," he admitted.

When he had gone,

"Nice boy," commented Mrs. Murdock comfortably, "and not a bit like what I thought."

"Boy?" asked Anne, laughing.

"Sure and they're all boys to me — the big men — from the cradle to the grave. There's no one younger than your father this minute. Sometimes he acts as if he wasn't out of shorts yet," Mrs. Murdock announced, "and the sooner women realize they grow up but men never do, the better off they'll be and the wiser."

She was no fool, was Molly. She had seen the light in Anne's eyes when Fellowes had entered the room; had seen the response in his; and her heart was troubled.

Yet she had no misgivings. She thought she

knew what she called a "decent man" when she saw one. She was only sorry for her child.

"A married man," she told herself, "and the girl thrown with him day in and day out. I should have guessed it sooner."

Upon the day that Anne came back to the office, Linda returned.

She was looking amazingly lovely, Fellowes thought, without the slightest acceleration of his pulse. Bronzed and rose, her eyes deeply, velvety brown — eyes like pansies — her lips red with healthy blood under the smooth caress of the lipstick. But she was nervous. He had never seen Linda nervous before.

He was determined to speak to her seriously, not about Jameson, but, as if the other man did not exist, of their own relationship. He had pledged himself to ask her: "Are you unhappy, and, if so, what can I do to set it right?"

But he knew that he did not wish to set it right. Yet he was an orderly man, and the complete disruption of anything as important and serious to him as marriage seemed an incredibly grave step. But if Linda wished it — then it should be so. His own happiness demanded that if she wished it he should accede. And surely if she cared for another man nothing was left to them save disruption?

But if she did not care for Jameson, and

was unhappy in her present life, could he offer himself to her again, for her happiness' sake? Could he say: "Shall we start over? I will give up my work. I will go where you wish, be your companion. We will play together. We will find new grounds of mutual interest."

He knew that he could not thus offer himself. Giving up his work would be suicidal to his soul. It would mean idleness, restlessness, boredom, misery. And it would mean losing Anne — the precious, treasurable little he had of her — entirely.

This he could not face. Could not demand of himself.

Having reached this mental impasse he sat there in the lovely library, watching Linda walk about — finger things, light a new cigarette and throw it away. He must ask her — now. He must ask her: *"What do you want?"*

But suddenly she had answered the unspoken question. For she stopped in front of him and, looking at him very directly, her nervousness under control, said, very simply:

"Larry, I want a divorce."

Chapter 9

The Newspapers Take a Hand

"I want a divorce," Linda repeated.

In the moment which elapsed before he answered, Fellowes felt a hundred conflicting emotions — relief, a wild hope, regret, and more. All his uncertain plans for reaching some sort of understanding with his wife were dissipated by that one clear demand. He had arrived, to be sure, by a long road, at the inevitable conclusion that Linda, his wife for ten years, was no longer necessary to his happiness, nor he to hers. Yet, at her abrupt challenge, sex pride, so essentially male and so illogical, lifted a bitter and angry voice within him. He was, for the fleeting moment, almost ready to believe that, had it been required of him, he would have been willing to make tremendous concessions, amazing sacrifices to secure Linda's happiness — the sacrifice of his work, of his emotions, of his veritable existence.

Almost — but not quite. The cool, ironic sense of humor which Anne had discerned in him came to his rescue, and with it his basic sense of justice and the knowledge that not for the empty complacent sake of a *beau geste* would he have been willing to throw away his hope of his own future happiness. For, with so single and so sure a stroke had Linda cut the Gordian knot of their mutual problem.

Women, in the majority, are less devious than men. They upset the apple cart with a steadier hand. They are less entangled in the past and the present. They live, as it were, in the future. In the first kiss of two young lovers, the girl, her lips still warm from the exquisite flame of that caress, is dreaming forward, while the boy knows only the captured moment. And now Linda, young love having failed her, was looking ahead, discarding all the past, repudiating the present in one frank demand for freedom.

"You no longer love me," stated rather than asked Fellowes, quietly.

Men are the sentimentalists. As he spoke, he re-experienced all the youthful, untested happiness they had known together — the early raptures, the initial benediction of their union. These things he relived with a poignant and aching regret that they should no longer exist. For the ephemeral moment he regarded Linda, the woman, through the eyes of the Larry who had been her lover. And those eyes were wet.

Linda answered, "No," thoughtfully enough, and sat down near him, composing her restless hands in her lap.

"I'm fond of you," she said, "and we're friends. That's what I rely on, your friendship for me. We've been happy — I admit. But for five years now — more than five years really — our marriage has been a makeshift sort of thing."

"You can't live on the heights, not always," Fellowes reminded her.

"No, I didn't expect to," Linda told him. "But — you've become more and more engrossed by business, you've had very little time for me. And in that time, I — grew up, grew up without you. We haven't anything in common. We've been quite as contented apart as together. I've run your house for you and made you, when necessary, a docile enough wife. There was a time, Larry, when I wasn't — just amiable. That time has passed. Nor do I feel that you've been unhappy at its passing. You've been as indifferent as I. A wife who trembled when you came near her, who was sick for your touch, for your desire, would have embarrassed you, faintly. At least I think so. No, you've been content with things as they are. But I'm not — not any longer. I'm young — I'm normal and healthy. I want life in all its fullness. I want

272

a chance to — to take the happiness my maturity offers me. Please," and she flushed slowly under the golden-bronze, "please don't think that I've gone off at the deep end over all, all the old catchwords — repressed desire, and all the rest. I'm not putting in a plea for the purely physical escape. I want it, quite frankly, but I want companionship most of all. You've worked and I've played. And I've played too long alone. That's all," she said.

"You've been frank with me," he told her, and spread out his fine hands in a gesture of utter futility. "I suppose it would be of no use if I offered to go your way — to give up the work which has kept me from you, to offer myself to you over again?"

"Too late," she told him quickly, almost harshly. "Larry, answer me with all the honesty in you — *do you want to?*"

She stared at him and his eyes answered her, before he shook his head.

"No," he told her, heavily, "I don't want to. I — I can't recall the boy who was your lover, Linda."

"You see?" she smiled sadly enough. "It's no good. And I'm not the girl you loved, the girl who loved you, Larry. Not any more."

After a moment he told her, gently:

"You were dear and wonderful — all a man could ask, and more. And you've made a magnificent wife, proud and loyal and above approach. There is, of course, someone else. I'm not asking you to confide in me, Linda. I think I know. I'm not censuring you, remember. If you would rather tell me nothing, if it would hurt you less to ignore this other factor, we will be silent."

The color rose again. But she said, instantly, her eyes unswerving:

"No, I was going to tell you. I owe it to you. It's Dick — Dick Jameson. I ask you to believe me, Larry, when I tell you I have not lent myself to a sordid flirtation — an — an affair."

"You needn't have said that," he replied at once. "I know you, Linda."

She smiled at him then and there was so much of authentic beauty about her that he caught his breath. What was he losing? Yet, in the same instant it came to him that he was losing — nothing. For this woman he had never possessed.

"He's cared for me a long time," she explained simply. "But he said nothing. I knew, of course. I'm not exactly a fool. But I thought — as women will think — that if I ignored my knowledge and never let him know, we were safe enough and I wouldn't be — encouraging him. That sounds very silly, but it's feminine reasoning. You see, it was pleasant to have somebody always there when you wanted him, someone who would rather be with you than with anyone else in the world, someone who kept silent, yet wrapped you around in an intangible warmth of devotion —"

"Ah, Linda!" said her husband.

"Don't — it doesn't matter. I mean, I — I didn't realize how much I had missed these things until they came to me again. I don't blame you, Larry. We married because we loved one another, because we felt for each other that perfectly normal, healthy pull of sex-attraction young people confuse with something enduring. Perhaps, in many cases, it does endure. But we never — built upon it. We were too young — not in years, perhaps, but in outlook — to see ahead. You went your way and I went mine; and the original bond slackened. I'm glad it did. I — I would have hated, some day, being held to you by that one thing alone. We've managed a decent friendship out of it, at any rate. And respect."

He asked, after a moment:

"And — Dick?"

"When we were all at Hot Springs — last fall — he started to say something. My fault, I suppose. I stopped him, but the damage was done. We were together a good deal at Palm

Beach — nothing was said, Larry, there wasn't a word or a gesture. But that can't go on forever. Down at The Homestead this last time — he did speak — fully — and I listened. And I knew what I must do. I had to come home and ask you to release me."

For a moment her eyes were veiled. Sharply, Fellowes realized that she had forgotten him, briefly, that she was thinking of Jameson — of the word given, the vow taken, the understanding reached. And he felt a curious retrospective jealousy — not for himself as he now was, but for the never-to-be-entirely-laid ghost of the man who had married Linda, ten long years ago.

He put out his hand and Linda, raising her eyes, leaned forward and gave him hers. He held it a long moment and then relinquished it, a symbolic sort of gesture.

"You must be free," he told her, "and — happy."

"Don't spoil it by — quibbling," she warned him. "Don't leave me the burden of doubt; don't make me reproach myself. Tell me; won't there be happiness for you, too, in — freedom?"

"Did I sound," he asked her, ruefully, "like a sort of sacrificial hero, a martyr? I didn't mean to. Happiness — for me? I don't know. I hope so. But at least no unhappiness, Linda.

276

So don't reproach yourself. Of course, it's never very pleasant to be faced with the fact that one is a failure. And I have certainly failed — you."

"No — not you. It goes deeper than that," she told him.

They remained for a long time without speaking. They were dedicating this ultimate moment to the past that had been, and the future which would never be. Months would pass by; Linda would obtain her divorce; papers would be signed and the legal formalities satisfied — but this was the true moment of their separation.

After a time, he said, wearily:

"Go to bed, Linda — tomorrow we'll talk over ways and means."

She nodded and rose to leave him. At the door she turned. He was sitting, his hands clasped between his knees, his head bent. He had a curiously defeated look. She wanted to run to him to say: "Don't! Don't! You'll be happy, too — so much happier!" But she did not. She could not, for she had no right to intrude upon his personal reticence.

In the morning, as they had agreed, they talked things over. Paris? — the day of quick Paris divorces was waning. "Reno," Linda said, firmly. "I'll take an apartment — stick it out there for the requisite time."

277

"I want to settle some money on you," he told her.

"No — please. You've been generous. I don't spend three-quarters of what you give me. There's more than enough."

"But," he spoke strongly, "the money — it's so much yours — all I've made in the last few years. You helped, you know."

"Helped?" She looked at him in astonishment. "I've never," she told him bluntly, "taken the slightest interest in your business, Larry, and you know it."

"Yes. But — there are other angles. The — the purely social side. You've been, in a measure, a working partner."

"I can't see it, I won't take money from you, my dear," she declared, firmly.

When everything was settled, she asked him a little embarrassed:

"If — if you'd care to see Dick? He wanted to talk to you."

Fellowes made a gesture of pure horror.

"No. I like Jameson," he told her simply. "We've been good, if not close, friends. God knows I bear him no malice. And you and I know, Linda, that this is no triangle-drama. I haven't the sensations of an outraged or deceived husband. You've given me no cause. You've been more practical than I. You haven't left me with any illusions about myself. I can't pretend, in the face of your honesty, which has served us both, to be martyred, to be 'giving you up for your own happiness.' But — leave me a few shreds of decent, if unnecessary, illusion. I'd rather not see Jameson, if you don't mind. Perhaps I'm not modern enough. Do you remember Harvey, who was best man at his wife's wedding to his best friend? People called it a marvellously modern gesture — a disinterested, ennobled act of friendship. I didn't agree with them. There is something indecent about a man slapping his successor on the back."

"Larry!"

"I'm sorry if I hurt you," he apologized, as he saw her wince. "I didn't mean to. But let's leave the baked funeral meats out of it."

Linda's removal to Reno was accomplished with very little fuss and no publicity. Her arrival there was not heralded. She had been in residence for some time before the fact became generally known. Her friends were more or less used to having her go away for protracted periods. There were no speculations about this particular absence, simply because there had been no rumors of a rift in the Fellowes' marital lute. Her closest friends, Mrs. Lucien, Mrs. Marsh, and one or two others, had been told the truth. But they were loyal women.

279

Fellowes went to his office as usual. Nothing was said, and nothing conjectured. But Anne, with her quick intuition where he was concerned, was aware that something was wrong. He appeared so abstracted and, as if purposely, he shut her out. Their business relations were unaltered, but the unacknowledged personal relation which was so strong, which each had guarded against as the tension between them grew, seemed finally shattered.

It came about because Fellowes was putting a closer control upon himself. Until his marriage with Linda was over and done with he was in honor bound to say nothing to anyone, least of all to Anne. He was not the type of man who says: "When I get my divorce, will you marry me?" He must wait until everything was clear and straightforward between them. Then he might go to her honestly and with no reservations, no *ifs* and *ands* and *buts*. Until the hour arrived he felt he owed it to all of them — to Linda, to Anne, to himself, to be silent. Linda had not been silent, but that was her situation, not his. His was entirely different. The girl he loved was working for him, in his office. He could not expose her to gossip, to speculation, until the quiet divorce was procured and the gossip and speculation might die aborning in the mere statement of a fact.

Besides, he could not know until he spoke whether or not she cared for him — enough.

There was a certain feeling of pride within him that he and Linda could face their problem and solve it with selfrespect and decency. Sometimes, thinking it over, it appeared to him that he could have been far more honest with Linda and himself had he told her frankly that he, too, cared for someone else. But that would involve Anne, and of Anne's reactions toward him he knew nothing, could only guess, ardently and with hope, wonderingly and with the see-saw extreme of despair.

And so, he kept his silence, and Anne was terribly troubled; yet in a way it was a sort of bitter relief to her to be treated in this new impersonal fashion — to have the scraps of intimacy, warmth, intimate friendship, upon which her love had fed even when she herself kept aloof, withdrawn from her. But she was hurt beyond relief. Had she done something? Had she — and here their respective positions, that of employer and employee, were clearly defined — had she in some way overstepped the boundary line?

It is probable that Mrs. Fellowes would have obtained her divorce and the public been none the wiser until the decree was a fact, if it had not been for a young woman who was also wiling her time away in Reno, upon the same errand, and for a second time. Her unimportant name was Hallie Martin, and she was, by profession, a newspaper woman, having long been employed by the *Daily Record* as a writer of special articles of the most "weepy," hearts-and-flowers sob-sister type.

She had served an apprenticeship as society editor; she was a clever woman and she never forgot a face; and Reno is not very large, although the idea persists that half our population congregates there at one time or another.

Mrs. Martin wrote back to her city editor: "Linda Schuyler Fellowes — Mrs. Lawrence Fellowes — is here. She has an apartment, a maid, a car and chauffeur and an Airedale pup. She keeps to herself and is never seen at parties and such. Perhaps the climate attracts her. Who knows? But there is something secretive about it. *Verbum sap* —"

The *Daily Record* wired Mrs. Martin *carte blanche* and sent a reporter to Fellowes' office. The reporter did not get farther than Anne.

Returning, he announced that Fellowes refused to be seen and that his secretary was "the prettiest little trick that these old eyes" — they were twenty-six years old — "have ever rested upon."

The city editor digested that in a profane silence. When Fellowes returned home that night he was met by the admitted connoisseur of genuine beauty.

"About your divorce, Mr. Fellowes?" began the reporter, briskly.

"I decline to be interviewed."

"But it is true, is it not, that Mrs. Fellowes is in Reno and has filed her suit?"

"Will you go out quietly, or must I throw you out?" asked Fellowes incautiously with a deceptive calm. He had had a tiring day and was in no humor to treat diplomatically with the Press.

The reporter went out quietly. He was accustomed to threats. But, as everyone knows, the high hand is no hand to play with the newspapers. For the *Daily Record* managed, generally, to have an ace up its sleeve.

"Nothing to be gained from Fellowes," reported the newspaper man, "but — well, it's always possible to dig up a little dirt."

Inquiries were made, and guardedly, at the office. It was a very large office. Not hard at all to find someone who had the entrée there, someone who worked there for a living. But quiet excavations could disinter nothing. The office — literally — knew nothing; and it was loyal.

It was practically established by Mrs. Martin's efforts that Linda Fellowes was suing her husband for divorce, but that was a tame enough story. It was necessary, in the behalf of the great reading public who hangs on straps in the subway or pursues the pictorial news over the coffee cups, to provide more than a bare statement of fact. Disgruntled wives, who dislike their husbands and who live with them for support of home and children, must be permitted their righteous moment: "Aren't these society people terrible!" And young girls going to work on misty mornings must be provided with their vicarious thrills.

Jackson, the menaced reporter, sleuthed a bit around town. He had nothing to go on but a hunch, and his hunch was a simple problem in mathematics — a wife in Reno, minus a husband in business, plus a raving beauty in the husband's office equals — divorce.

Equals, also, scandal.

He was able to learn how long Anne had worked for the agency, how long she had been in Fellowes' private office. He became more friendly with an acquaintance of his own in the office, a young man in the art department, rather a newcomer. Through him, he met Polly, and Polly, who was "crazy about literary people," talked rather freely. And young Jackson went back to his job and announced that Mr. Fellowes was pretty thick with his red-headed secretary.

That was enough to work on.

BEAUTIFUL SECRETARY STEALS RICH HUSBAND FROM SOCIETY WOMAN was the way the *Daily Record*'s mind worked.

Jim Murdock was called in. Jim was the boy to handle undeveloped scandal and handle it within the libel laws.

"Lawrence Fellowes," he was told, "of The Fellowes Advertising Agency, is getting a divorce — or rather, his wife is, very quietly. There's been nothing said, nothing has broken, but it all leads up to a girl in his office — his secretary," said Jim's chief, vaguely, and frowned because her name had slipped his mind. Which was just as well.

"Go out and find out what you can. See the girl, if possible. Make her talk. Take a photographer with you," he concluded.

Jim walked out of the office. He had learned to control his features, and his apprenticeship in repression stood him in good stead now.

A girl in Fellowes' office? His secretary? That could only mean — Anne!

His first emotion was anger — violent anger against Anne's employer, anger against herself. Then, he cooled down.

"Give the kid a chance," he told himself. "You know what a lot of hokum this business is. It may be a flop. God, I hope it is."

He went directly to the agency and walked into Anne's office. He'd never been there before, but he brushed by the reception clerk with a mere "Miss Murdock's brother," and left her gazing after him in some bewilderment, shaking her black head, and wishing he hadn't been so brief.

A personable young man — Jim.

Anne was not in her office. She was with Fellowes in his. She held a newspaper in her hand, and was saying, in genuine agitation:

"I'm so sorry . . . so *sorry*."

Fellowes looked at the item, FORMER SHOW GIRL TAKES POISON, and read the name and the brutally frank description.

"Dolly — Dolly Davis?" he asked sickened and incredulous.

Anne answered, half crying:

"Yes. Do you know — I — I *liked* her. There was something honest about her —"

Fellowes said, blankly:

"I wonder what happened?"

"Oh, that man," Anne told him with a gesture of disgust. "And they didn't marry, after all. There's nothing about a husband here. Of course her colored maid has told pretty much all she knew."

She shuddered and Fellowes put his hand on her shoulder. There was comfort for both of them in that contact, a sense of understand-

286

ing, and the quick uprushing warmth of a flame leaping.

He dropped his hand as if he had betrayed himself; said, steadying his voice with an effort: "I'm sorry, too — damned sorry." Then, looking at Anne's quivering mouth, he said, inadequately: "So sorry that you should have been brought close to anything like this." Then he wondered suddenly if, after all, the restrictions he had placed upon himself had not been unnecessary. "Anne," he began, with a breathless awareness that his entire happiness would hinge on this moment — *"Anne — ?"*

But when she looked up at him with questioning, waiting eyes, the scarlet flooding her face and neck at his use of her christian name, he thought swiftly, "Not here!" He couldn't bear to tell her here. He'd go see her; he'd take her out; they would have dinner together; they'd go back to her little flat, and he'd reach out his hungry arms and ask her —

But there was a step in her adjoining office, a man's step. Anne turned before Fellowes could speak again and walked away. Her hands were cold. What had he been going to say — in that shaken tone? And so, her eyes dim and her heart choking her, she walked directly into her brother's arms.

"Jimmy! What on earth!" she gasped and then, looking at his troubled face, she clutched his arm, suddenly. "What's wrong! Mother — Kathleen — Dad?"

"No, don't get excited. They're all right. I want to talk to you, that's all. Can we go somewhere and be alone?"

She nodded, sick with anxiety.

"The conference room — it's empty."

He followed her in there and sat down with her at the long table.

"Jimmy, what *is* it?"

"This," he told her. "Fellowes' wife is suing for divorce in Reno. Very quietly, see? But the papers have got wind of it and — of you."

"Of — *me?*"

She could hardly credit her ears. Fellowes' wife — divorce — herself —

"Of *me?*" she asked again, incredulously.

"Yes. Oh, I know there's nothing in it. But — you are his secretary; you are with him all day and sometimes part of the night; you've been away with him and his wife; you've visited them on Long Island. Can't you see what a pretty slick case can be built up against you, Anne? And," he added, "you're so confounded good looking!"

She was twisting her hands together, her eyes enormous.

"But — but — it mustn't — They can't

print anything like that. It would ruin him — the publicity — It mustn't be. Jim, you've *got* to stop it!" she said, frantically.

Her brother leaned over and took the nervous little hands between his big palms.

"Anne, look at me! You're thinking of him — not of yourself. Answer me one question. Do you, are you in love with him?"

The hands grew quiet in his own — quiet and cold. Then she said, in a small, clear voice:

"Yes, Jimmy."

"My God!" He stared at her a moment, then said violently: "The damned scoundrel!"

"No — no — he doesn't know I'm alive. I couldn't help it, Jimmy," she implored wildly. "He's — he's so much the biggest thing that's ever come into my life. I never dreamed — about him and his wife. I thought they were devoted —" she said not quite truthfully. "I never knew there was anything wrong. Jimmy, you must stop the scandal, you must! I'll — I'll kill myself! I'll do anything! You mustn't let it hurt him —"

"Don't be a fool," he told her, brusquely. "Don't get up in the air. I'll scotch it. Never mind that part. Resign from this job at once. Tell him you're sick, and go home today and send in your letter."

"I can't. We're so busy. It would be disloyal. It isn't possible."

"He can worry along without you. Go home, I tell you. I'll see you tonight."

He rose and Anne rose too.

"Jimmy — Jimmy —"

Suddenly he put his arms about her. She was very dear to him.

"Don't fret, honey," he said. "I'll see you through. I know you, Anne. Don't think I blame you. It's just one of those messes —"

After he had left her, she sat there in the big, empty room and tried to think.

Linda — a divorce — and herself somehow implicated —

She held her head between her palms and felt faint for the first time in her healthy young life.

Linda —

Resign, Jim had told her. Leave him — leave him thinking her disloyal and ungrateful. For she couldn't tell him, she couldn't face the telling.

If she did tell him she knew him well enough to know what he would say. He'd tell her to stay in the job rightfully her own — and to the devil with newspaper talk.

Yet publicity was the one thing an advertising man couldn't afford.

If Jim had seen them standing together. Of course he had seen. But it had been so innocent a contact, she had been upset about Dolly.

"Oh, poor Dolly!" her tormented mind had time to cry — the seeking, unhappy, flickering eyes closed in death, the loose, pretty mouth burned with a deeper stain than paint, the restless, passionate foolish heart stilled —

She rose, after a time, and went back to the office and found Fellowes looking for her.

"Where did you disappear to? Why, what's wrong?" he ended instantly.

"My brother — came. I've bad news," she lied valiantly, yet, after all, was it not the truth? "If — could you spare me?"

"Of course. Is there anything I can do?" he asked, aware of rebellion, through all his concern for her, that the moment had passed, that he could not now ask her to meet him somewhere after office hours, that he would have to wait — a little longer.

"No, thank you. It may not be very serious," she said and tried to smile.

"My car's outside," he told her. "Please use it."

"Thank you, no — Jim's waiting for me."

"I'm so sorry," he said, as he had said a few minutes earlier. And was so much more than sorry. "Please, if there is anything at all I can do to help, will you let me know? You promised once," he reminded her.

Anne — he had called her — *Anne*, a few minutes ago — and she had wondered — and feared and hoped — and been blind with uncertainty and the desire for flight — the desire for escape, to dream over the implication in his shaken voice. Now, she mustn't think of anything but his danger, of the present situation.

"It's all right," she said. She moved to the hat stand and took down her things. "Goodby," she said, and did not look at him.

But when she reached the door she turned and looked about the office. For the last time — for the last time. And her eyes met his own with a frantic, so tragic a glance that he took a hasty step forward. Not to be able to help her in this unknown emergency, not to have her full confidence — always that hurt him bitterly. And he spoke her name again, urgently:

"Anne?"

Somehow she managed to smile again.

"I'll be all right. I'm sorry," she said, "to leave you like this."

She closed the door, softly. He stood there staring at it, remembering her eyes.

She was in trouble. She was his friend. He — he loved her, loved her. And he was letting her get off like this — alone.

He went back to his desk and sat there thinking.

Why hadn't she told him what the difficulty

was? Couldn't she admit him that far into her confidence?

Anne went home. By some miracle, Kathleen was out. She had the little flat to herself. All the rest of that day she lay unstirring on her bed, trying to face her exile and her grief.

Jim came that night.

"It's all right," he told her, at once, when, white and haggard, she met him at the door. "The thing's squashed flatter than a pancake. No, no one knows my relation to you except! my chief. He's human enough, although you'd not think it. I told him frankly who you were. I said there was nothing in the story — office gossip, malice, that's all. I told him you weren't satisfied, that you had given in your resignation some time ago — and that you were engaged to be married."

After a moment, he advised, gently; watching her startled face:

"Wouldn't that be the wisest thing to do after a while? You — you'll get over this. It's glamour," said her brother, unhappily, "and being thrown so much with a man of Fellowes' stamp. You'll get over it, and marry some one who — who's in your own class, Anne, who'll love you and work for you — and you'll forget this nonsense. You must!"

She did not answer but after he had gone she went to the desk and with shaking hands started her letter to Fellowes.

"Dear Mr. Fellowes," she began without formality, "I'm so sorry to have to give you my resignation, to take effect at once. There is illness in my family and —"

Oh, but he'd find out — he'd know she'd lied!

"Dear Mr. Fellowes," she began again. "I am forced to hand in my resignation to take effect at once. I can give you no reason —"

She stopped writing and put her head down on the desk, but her heart formed the phrases —

"Oh, my beloved," cried Anne's heart, "I am leaving you because it is better for us both — because I would only harm you if I stayed. I am leaving you, because I love you."

Kathleen, coming back from the theatre, found her there, at the desk, her head on her arms, sleeping, with the tear marks on her face and the letter paper sodden under her cheek.

Chapter 10

Miss Murdock Accepts a Proposal

Kathleen touched her sister on the shoulder. There was no response. Anne was sleeping in the abnormal, fathoms-sunken way of utter mental exhaustion. Suddenly sickeningly afraid Kathleen called "Anne!" sharply, and shook her hard. After a moment, Anne's breath escaped her in a little tired moan and she opened her eyes and stared blankly at the other girl.

"It's late," Kathleen told her. "Come to bed, Anne, you look all in."

Her eyes dropped to the desk. Blurred, the words running together, she saw the letter, the last Anne had started to write: "Dear Mr. Fellowes —"

"What's happened?" Kathleen asked quickly.

Anne shook her head and her lips trembled. Regarding Kathleen, she observed with a curious impersonal detachment how pretty the younger girl was. She had returned home directly from the theatre, where she was playing in that prodigious Broadway hit, "Sunny

Skies." There were faint smudges of make-up discernible on her lashes and eyes, and her clear, gloriously youthful skin had a fresh, glowing look.

"Well," Kathleen ordered practically, "whatever's happened you're going to get into bed — immediately."

Anne rose. She was stiff and cramped. She followed Kathleen into their bedroom and docilely permitted her sister to put her, practically, to bed. Then Kathleen turned out all the lights but one and went, with her light, buoyant step, into the kitchen, where she heated some milk and brought it in to Anne.

"Drink this," she commanded, rather enjoying her rôle of nurse-guardian to the older girl who had always played just such a part with her. Now, momentarily, the tables were turned.

Kathleen sat down on the bed, slim hands clasped about one pretty silken knee.

"Tell me," she commanded, and added, "You'll never get a good night's rest until whatever it is is off your chest."

After a moment Anne told her, in a low, monotoned voice.

"I'll resign, of course," she ended wearily. "Jim's right. It's the only thing to do. The only way I can protect him."

"He's a man," Kathleen told her, scornfully,

and her eyes flamed. She'd acquired a pretty poor opinion of most men lately. "Why should you worry about him? He'll come out all right. It's not fair that you should lose your job and have to look for work just because Fellowes and his wife disagree. Talk about an innocent bystander!"

"You don't understand," Anne told her, patiently. "I've always protected him. That sounds crazy, but it's part of a good secretary's job. Well, this is the last thing I can do for him. Besides," she added with a bitter honesty, "it had to come sooner or later. I had to make the break — I've shilly-shallied long enough. In this way, I'm forced to it."

"I see. Well, it's your own funeral," Kathleen commented with calculated callousness. She looked anxiously at her sister. "And you look just about ready for flowers and the silver handles. But, Anne," she went on, "you can't write Mr. Fellowes and tell him you're leaving for no good reason. You owe it to yourself to tell him the truth."

Anne answered, after a moment:

"I know it. And I owe it to him, too. But, can't you realize the whole situation, Kathleen — the agonizing embarrassment of it?"

"I do. It's funny," Kathleen remarked thoughtfully, "how quick and clever you are at straightening out other people's difficulties for them, but when it comes to your own you go all to pieces. You've given so much to that darned office of yours, you've nothing over for yourself, Anne."

"I suppose so," Anne murmured.

After a moment, Kathleen said, and shuddered a little:

"Dolly Davis — I — I saw it in the paper, Anne. It was too awful!"

"Yes."

"We — haven't talked about — George," Kathleen told her. "I've never told you how grateful I am. At first, I almost hated you for interfering. I don't know what happened to me — why I went off my head like that. The newness of everything, the excitement. Of course, I knew that a lot of rotten stuff went on in that crowd. I honestly didn't believe it about him and Dolly — but there were others. And — I don't know why, but all that attracted me, fascinated me, the way fire used to when I was a kid. I didn't want to get burned myself; I was afraid. But there was something about the danger and — yes, the sort of careless, masked shickering *evil* of the whole thing that made me feel — terribly grown up and on my own. I can't explain. I'd use all their catchwords and phrases as if I were playing some sort of a part. But after — after you talked to me, and George pulled out, and I got over it — the infatuation and the hurt vanity — I began to see things pretty straight. The bunch I know best with the show now — some are good and some are bad, and some are indifferent enough — but I guess I've got my balance. I'm so grateful," she told her sister again. "You saw me through that bad time, just as if I'd had some illness, and you were taking care of me. I don't suppose," she ended, wistfully, "that I can do much for you now — but I'd like to."

Anne leaned over to her sister, kissed the flushed cheek. "You have helped me," she told her. "You've pointed out to me where I was wrong, where I was cowardly, and what I must do."

The next morning she went back to the office. Opening her own door gave her a curious sensation. She had been so sure the day before that when she shut it she had closed it for the last time. Now, here she was walking in, taking off her things, looking over the mail, answering an early 'phone call, as if nothing had happened, as if the world hadn't come to an end.

She was unable to see Lawrence Fellowes alone until late afternoon. She was with him, of course, in the daily progress of her routine duties; she sat with him on a conference; she waited in the outer office while he kept appointments. But not until something after four was she able to go in and shut his door and ask if she could talk to him for a little while "on a personal matter."

Fellowes looked up from some proofs which lay on his desk. He had asked her, when they'd first met that morning, how she was, if everything was all right. Now he said, meeting her grave eyes:

"You weren't telling me the truth this morning, were you? What's the matter and how may I help?"

Anne sat down in her own chair and leaned her elbow on one broad arm.

"I didn't tell you the truth yesterday, either," she answered, quietly. "But I shall now. Mr. Fellowes, my brother came to me yesterday — he's a feature writer on the *Daily Record* — *and told me that the newspapers have found out that Mrs. Fellowes is in Reno* —"

"Hell!" Fellowes said, quite simply. "I thought I'd put a stop to their speculations. I kicked one bright lad out of the apartment lobby the other day — or practically kicked him out."

"That wasn't very wise," Anne told him frankly, "because they went to work and found — me."

"You?" He looked at her in astonishment and a sense of impending trouble. She flushed, but went on bravely:

"Jim was sent out on the story — you can imagine the sort of thing they wanted — secretary — employer — employer's wife. They could build up their story on the flimsiest sort of evidence. The editor had no idea Jim was my brother. Jim's been to him since and told him that I'm leaving the agency — that I sent in my resignation some time ago. It was the only way to stop it."

Fellowes said furiously:

"I'll not have you hounded out of here! I'll not lose you through any dirty trickery of the press!"

"But you must," she told him intently, "and I must go. You can't afford the publicity, even though there's no truth in it. You'd never live it down. It isn't fair to you, nor to Mrs. Fellowes."

"Linda will understand," answered Fellowes instantly, "and I can stand the gaff."

"No . . . I'm leaving," Anne told him, and hated herself because her voice shook so. "If I didn't, and the papers went out after the story again — oh, it would be impossible — impossible! All the gossip even here in the office —"

"I'd put a stop to that," he told her, angrily.

"You couldn't. You can't stop people talking by telling them to," Anne informed him.

"You're not thinking of yourself, are you, Anne?" he asked after a while.

"Of course I am," she lied.

"No, you are not — only of me — and Linda," he added, as an after thought.

"It doesn't matter about me," Anne said, throwing discretion to the winds, "but it matters terribly about you."

That struck him. But he hadn't time to think it over, then. Later he could think about it and all its implications.

"Just what have they got on us, exactly?" he asked with a wry smile.

"Nothing. Everything. Just the fact of — of Mrs. Fellowes going out West and — all the secrecy there must have been — and the long time I've been with the agency — the year and a half I've been with you. They know that I work with you, at night. They could find out, Jim says, very easily, that I was at Hot Springs with you and Mrs. Fellowes; that I've been at your home. There's nothing tangible — nothing that by itself doesn't look perfectly natural and innocent. But taken all together — can't you see? I've talked with Jim. I've been thinking. There was the time we were both absent from the office — I, in Chicago, you in Washington. If they should get hold of that — through some one in the office, some one probably quite innocent of malice —"

"That's absurd," Fellowes disagreed, hotly. "It would be the easiest thing in the world to prove where we were — I've a dozen witnesses and a hotel bill for my part, and you have Mr. Lawson for yours."

"Oh, *proof*, that doesn't count!" Anne told him wearily. "I know something about newspapers. They can print a speculation, leave the question open to the public, and still be within the law. And we could furnish proof until judgment day. They would print our statements and make their apologies, but there would always be people who'd think the paper had been coerced or fixed in some way. There'd always be people ready to believe the worst — to whom proof didn't matter, who'd shut their eyes to it. And if this ever gets out, Mr. Fellowes, nine-tenths of the people you know, and don't know, will believe that Mrs. Fellowes is divorcing you — on — my account," Anne ended, very low.

"But that's damned nonsense!" Fellowes shouted, so loudly that Anne looked apprehensively at the closed door. "Damned nonsense," he repeated, a little lower. "Mrs. Fellowes is divorcing me on routine grounds."

After a moment, Anne answered:

"I suppose so. But no matter what reason she gives in her suit, someone will always think it's another woman — and that she was just being — decent about it."

The ivory paper cutter Fellowes was holding between his fingers snapped suddenly. He laid the broken pieces on the desk and fitted them together with meticulous care — then swept them into the waste-paper basket.

"Look here," he said, quietly. "We've been good friends, you and I. No one in the world, not even my wife — my former wife," he corrected himself carefully, "knows me as well as you do. You know things about me that are a sealed book to my closest men friends. I've not had to camouflage with you. I've taken all this knowledge more or less for granted, just as I've taken your hard work in my interests, your diplomacy and your loyalty. Well, I'm remembering these things now — I'm taking them for granted no longer. I wish I'd told you about Linda's move before this. But, for a time, my pride was involved. I'd failed — as a husband. That hurt like the devil. Linda wasn't happy with me. I wasn't giving her what she needed, what she wanted — companionship, and — and love. We'd grown away from each other. And it was too late to return — even if I were willing to give up my work and start out all over again. And I was not willing. She was honest with me — she asked me to let her go — she knew that she was no more necessary to me than I was to her. I wish," he said again, "that I'd told you. Perhaps, I don't know, we might have foreseen just this. Though I don't see how we could. And I want to tell you one thing — I'm perfectly willing to stand anything that may come of this mess, but I'm not willing to stand losing you, Anne. You — you are far too necessary to me."

She said, very white, clutching the desperate chance, trying, womanlike, to let him convince her:

"I shouldn't let you do it. Yet — if you are willing — I am, too."

He looked at her, arrested. Then he realized what he had only thought of, momently, when he asked her; "You're not thinking of yourself?" He realized her side of it. He could stand it. He was a man. To the devil with the publicity and unpleasantness! Linda? Linda would be safe with Jameson before long — it wouldn't matter to her. Although she'd be sorry enough and would deny it for his sake. But Anne would bear the real brunt.

After a moment, he told her:

"I've been a fool. And selfish — my God, how selfish! I was thinking of — Lawrence Fellowes — and feeling rather set up about it — feeling I was the devil of a good fellow to be willing to see this through in order to hold your job for you. And yet I wasn't thinking of your job at all, except as it affects me. I wasn't thinking of you. You'll have to go, Anne," he told her. "You have your people to think of — and yourself."

"My people won't believe anything against me," Anne argued. "If you say the word, I'll stay."

"No —"

He rose and held out his hands to her. She put hers in them wonderingly, felt them close down hard, painfully hard. He drew her to her feet and held her there, at arm's length, linked by their clasped hands, looking down into her eyes.

"I can take chances for myself — I won't take them for you," he told her. "You can't afford to have a rotten filthy newspaper story connected with you. I accept your resignation," he ended, very low.

He dropped her hands and turned away for a moment. When he swung back to her his mouth was contoured to a smile, but his eyes remained sombre.

"You've been the best secretary and the best friend a man could wish for," he told her.

She shook her head, like an unhappy child, and turning, went into her office almost blind with tears.

And that was all that passed between them until she was ready to leave. He was still at his desk when she went in, her hat and coat on, her handbag under her arm.

"Good-by," Anne said, with difficulty. "I — if I were you, I'd use Miss Danton until you fill my place. She's quick and she does good work. If you like, she could come to see me any evening, and I'd tell her as much about the routine and all as I can."

Fellowes said, quickly:

"But it's *not* good-by. You'll let me see you? We're *friends,* aren't we?"

"Of course."

"I may come to your apartment?" he asked, like a boy. "You'll have dinner with me — often — we'll talk about the work and — ourselves?"

Anne shook her head.

"No — not yet. Can't you see," she asked, in despair, as she saw his face darken with disappointment, "how that would ruin everything — if people saw me with you outside? There wouldn't be any use in leaving the office — no use in anything," she told him.

"But I *must* see you," he argued, stubbornly.

Anne said, in a panic:

"Not — yet. When everything's settled — but — not yet."

She held out her hand. It was an effort to

her to lift it. She felt as if it were as heavy as her heart.

"Good-by," she said again.

He took the hand in his own, held it a long moment.

"I won't say it," he told her.

When she had gone, he stared blankly at the closed door.

Gone — for good — little lonely, competent Anne. Anne who carried so many of his burdens on her slim shoulders — Anne who was as necessary to him as the air he breathed. But you didn't think deeply about the vital need of air until it was denied you.

He said aloud, still standing there, staring:

"But I need her. I can't lose her. I *love* her —"

She had forbidden him to see her. He recognized, with rebellion, how wise she had been. Not for himself — though she had thought only of him — but for herself, and he must think of her. He was bitterly regretful for his own sake that he hadn't told her how things were with him. If Jim hadn't come in — damn him, anyway, good fellow though he undoubtedly must be — but if Jim hadn't come in, he would have spoken. Now, for Anne's sake, with this particular trouble brewing, he must follow his original plan and say nothing until the case was over

— and forgotten.

Then he could go to her, tell her that he loved her, ask her to come back to him — not as the — what had Linda called her? — the office wife, working for him, guarding him, giving him all her energy and devotion — that would be impossible, he could no longer endure to have her near him in that capacity — but as — the wife in his home, the one woman, *his* —

"Anne," his heart cried out after her, "wait for me, believe in me, love me!"

"It doesn't matter about me," she'd said, "but it matters terribly about you."

There'd been confession in that. He'd known it at the moment of her speaking, but had put it aside for the moment as something to treasure secretly, to marvel at, to think about. Confession, not of simple loyalty, but of the last tenacious loyalty of a woman's soul, confession — of *love*. And on the heels of this realization he knew a humbled gratitude, a shaken wonder and a rapturous certainty.

But there was one thing he must do, to be sure for her sake. He went personally to the office of the *Daily Record* and demanded to see the editor-in-chief. After a little talk with that curiously courtly and rather charming individual, he was turned over to Adams, the city editor, and stated his errand to him briefly enough.

"Oh, that's all washed out," Adams told him in some disgust. "Nothing in it. Don't worry, nothing will be said — simply the bare statement of your wife's suit. You'll have to stand for that, Mr. Fellowes. It's usual enough. People can't get divorces nowadays without telling the world."

"I didn't expect it would be kept from the press," Fellowes informed him. "But neither Mrs. Fellowes nor myself desire any advance publicity. You appreciate my position?"

"Oh, quite," Adams answered, carelessly, "but news is news. If John and Mary Smith decide to separate, that's one thing — nothing to addle the morning eggs, you know. But if Lawrence Fellowes of the Fellowes Advertising Agency and his wife, the former Miss Schuyler, agree to disagree after ten years of married life — that's another. That's NEWS. You business men look with scorn and loathing at us nosey newspaper lowbrows — until, perchance, you may need us for something; when it's a different story. But you forget that we are pledged to furnish a very vast public with — news. So we furnish it, and you people who furnish us with the means can go jump in the lake."

He grinned rather agreeably. You couldn't get sore at him, reflected Fellowes, hopelessly.

"Yes, I get all that," he agreed, "but the point is — why on earth try to drag a perfectly innocent woman into it? You'd nothing to base a story on, much less a sensational one?"

"Oh, yes, we had," yawned Adams. "I see you don't follow the drift of the newspaper mind. Look here, I'll show you. You and Mrs. Fellowes had a large, splashy wedding — that was news. Your position, your inherited money, Miss Schuyler's name — that was news. Then, for ten years, you led a most exemplary life. Sob-sisters, doing society sketches, were always citing you — that was news in this day and age. Mrs. Fellowes was continually before the public — that was news, too. Then, suddenly, she beats it for Reno — news, more news. Now, why? The newspaper mind gets to work. It works like a detective — *cherchez la* — anything — man, woman, child. In this case we appeared to draw a blank. Mrs. Fellowes' name has never been connected with anyone." He paused, chewed his cigarette, and looked sharply at Fellowes. Fellowes' face was a mask, but his heart pounded with relief. At least that much was gained — they wouldn't start hunting down Linda and come on Jameson's trail.

"In your case," went on Adams, after a moment, "we drew an equal blank, until one of our bright young men noticed your secretary.

It was reported to me that she was an exceptionally pretty girl. Now wives and husbands, employers and secretaries — these are old triangles. They happen not only in the news but in real life. Why not? A busy man is thrown continuously into the society of a pretty and intelligent young woman; a young woman who understands his business — and incidentally himself — one thousand per cent better than his wife does. His wife is connected in his mind with — what? With bills, expenses, domestic difficulties, servant problems, money . . . always money. His secretary, on the other hand, is connected only with his business troubles — and she shares them, she does not create them. She works in his interests, not against them. His wife sees him in — mental undress. Sees him tired, irritable, crabbing about something, too busy to take part in whatever little schemes and interests she has. His secretary, however, may see him bad tempered, impatient, or as a slave driver; but she sees also what he accomplishes and how he accomplishes it and why. He becomes, in many cases, a sort of god to her. And he knows it, after a while, if he isn't a fool. Given all this motivation, as we say up at The Algonquin — and add to that a secretary who is very easy on the eyes — well, have you arrived at the result, which is, rightly or wrongly — NEWS?"

He grinned again and added:

"I don't often waste my time explaining to people why they are grist for the mills of the press. But if you'll excuse me, Mr. Fellowes, it seemed to me that somebody ought to put you wise to things that any smart kid in high school knows all about — thanks to the papers."

"I do see your point," Fellowes said, slowly.

"Of course you do. You'd be a fool if you didn't, and fools don't usually reach the position you hold, as it happens. But a man," Adams said comfortably, flinging the dead cigarette on the floor and reaching for a new one, "a man may become the Lindbergh of the Advertising Business and still be pretty damn dumb about some things. I'm sorry we jarred you about this business. Before I saw you my chief told me to reassure you. You don't buy much space, but you buy enough to make it worth our while not to antagonize you when we are able to placate you without any real news-loss to ourselves. We were quite justified in trying to smell out a good story — even if the scent was rather thin. That's out now. It was a coincidence that Jim Murdock happens to be your secretary's brother. Of course, he'd protect her — and we think a hell of a lot of Murdock down here — but, as it happens, his story seems pretty straight. For it's true, I suppose, that she resigned some time ago?"

"True enough," Fellowes answered.

"And that, coupled with the fact that she's to be married, makes our story deader than last year's murder," said Adams.

Fellowes, by some miracle, kept his face blank. But his pulses hammered at his temples. Married — *Anne?*

"Oh," he commented, and somehow succeeded in smiling, "I see that her brother told you — it was to be kept a secret for a time."

"We'll keep it, never fear," laughed Adams. "*That's* not news — it boils down to a quite unknown girl getting married. What's that to the public? No, with her skirts clear of your pending divorce case, Miss Murdock no longer interests us."

Fellowes went back to the office. Miss Danton was at his disposal, and he admitted to himself that she was alert enough, worked hard, and appeared to take an interest. But she was short and dark and wore a trying shade of tan and had adenoids. Also she fluttered a little because of nervousness.

"Miss Murdock," she told him, "left word I might come to see her and she'd help me fit in more quickly, Mr. Fellowes."

"By all means," answered Fellowes vaguely,

and bit back a savage, "Felicitate her for me, won't you?"

It did not occur to him at once to doubt Adams' veracity or Jim's. What an ass he had been! Taking her love for him for granted, just as he had taken her work, her business integrity. Why should she love him? Like him, yes, as a good employer, as a sort of friend. Adams was all wrong. He'd let his story sense run away with him. Daily contact in an office did not engender any godlike illusions in a girl's mind. Her employer was her personal concern — in office hours. Afterwards, she was through with him; she'd turn to a young man for love, to a man she'd not seen in mental shirt sleeves, wrestling with phrases, with problems, nervous, impatient, egotistical. She'd want youth and laughter and the things furtherest removed from an office existence — the sunny carefree things; she'd want dinner for two, dance floors, the curtain rising, flowers and engagement rings; and eventually a flat somewhere or a suburban cottage, a gas range, a backyard — babies.

His heart hurt him until it was physical agony. To love her — and to lose her. The whole story. But he'd never had — *Anne*. He'd just had — Miss Murdock, Secretary to the President.

But she might have told him! She'd prom-

315

ised she'd tell him if ever the situation arose. Surely they'd been good enough friends for that much confidence! She should have told him, not let him hear it in that noisy, smoky, glaring newspaper office from that fat, sweating, sardonic fellow who enunciated out of the corner of his mouth and chewed cigarettes while he talked.

It hadn't been square of her.

He'd not thought of himself as a vain man, yet this had proven him vain to fatuity, he told himself bitterly.

That evening he worked in the office until seven and went out, selecting a restaurant at random, to a solitary, tasteless dinner. He presently pushed the thick plates and cup away, and began to think, to seek loopholes, to make excuses. Perhaps after all Adams had misunderstood something Jim Murdock had said to him; perhaps there was no truth in the rumor.

There was only one thing to do, and that was to find Anne at once and ask, no, *demand* an explanation. Half an hour later he was ringing at her door with a sort of sustained savagery.

She opened it to him and fell back a step at the sight of him, the estranged, demanding eyes, the set mouth, the outthrust jaw.

"I asked you not to come — you shouldn't

have —" she began, but he ignored her and pushed past her into the living room, flung down hat and coat, anywhere, and turned on her, looming very big in the small space.

"I had to come. Look here," he began, half incoherent. "I've heard — Anne — you can't leave me — you've got to stay —" he began, and when she stood there, helpless under the sudden onslaught, he took her by the shoulders in the gesture she remembered so well. "You've got to stay!" he repeated.

"But — after what we agreed?" she said, stumbling, almost dizzy with his nearness, the feel of his hands on her flesh.

"It doesn't matter what people say or think. You were willing to leave for my sake. Well, don't worry about that any more. I was willing to let you go for your own sake. I've gotten over it. You *must* stay."

Then, abruptly, he dropped his hands from her shoulders and took her wholly into his arms, roughly, completely.

"I've got to have you," he told her hoarsely. "I'm mad about you. You know it, Anne — you know you belong to me!"

He forced her chin up with his hands and bent to her mouth and kissed her hungrily and demandingly and deeply. They were alone in the apartment. Night encompassed them, pressing in at the windows. Night with its

darkness, its promise of tenderness and nearness and violence. They stood isolated, in a
small circle of brave light, lost and destroyed,
mind and body in that desperate embrace.

She was so shaken she thought she must
drop but for his arms about her. His arms
were danger and support. So while she cried
out, repudiating him, for both their sakes, she
yet clung to him with a remnant of strength.
It was pain, it was agony, it was peril and
madness, it was a dream come true, and it
was rapture to be held like that.

Fellowes said, huskily:

"You do care for me — you do!"

That brought her to her senses. She did care
for him. Too much. If she surrendered to the
demands of her own flesh and blood and his,
they were lost. She could not harm him consciously, as unconsciously she had been near
to doing.

She did not answer. Slowly Fellowes withdrew his arms and stepped back and faced
her, his gray eyes dark in his white face.

"So it's true, then —"

"What is true?" she managed to ask him.

"That you're to marry O'Hara. That man
Adams told me so at the newspaper office.
I didn't believe it. I couldn't. Not wholly."

For an instant she wondered if she were
going mad. Adams? She put her hand to her

eyes in a little gesture of blindness. Jimmy must have told Adams that she was engaged, as he had suggested. He would go to any lengths to make the insinuated association with Fellowes as impossible as he could. And Fellowes had jumped at obvious conclusions.

Well, it was a way out. She'd tell him it was so, and then he'd leave her and she'd never see him again — never see him again.

"Is it true?" Fellowes demanded again.

"Yes," said Anne, in a small tired voice, "it's quite true."

After a long moment, during which they stood staring at each other, he said:

"Well — my mistake. I thought — it doesn't matter what I thought. I won't ask you to forgive me for what I did just now. I'm not sorry," he said, and turned and walked to the door.

A moment later it shut behind him. Anne ran to it, her arms outstretched.

"Only come back," she pleaded with the empty hall, "— only come back. I'll do anything — give anything — be anything you want me to be — only come back!"

But nothing answered her save the echoes of her own desperate weeping.

Fellowes hailed a taxicab and climbed into it wearily. He felt bruised, like a man who has taken terrific punishment. He'd gone there to tell her he didn't believe Adams' casual, world-shaking statement, to tell her he loved her, to ask her to wait until he was free, to ask her to give herself into his keeping, forever — and he'd not said a word of all this, because his need was so great that he'd taken her in his arms and held her close and kissed her and lost himself in her imagined response. Now he was glad he had not spoken, for what Adams had told him was true and she was to marry O'Hara.

Later that night Fellowes went out, hunted up some men he knew slightly, for whom he cared even less, and proceeded to get deliberately drunk, something he'd not done since — since the Dolly days. And somehow there was a night club — and there were women there — and one of them was small and blonde in a fragile sort of way — and somehow — and somehow —

The next morning he was sick with disgust at himself. The gradual drifting away of the other men, the sullen sitting there at the table with the girl clinging to his hand — "You're very strong, aren't you, and," she laughed thinly, "very rich? And I like you. I — I could be crazy about you, Big Boy. Can't you laugh just a little — for Nona?"

So he had laughed for Nona . . . more than a little.

And that next morning found him dismissing the trainer: "No, I'm not up to it today. A shower — black coffee — that will fix me up —" and then sitting there at the breakfast table, his head in his hands, thinking — remembering.

By God, there was something funny about it after all. Linda had said he'd no sense of humor — the custard-pie sort. No, Anne, had said that. Well, he mustn't think of Anne. But — "Isn't it funny, Anne, after all, Linda needn't have gone to Reno for her divorce. She could have gotten it right here and welcome. After all these years, and being cautious, and not taking the fruit offered, and feeling rather smug about it, and now — and now —"

Nausea rose in him. That cheap little girl, and the scented stuffy flat, and the savagery that had taken him, the madness to blot out everything, to forget, to go berserk —

But the thing that remained to torture him was the feeling that he had not been unfaithful to Linda, who was still his wife, but to Anne, who had never been his wife. Anne, who was to marry another man.

He wondered what Anne was thinking — if she laughed to herself at the remembrance of his madness, or if she had forgotten it in O'Hara's arms.

He did not know that she was almost beyond coherent thought. He did not know that she was tasting the bitterest fruit of all, the fruit of a dead desire, of something once longed for which has come, too late. For just such a face as he had shown to her last night, just such avowals of hunger, were what she had once longed for, with her body and with her cool mind, which once had thought itself so wise.

For Anne, believing that the passion Fellowes had brought her during those few terrible moments in the quiet room was the half loaf, Love's little sister, knew, as she had known at Hot Springs, that she could not accept it — wanting so much more. Yet once she had thought to invite it. Now, although every fibre in her cried out for surrender on any terms, she had fought her way to sanity and seized on his misapprehension as a way of escape. That he cared for her she did not believe; that he wanted her, she knew; but it brought no comfort, only an acrid shame that his wanting should be so much less than her own.

And because if, in seeking her escape, she did not bind herself to it, did not make it reality, she knew she would be taxed beyond her strength, she went to the telephone and called Ted O'Hara. That night, Ted O'Hara, reaching home found a scribbled message. "Call Miss Murdock at her house," it read.

Ted had been away on business for a week, sent by Sanders to talk over some copy with a Western client. It had been his first important responsibility; the affair had been concluded satisfactorily, and he was back again, having reached home after dinner time and going straight to his rooms.

He rang Anne up. Her voice came to him, a voice, he thought instantly, with a difference in it.

"Ted? Could you — come down tonight?"

Could he — !

He was there in less than an hour. Kathleen was at the theatre; Anne was alone. He was so glad to see her. She made a fool of him a dozen times a week, he told himself, but there was no one like her.

"I've left the office," she told him, almost immediately.

Ted's mouth fell open, stayed there, frankly.

"Oh, do close your mouth," she said, laughing in spite of herself, "unless you breathe better that way. What's so remarkable about it?"

"Nothing. Only I thought you were a fixture — a little Rock of Gibraltar."

She reflected, swiftly. Of what use to tell

him half truths? Nothing would reach him, at the agency. She might as well lie and be done with it.

"I was tired of it," she answered lightly, "and Jim had heard of an opening with the Burroughs people —"

"Anne!" His face was radiant. She had left — Fellowes. There wasn't any truth in that old gnawing anxiety of his, after all. "Anne," he repeated, "don't take another job. Take me — instead!"

She lifted her hand, spoke the routine warning and waited, knowing what would follow.

"Teddy!"

"Oh, I know, but you've got to listen to me. I'm getting along like a house afire. I think — this is under your hat — I think that Sanders is going to have an assistant, and that assistant is going to be me. Assistant to the vice-president! Sounds pretty darned good, doesn't it? There'll be a raise presently. Anne, cut out the work and take a partnership job. I love you — I want you — there'll be no stopping us. We'll get to the top, the two of us — together."

She looked at him a moment in silence — the eager, attractive face, the frankly red hair tossed as he ran his fingers through it.

"Anne?" he asked pleadingly.

Well, why not? There wasn't anything left

for her any more. The job was gone — the job that had meant so much. Fellowes had gone — she'd let him believe the lie —

Well, she'd make good.

"Teddy," she said, and smiled a little, "you're such a dear, and I'm so fond of you — but — I don't love you —"

"It's enough to go on — you'll love me," he told her confidently. "You'll have to love me — I'll *make* you! You — haven't had time for love; you haven't learned how," he went on, "giving every minute of your waking time to your job. You — you got sort of single-tracked. Well, to the devil with the job — I'm offering you one for life."

She rose and went over to him and sat down on the arm of his chair, and put her hands on his shoulder.

"If I say 'yes,' " she asked him gravely, "you'll be patient with me — and not expect too much — ?"

"Anne!"

He pulled her down to his lap, kissed her eyes and her mouth with a young, ardent hunger.

She liked him, she was fond of him, her senses were as young as his. She was ardent and unspoiled; she had the imagination which makes a woman that rare thing — a perfect lover. And she was tired, beaten to the ground with emotion and grief and the aching sense of loss that was irreplaceable. It was comfort, sheer physical comfort, to be in the arms that held her so closely, that loved her so eagerly, to hear Ted's broken vows and fantastic promises, to know herself beloved and enduringly desired.

For she had been so terribly hurt.

She closed her eyes and tried to forget herself in Ted's kisses. But closing her eyes was a dangerous procedure. She could imagine, with her white lids folded, other arms about her, another mouth laid close on hers — remembered pressure, remembered passion.

"Is it always going to be like this?" she asked herself, in a sick panic — "Oh, God, *don't* let it always be like this!"

She opened her eyes and looked straight into Ted's. Of course it wouldn't always be like this! She'd — she'd grow to find release and comfort in Ted's caresses because they were — Ted's. Not because they were just kisses — a man's, any man's kisses, that she could dream to — substitutes, narcotics.

"I'll marry you," she said.

Chapter 11

And Breaks an Engagement

Kathleen, coming in rather late, found Ted still there. He was walking the floor when she entered, in a blaze of excitement, ready to take the world by the throat and choke from it the answer to his demands, his desires, the realization of all his dreams. Anne, curled up in a chair, a little pale, her eyes drowsy, was watching him, smiling a little. And as Kathleen, entering, ejaculated, "Why the oratory? Where's the soap box?" Ted seized her around her supple waist, implanted a resounding kiss upon her smooth cheek, and announced gaily:

"Congratulate me — sister!"

Kathleen promptly extricated herself and looked over at Anne.

"Has he gone cuckoo?" she asked, astonished.

"On the contrary," Ted answered for himself. "I'm sitting on top of the world. How'd you like to maid-of-honor at a quiet home wedding?"

"Not — really?"

She ran to Anne, stooped to kiss her. Anne nodded.

"Yes — really!" she answered. "Ted, do go along home — I have to work tomorrow," she added, mechanically, and then stopped and bit her lip.

"No, you don't," Ted told her, "never again. Kathleen, will you leave the room or must I embrace my affianced bride before an audience?"

Having received her cue, Kathleen departed. Ted, lifting Anne to her feet, held her a long moment and then kissed her with, she thought, wearily, a new reverence, new sweetness.

"Good night, dearest," he told her, "you've made me very happy."

At the door he turned. She was standing there, her hands clasped in front of her, looking at him with a most curious expression — one which he could not read, happiness having blinded him to its mingled fear and regret and wistfulness.

"May I tell people?" he asked, as simply as a boy.

She hesitated, and then nodded. Well, why not?

When he had gone, Kathleen came back into the living room in a wisp of lace and sheath of satin. She curled herself up in the big chair and ordered, severely:

"Come here at once!"

Anne went to her and perched on the arm of the chair where so lately she had sat with Ted. Kathleen asked her, gravely:

"It's true, then?"

"Yes."

"Anne, you're not happy — you don't love him!"

"I do," Anne answered stoutly. "I'm awfully fond of him."

"It's not enough," Kathleen answered out of a new wisdom. "Being 'awfully fond' isn't enough. Nor yet — being crazy about a person. I think I know now," she went on, a little dreamily; and Anne was too preoccupied with her own problems at the moment to wonder how Kathleen "knew," in what way and through whom knowledge had come to her. "Anne, you can't marry Ted with another man in your heart," Kathleen concluded.

Anne lifted her head high, gallant. She said, after a moment:

"I won't. I'll —" she stopped and in a low voice went on, "I promise you, Kathleen, I'll make Ted a good wife —"

"Who," asked Kathleen scornfully, "wants a 'good wife'? Anne, we've got to have this out. You're in love with Lawrence Fellowes and you're going to marry Ted O'Hara.

329

It's not fair to you nor to Ted."

"I'll *make* it fair!" Anne cried, childishly. "The other was madness, insanity! I'll cure myself. I'll forget."

Kathleen looked at her a long moment. Then she said, rather abruptly:

"I advise you to make the cure thorough before your wedding night."

"Kathleen!" Anne cried, and then was silent, flushing. Her — wedding night?

"Oh, Anne," Kathleen told her, in affectionate exasperation, "get wise to yourself! You are grown up, you've worked for your living; you've seen what life does to people, what marriage does to them. You — you don't believe in Santa Claus any more, do you? Face things — don't hide around corners from them!"

She put her arms around her sister and leaned her cheek against Anne's shoulder.

"I want you to be happy," said Kathleen, very close to tears.

"I will be — I *must* be," Anne reassured her.

But all the will and must in the world couldn't make her so.

Time went on. The family was told and received the news without much astonishment. Mr. Murdock was frankly pleased.

"I hope," he told Ted, dourly, "you can

manage her better than I've been able to."

But Mrs. Murdock was grave. She liked Ted; she had hoped for just such an outcome to his devotion to Anne, but — she was anxious. She asked her daughter, that first Sunday when the entire family reunioned in the little brick house: "Anne, tell me, girl, are you *sure?*"

"Quite sure, dear," Anne told her steadily.

"You must be," her mother said, a worried line between her kind, gay eyes. "Marriage is hard enough even for people who — who love each other very much."

Jim was not quite satisfied, either. He got Anne away from Sara's congratulations long enough to ask:

"Is it all right, Sis?"

"Of course it is. Don't be silly. Don't you like Teddy?"

"Sure, I like him; he's a good scout. That's not the point. I mean — what you told me —" he floundered, "and what I said up at the office. That hasn't forced you into anything you'll regret, has it?"

"No. Please don't worry about me. What — what I told you was true enough, only — can't you see," Anne denied her heart, "can't you see it was just what you said — glamour, propinquity, a sort of crazy hero worship? This is different — real — very day."

And with that he had to be content.

Ted's news was not long in spreading over the office. Betty Howard was the first to know and to be genuinely happy about it. And then Sanders, who sighed and said, "Another good man gone wrong! Well, she's one in a million, O'Hara. We'll have to do something pretty good for you both." Then Polly, whose eyes were red for a week thereafter, and whose congratulations, extended to young Mr. O'Hara himself, were compounded of honey and gall. And finally, of course, Lawrence Fellowes.

Well, that he had known it for some days was no consolation. Nor that he had made a fool of himself.

Ted was insistent in his demands for an immediate wedding.

"No," Anne told him, "not until — next fall."

"Next fall!" Ted exclaimed, in horror. "A year away!"

It was then early autumn, a year from the time she had gone to Hot Springs with Fellowes and Linda.

"Yes."

"But what's the sense of waiting?" he wanted to know, in despair.

"All the sense in the world. I — want to get my clothes ready," Anne told him, fran-

332

tically hiding behind one of the oldest of all feminine excuses. "We must take time and look about for a place to live — and I want to go back to work."

"Work? But you promised —"

"No, I didn't. Ted, please don't be angry," she begged him. "I — can't be rushed into things. I must have time. You said you'd be patient —"

He was terribly disappointed but there was no moving her. He went, in a vain hope of support, to Mrs. Murdock, to Kathleen, even to Jim. And all gave him the same advice:

"Don't hurry her. She's been independent too long. All the arguments in the world won't budge her."

So he had to accept her decision. She took a job very soon thereafter with the Burroughs people, the opening of which Jim had spoken to her a short time before, and went to work, secretary to the general manager of the concern, and tried to believe that she was happy there, and contented.

She had been frank with the new boss, Mc-Pherson.

"I'm engaged to be married. Will that make a difference?" she asked when he interviewed her.

McPherson, young but graying at his lean temples, looked at her in vexation.

"Of course it will. That's the trouble with you women — you're always getting married," he grumbled, and added, as if to himself, "just when I thought I'd gotten somebody who'd yank me out of the angles six incompetent women have gotten me into!"

She said, smiling faintly:

"But — it won't be for a year yet — perhaps more —"

McPherson threw up his hands.

"Can you promise me that?"

"Yes, Mr. McPherson."

She had known of him for some time. A clever man, a keen one. She had even met him — "My secretary, Miss Murdock," Fellowes had said proudly, as if he were introducing his competitor to a phenomenon.

"Well," McPherson told her, "you've got me where you want me. I must have someone — quick. Someone who understands this game. And you're the only possible person so far. I know how efficient you are. I know all about your work. I was ready to give you a life job if we got along together. However, a year — Lots of things can happen in a year," he added, hopefully. "Not that I wish your young man any hard luck, of course, but if he breaks his neck or runs away with another girl I wouldn't shed any tears."

So Anne went to work. She liked the position; it was much the same, in a way, as her work with Fellowes. But McPherson was a very different chief. He treated her in a rather more personal manner, and yet as if she were an intelligent boy. There was no consciousness of her sex in his attitude. Half the time he called her "Murdock." Sometimes he swore, not at her but at life in general, when things were going badly. Often he praised her in his blunt, forthright manner, and he stood on no formality whatever. He treated her as if she had been in his employ for a great many years. He did not brook the slightest stupidity; he was intolerant of mistakes — even minor ones — and not as open to her suggestions as Fellowes had been. However, he was just, and Anne liked him.

But she was unhappy.

After all, she told herself, it *had* been the man and not the job. For all the excitement had gone, all the thrill, all the feeling that she was a part of the work, that she counted. All the joy had departed. It was simply a good job that she tried to do well.

That was the autumn in which Linda Fellowes, having completed her residence in Reno, procured her divorce and sailed, immediately, for Europe. The papers announced the conclusion of her suit and her departure, and that was all. The incident was closed.

Once, during that winter, Anne saw Lawrence Fellowes. He had heard of her new position. For weeks he fought against an overwhelming desire to drop into the Burroughs office — casually — and see her. Of course had it not been for the fact of her engagement, the moment he was free he would have gone to her — but, she no longer was for him, even remotely. He told himself that it would be sheer madness to attempt to see her, that the small comfort which her physical presence, the assurance of her reality, would bring him would not compensate for the bitterness concomitant with that ephemeral happiness. Better to forget her. He had tried to, in a hundred futile ways — working hard, playing harder —

On this occasion his appointment with McPherson was not, he reminded himself, of his own seeking. He came to the office, therefore, schooled to the encounter; yet it was with a sense of absolute shock that he walked in, unannounced, as it happened. "Mr. McPherson expects you," the reception room clerk had told him, and he'd said, hastily, "I know the way —," and then he saw Anne sitting there at the typewriter. She was alone in the big room and as he came in she lifted her hands from the keys, dropped them in her lap and drew a deep audible breath of weariness.

Standing there in the doorway, Fellowes experienced a tremendous surge of emotion. She was — just as he had seen her so many times, day in, day out; just as she was in his dreams and his heart, since she had left him — little and lovely, the sunlight on her hair, the small face a trifle thinner and more colorless than he remembered it, the slim, round figure, the simple, smart frock.

"Anne?" he said and his voice shook.

She had not heard him come in, so many miles had she been from the office, from the work just completed. Now she looked up and saw him, and he watched the color flood her face and throat, and die away, leaving her whiter than ever.

But her verbal recognition of his presence seemed perfectly composed.

"Mr. Fellowes," she said, and rose, "I'll find Mr. McPherson."

Fellowes came nearer and held out his hand.

"Aren't you going to shake hands with me?" he asked. "Haven't you forgiven my stupidity, my second blunder?"

She laid her hand in his. Why, she wondered, in terror and agony, had this encounter been forced upon her? So hard, so terribly hard. And she had been trying, with every ounce of strength in her, to forget, to cut him out of her mind and heart, and to turn that mind and heart, shriven and clean, to Ted.

He said, releasing her hand abruptly, because he so much longed to hold it, to bruise it with his strength, to put it in his own, for ever:

"I heard that you were here. I wondered. I thought, of course, that you and O'Hara —"

She raised her head in that spirited way he remembered so well, and answered briefly:

"We're not going to be married for some time."

"I see. He's a very fine chap," Fellowes admitted, and hated Ted O'Hara as he spoke as he had hated no other living person. "I don't suppose it's the book of etiquette to congratulate the fiancée, but I do —"

"Thank you," Anne told him, and made an effort at smiling. He looked at her a minute and if her own eyes had not been so blind with terror she must have seen that which was naked in his own.

"Have you forgiven me?" he asked again.

Anne nodded mutely and stepped back a pace, twisting one hand in the other. If McPherson didn't come in, if Fellowes didn't go, she'd scream, burst into tears, run away, escape somehow —

But McPherson arrived in time. As his tall shadow darkened the doorway Fellowes said, low, hurriedly:

"Anne? I hope you're happy, I want you to be —"

"Oh, I am!" she assured him and smiled brilliantly. What was it to him if she were happy or miserable? If he had cared for her, he had recovered, soon enough. All his caring had been based on one appeal only, an appeal she had once tried to invite and make use of, and which had almost destroyed her — and him. Her face felt stiff as if she were dead. She moved her lips and spoke her lines, and yet she was a dead person. Happy? Less happy than ever, now that she had seen him again.

She gathered up her papers and left the two men together. Fellowes stared after her and McPherson spoke to him twice before he answered. She'd said she was happy. Well, what was it to her how he felt?

Anne went into the lavatory and put cold water on her wrists and forehead. She saw in the long mirror over the washstand the blue eyes that had darkened to black and were blazing with excitement; she saw the red lips that shook and the cheeks that flushed and paled.

"Fool — !" she told herself.

She had not seen him since the day she left his office. Not many weeks, as time had counted, yet an eternity, and still too soon, too soon for her peace of mind — and for Ted's peace of heart.

When she returned to her desk he had gone.

McPherson remarked in that careless, familiar yet indifferent way he had with her:

"Fellowes looks badly, don't you think?"

She responded that she had not noticed, wondering that McPherson couldn't see that she lied. For was not every altered line, every haggard trace in Fellowes' face known to her in the first moment she'd looked at him again?

"Funny thing," went on McPherson, casually, "that wife of his divorcing him so suddenly and quietly. Good looking woman. I met her several times before his uncle's death, at a time when he took her around a good deal to dinners and whatnot. She stopped that, when he reached his present job. I hear he's been hitting it up since she left him. One wonders what's in back of it. Well, I suppose he'll marry again, after a while," speculated McPherson, "and some little snip, pretty as paint, and shallow as a saucer."

"Why should you suppose that?" Anne wanted to know, in a tone not commonly used between employee and employer.

McPherson noticed it, of course, but it was not apparent in his easy reply.

"Oh, because that's the sort of thing men, nearing forty, usually do. It appears to be routine. They marry, quite young, a perfectly

340

suitable wife. Then, for some reason or other, they dissolve the marriage. And they're lonely. So they look around. And there are plenty of girls waiting for just such a psychological moment."

"That," said Anne shortly, "is a generalization. And generalizations are apt to be wrong."

"Well, you know him better than I do," McPherson admitted, carelessly.

Anne was astonished and angry at herself for her lack of discretion. But McPherson had stung her into admitting to herself something she had tried not to face. Of course, now that Lawrence Fellowes was free it was on the cards that he would marry again. Anne had never been jealous of Linda in a bitter sense — save during that time at Hot Springs — and even then her jealousy had been more a wounding self-tormenting agony, and had not affected her genuine liking for the woman who was then Fellowes' wife. She had never hated Linda, had never wished her evil. But for that hypothetical, shadowy unknown woman who might enter Fellowes' life intimately, now that Linda had left it, she knew a devastating hatred, a savagery of emotion that was almost murderous.

And McPherson, who had been watching her face, repeated reflectively, slowly:

"Well, you know him better than I do."

Anne said nothing, and there it ended as far as conversation was concerned; but McPherson was left with a gnawing curiosity. For he was a very curious man and had an almost feminine prying quality of mind. Anne had not given him any very adequate reasons for leaving Fellowes' office. She had merely said that she wished to make a change. Had there been anything of a personal nature between her and Fellowes? wondered McPherson. She was, of course, an extravagantly pretty girl, a girl any man might notice, with whom any man might permit himself to fall in love — and looks were no drawback in a secretary provided brains went along with them.

He could see through a stone wall as far as most men, and could manipulate two and two until the sum read five or six. Was there, he asked himself, not really caring, but always ready to set himself a problem, any connection between Anne's resignation and Mrs. Fellowes' divorce? But if so, where did Anne's young man come in? And why?

These speculations rather increased his interest in Anne, but the interest was neither personal nor emotional. He was a rather cold man and definitely cynical. A very unfortunate matrimonial experience in his early manhood had left him most cautious where women were concerned. He called it being without illusions, and did not realize it was a more positive than negative reaction — a caution dictated by fear.

If, as he conjectured, there had been some sort of a mix-up in Anne's former job, then Anne had all the potentialities of a stick of dynamite.

Not that he, of course, was in any danger. She did not hold the position of trust with McPherson that she had held with Fellowes. Mr. McPherson's personal checking account was his own concern. He employed a secretary to protect him from importunate callers, to reply to his letters — he always dictated them and never left them to her discretion — and to see that the general office routine ran smoothly. Now, coming to the conclusion that she had been more than ordinarily in her former employer's confidence, it occurred to McPherson that it would be amusing and perhaps profitable to pump her a little regarding the other agency.

Here he was consciously neither dishonest nor unethical. He did not endeavor to discover any matters of great importance affecting the good-natured rivalry and competition between the two firms. It was simply all of a piece with his unbridled curiosity. And Anne, who sensed something of this, was not particularly concerned. When she could answer his careless questions without affecting her loyalty — a loyalty which remained as strong and unbroken as if it had been born in her — to Fellowes' business, she replied. When she believed that McPherson overstepped the mark, she evaded or said briefly that she was unable to answer the query.

Toward summer, however, a large, newly organized company, having set aside an unusually large appropriation for the launching of a new razor, teetered, rather coyly, between Fellowes and the Burroughs when it came to a question of selecting an advertising agency, the members of the firm disagreeing.

McPherson, with his uncanny scent, got wind of this, and warily began to question Anne as to certain policies of the agency whose employ she had quitted — policies which it would be rather well for Mr. McPherson to know were he to be fully equipped to meet all the demands of the possible client.

Anne answered him with a blunt denial that she knew anything at all. And McPherson asked her, quite kindly, if she was still employed by Mr. Fellowes or drawing her salary from the Burroughs concern? Her answer to that was her instant resignation.

She went home, worn out with wondering whether she had been right or wrong. Strictly speaking, she would have been betraying no trust had she replied — as she could have — fully and with absolute knowledge to McPherson. He had asked her nothing which he couldn't have found out himself. The question was not one of any secret formula to success. But Anne, apparently, had not been able to free herself from all her old associations. Her heart was not in her work for Mr. McPherson, right-hand man of the more important Burroughs. Her heart was back where she had left it, in Lawrence Fellowes' private office. And nothing that she had learned in the Felllowes Agency during her long apprenticeship, or her personal closeness to Fellowes himself, could ever be passed on to a competitor either to satisfy one man's feline curiosity or, by an inch, to better his firm's chance.

Ted was overwhelmed with delight when he learned that she had relinquished the position. She did not tell him the reason — Ted too, was connected with Fellowes; she could not afford, she knew, to give herself away — she merely stated that she did not like the job and was already tired of it. His natural reply was to urge marriage upon her.

"I'll get a vacation during July," he said. "What's the matter with making it a honeymoon?"

345

Anne put his eager hands from her and turned her cheek to his kiss.

"No — I said in the fall. Give me this summer," she begged him.

"But what will you do?" he wanted to know, reasonably. "You might just as well marry me. You'd just be hanging around. You wouldn't take a summer job. What's the matter, Anne, can't you make up your mind?"

"I made it up," she answered, "for — next autumn. Oh please, dear, try to be patient! I want to go home and be with Mother for a time. Kathleen's going on the road. I give up the flat — she can make other arrangements when she returns. I'd like to — rest," Anne said.

"You don't care for me, at all," he told her, wounded.

"Yes, I do — only — only —" and here, to her intense surprise and horror she began to cry, as frankly and wholeheartedly as a child.

Ted was seized with instant remorse. He took her in his arms and tried to comfort her and all but cried with her.

"It's all right," he said, over and over. "You're just tired and nervous. I'm a brute to nag you so. Forget it and make your own plans, and I won't say another word."

She thought afterwards how sweet and how

mistaken he had been. Mistaken, that was, as far as his own good was concerned. For she was in so emotional and unsettled a state of mind that if he had ignored her tears and her entirely feeble excuses, she might have, for the sake of peace, for the sake of having matters taken out of her tired hands, surrendered to him, given in and married him, for better or worse.

The flat was closed. Kathleen went off on the road, her heart high with a sense of adventure, and yet a little low because of some one she was leaving behind. Frank Young, the impetuous and clever boy on the *Times*, whom she had met through her brother, had become a large and emotionally perilous factor in her life. She admitted as much to Anne.

"That's one reason why I'm taking this road company job," she said frankly. "It will keep me away all summer . . . and by then I ought to be sure. I am sure when I'm with him — but — I've been that before," said wise Kathleen, "and it's being away that counts. If I get along all right without him, if I don't miss him as much as I'm afraid I'm going to — why that's proof enough."

"Has he asked you to marry him?"

"Yes — course he has — the first time I met him, for that matter!"

"If you marry him, will you stay on the

stage?" Anne asked, feeling that this young sister of hers had matured amazingly in the last year.

"Of course. Frank doesn't mind. He likes it," Kathleen told her in some astonishment. "I'd like to have a baby," she announced further, with perfect honesty and no reticence, "but there's plenty of time for that. We've talked it over."

"You've talked it over! and still haven't said you'd marry him?" Anne asked.

"Not yet — not until I get back from the road. Not until I'm sure," Kathleen answered. But her eyes were sure as she spoke.

Kathleen gone, Anne closed the flat which she had on a month to month lease, stored the little furniture, and moved back home to the red brick house.

Her mother told her, flatly:

"You're not happy."

"Of course I am. What makes you think such a thing?"

"You're not," her mother insisted, "not the way a girl should be who's looking forward to her wedding."

"Girls don't sit on silk cushions and hem napkins and dream and flutter, and swoon the way they used to," Anne told her. "I'm perfectly happy — and Ted and I understand each other."

348

"I doubt that," Mrs. Murdock denied instantly. "There isn't a man and woman living who understand each other. If they did," she added with unconscious cynicism, "they'd never fall in love, much less marry. Of course, it's natural to a girl to have — misgivings. All of them do. I did. But I married your father and I've never really regretted it — although I used to think I did when you were all small and there wasn't much money, and it was summer time and hot in the kitchen, and I had an ailing baby or two to look after and fret over. But that wasn't regret, really — it was lack of faith in my own strength. You'll know, some day, when you've children — of your own."

Children?

Ted "liked kids." He said so — he acted as if he did. Anne had seen him with Jim's uproarious pair.

Children — hers and Ted's!

She tried to face that veiled future. Kathleen's open discussion of it had brought the matter too close to Anne. And now, here her mother was talking — hinting —

But Anne's first response to Ted's lovemaking had vanished. It had produced in her a genuine if ephemeral emotion, born of her loneliness and her tired heart and her grief, born too of the natural demands of her un-

349

blunted senses. His kisses, his arms about her, had brought her a certain amount of physical comfort. And she had thought, her lips warm under O'Hara's and her heart longing for Lawrence Fellowes, that forbidden dreaming, that perilous making-believe, would lessen, would vanish, and leave her wholly Ted's. But it had not.

This she had faced, as the weeks went by, and had faced also that dreams were not nourishment for healthy young appetites. There came, inevitably, a time when Ted's arms and Ted's lips were, as she had hoped, just *Ted's* — and not, in imagination, another's. But the reaction to that apparent victory was not as she had, also, hoped and prayed. Once released from her imagination, once robbed of their dreaming, deluding quality, they left her indifferent, completely cold. And Ted, lately, had complained bitterly.

"Why won't you kiss me? Why do you always turn away? Why do you always put me off?"

She knew why and could not answer, could only continue to evade, to excuse, to make herself appear fatigued, petulant, "not in the mood."

"But you never are!" was his answer to that.

If, she now thought, she was so numb to Ted's ardor — what would become of her as

Ted's wife, as the mother of his children?

She did not want Ted's children. . . .

Essentially, she was not maternal. Essentially she was a lover. Children to Anne would come as the perfect complement to love, as love's flowering. They would never be valuable to her for themselves alone. They would be valuable, treasurable, infinitely desirable as the shared possession of herself and her lover.

This realization came to her, not suddenly but painfully and slowly, over the first part of that summer in the sweltering red brick house. And when it could no longer be evaded, when it had to be faced and thought out and exposed in all its implications to the strong light of honesty, she knew that she could not marry O'Hara. And after a time she told her mother so — and told her why — in part, with no mention of Fellowes.

Mrs. Murdock was unastonished — but indignant.

"I knew it," she said, "and you knew it — all along. It's not been like you, Anne, to keep the boy dangling like this, to tell him you cared for him, to promise to marry him."

She was ashamed of her daughter, and said so — and Anne answered humbly:

"I don't blame you. I — I've been dishonest with Ted and with myself. It was — a way out, an escape. I truly thought when I said

I'd marry him, that, being so fond of him, knowing him so long, I could come to care the way I should — the way he wanted me to —"

"You must tell him at once," said her mother.

Ted was taking his vacation. He had not left the city, but was staying with three other young men in a bungalow at Manhattan Beach. This was in order to be near Anne, and to get the exercise he loved — tennis, handball, swimming. He had spent several vacations in this fashion, and Anne had urged that he so do "for the last time." He could drive in and see her — they could be together as much as if he were still in the heart of the city.

The evening of her talk with her mother, Anne was terribly restless. Having made up her mind, she was like a great many women — impatient to have the whole thing over and done with — settled. Ted had said something about a party — moonlight swimming — that night, and had offered to drive in and take her down. She had refused, and he'd been hurt and angry about it, and they had parted, not on the best of terms.

Soon after dinner, she had asked Murdock if he was going to use the car, and had been told that he was not. She put on her hat, slipped a white flannel coat over her sheer, sleeveless dress and spoke, privately, to her mother.

"I'm going to drive down to the beach and talk to Ted," she told her. "I — I must. I can't go on a minute longer."

"You've gone on — the better part of a year," her mother informed her. "Can't you wait until tomorrow?"

"No — please — please understand," Anne begged. "I've been such a fool, and so unfair. I can't go through another night, thinking — thinking —"

"You can't go down there alone — with a party going on," forbade Mrs. Murdock.

Anne argued that she knew Ted's friends — they wouldn't think it strange. The party didn't amount to anything, just a few young people going for a swim and building a beach fire and having supper.

"I'll be going with you," said her mother. And that was that.

They drove down in absolute silence, Anne handling the rather rickety car safely and surely, driving through the stupendous massed traffic of a hot summer's night with mechanical precision.

When they reached Manhattan Beach the wind was cool and salt and the rows of bungalows — some pretentious, some merest shacks — blazed with light, resounded with voices and laughter, the music of phonographs and radios. The bigger houses were lighted, too, set back among big trees in their own pleasant, flower-scented yards. Beyond, at the end of each side street the ocean rolled in, calm, dark, mysterious, with the promise of light that the rising moon held out to it.

The bungalow Ted shared with his friends was at the extreme restricted end of the beach. That, too, was brilliantly lighted and the phonograph was playing on the little porch. "That's fine for you, but how about me?" it was inquiring plaintively.

Anne parked the car. Her mother, speaking for the first time, said, "I'll wait here," and settled back to watch the ocean and the rising moon, and think her own silent, wise thoughts.

Anne went in. Half a dozen young men and women, all of whom she knew, looked up at her entrance. They wore bathing suits, and had been dancing. There was something to drink on a wicker table in the corner, and some one had been busy in the small kitchen, judging by the confusion Anne saw through the open door.

Harry Peters, Ted's closest friend, came forward hastily.

"Anne! What a piece of luck — did you bring your suit?"

"No, I'm not going to stay." She greeted the others, smiling. "Mother's out in the car. We just went for a ride," she improvised, "and I want to speak to Ted."

"He's down on the beach," Peters told her, rather hastily. "I'll go get him."

"No, I'll go."

"Please —" Peters stepped forward, his pleasant face a little worried. "You'll get your shoes full of sand. I'll call him."

But she had run out, saying over her shoulder, "Thanks, Harry, don't bother."

There was a silence of voices after she had left, and the phonograph went on asking its mournful questions. One of the girls remarked, resignedly: "Well, that tears it — probably."

Peters said:

"Oh, I don't know. Anne's sensible. She won't see anything in it. Still, Jane, you shouldn't have brought her down."

"Why not? She begged to come. It isn't my fault that Ted gave her one sort of rush last year, and the bum's rush this," answered Jane, coolly, with a toss of her bright head. "*I* should worry!"

Anne went down to the small private beach which adjoined the bungalow. She called Ted once, and saw, as she called, a dark blur near the driftwood pile, which was ready, waiting

355

for a match to flare it into amazing, changing beauty.

She walked over, thinking he had not heard her. The wind blew hard here, and in the wrong direction.

She stumbled upon them — they were not more than a few yards away — Ted with a girl in his arms — Ted, saying over and over:

"I'm sorry — I'm sorry — I didn't know —"

Anne stopped, stock still. She wanted to put her hands over her ears — she wanted to run — she wanted to die of shame at her involuntary eavesdropping. But she couldn't move.

She heard the girl's voice answer — a voice familiar to her:

"You did know. I've loved you all along. You cared, once, a little — or said you did. I can't give you up, Teddy — I *won't* —"

Anne said, quietly, walking nearer:

"You won't have to, Polly."

Polly Ames pulled herself out of Ted's arms with a little shriek. She was wearing, Anne noted, with that absurd attention to detail which occupies minds at important moments, a scant silk bathing suit of a dark color — and over it a coolie coat. Her fair hair curled tightly, damp with the salt air, on her forehead.

"Anne! For God's sake!" Ted exclaimed.

He moved forward, angry and yet at the same time abject. The moon, sailing out from under a cloud, flung a silver arrow on the scene — the driftwood pile, the two girls and the man, the white, shifting sand.

"It doesn't matter. I came here to see you," Anne began.

"I can explain," Ted said, unhappily. Polly, since her little shriek, had not opened her lips.

"You don't have to. I came down to break our engagement. I hadn't intended to do it before an audience," Anne went on, feminine enough even through her very genuine relief, "but that doesn't matter either. I don't love you. I've told you so. I told you I thought I'd care — some day. I've found that I can't. This," she indicated Polly by the merest gesture of her hand, "this accident has nothing to do with my decision. I came on purpose to tell you that I was sorry — that you must let me go."

Polly Ames stepped forward before Ted could answer, and spoke, anger drying the tears in her eyes, anger lending force to her words:

"You're a selfish woman, Anne Murdock," she accused her. "You used Ted just as long as it suited you, and now you throw him over because you no longer need him. What's the answer? Did Mr. Fellowes give you your job back?" she asked. "There isn't anyone who doesn't know that you're crazy in love with him, that you just took Ted because you hadn't a chance —"

"Keep quiet," Ted ordered, turning on the other girl savagely. "All this is none of your business."

"It *is* my business; I'll make it so," cried Polly furiously. "Listen to me, Anne. All the time Ted was going with you at first, he was going with me, too. Oh, I know I had your leavings — that when you broke a date with him he came to me to have his vanity bandaged. But I didn't care. I was in love with him — really in love. I thought he'd come to see it, to see how little he meant to you, how much he meant to me. I wanted him, I tell you. Not as a convenience, but as my own. I wanted a home and babies; I wanted Ted, and, because I did, I let him make love to me; I let him kiss me with you in his mind. I thought, perhaps, some day, he'd forget you and turn to me. Well, when you lost your job and saw that your boss had no further use for you, you gave Ted his chance. Some chance! A fine life he would have led with you — always looking down on him, always comparing him with another man. Don't I know what a life it would have been? Hasn't he played a little of the same game with me?

You make me sick, you business women, competing with men, thinking yourselves so superior, always aiming to get the man higher up, not giving a snap of your fingers for the man who hasn't got there yet! You wouldn't be willing to work for a man — you'd always be thinking of yourself, throwing up to him how much money you could make, how important you are to your job. Work!" said Polly scornfully, "what does that amount to — to a real woman. It's just time until a man comes along who'll work *for* you, who'll make a home for you, a man who'll come to you, not for business conversation, but for love — for comfort — for babies. A man who'll be head of his house, not just tolerated in it."

She fell, a soft heap of curls and rage, on the sand and with her face on her arms began to cry bitterly.

"She's right," Anne said, her voice shaking. "She speaks for her type, I guess, and puts mine pretty well in its place. I — I'm sorry this had to happen," she told O'Hara. "But — please believe me, it isn't because I saw Polly with you that I told you I'd — quit. I'd made up my mind to it before I came down. She — hasn't made any difference, except that she makes me see myself a little clearer."

O'Hara was in as undignified and unheroic

a position as a man could well be. He looked down at Polly and then across at Anne. He said, with utter wretchedness:

"I've known — for a long time — pretty much how you felt about me. But I cared for you so much, Anne, — it's you I love! — that I was willing to take the chance."

"I'm not willing to take it for you," she told him. "Good-by," she said, and lifted her hand and then dropped it to her side. Of what use, the commonplace gesture? "Good-by."

She turned and walked away. Ted, walking over to the pile of driftwood, cursed — and aloud — for some moments, and kicked at the logs with his sandalled fee, as sullen as a boy.

She'd found him in a ridiculous position. She'd let him down before another woman. Not that that was her fault, however, he was forced to reflect. A woman who loved him. Well, she'd heard that much — that some one cared for him. That was a sort of stinging salve to his pride.

Polly — it hadn't been her fault, either. It had been his, from the beginning. But a man couldn't be blamed for going where he knew he was wanted. Of course Polly had made an unholy mess of this — and he'd never get over Anne — but still Polly loved him, and she hadn't been exactly responsible, and he had taken her in his arms and kissed her after she'd asked him when he was to be married, and had started to cry when he told her.

No, it hadn't been Polly's fault. She was something of a little fool — the sort of a girl a man laughed at a little, but wanted to take care of. She didn't make you feel — inferior and schoolboyish. She made you feel every inch of your height and every pound of your weight, and every atom of your strength, and perhaps a little bit more.

Anne? He'd lost her. He'd never had her — not really.

After a moment he walked back to Polly, and, stooping, picked her up and set her on her feet.

"It's pretty much of a mess, isn't it?" he asked quite gently. "Come on, let's go back to the house."

"Please," Polly begged him, "please forgive me"

"It doesn't matter," he said, casually, and went with her back to the bungalow, forgetting to suit his steps to her shorter stride, letting her almost run in order to keep up with him. He was not thinking of Polly then; he was thinking of Anne. It would not be until much later that he would realize how completely, how gladly, how gratefully he had come to forgive them both.

Chapter 12

And Decides on a Different Career

When Anne returned to the car, she found her mother waiting for her, her hands folded in her lap, her entire attitude one of patience and serenity. She looked briefly at her daughter under the light of a single street lamp, and asked merely, "Is it — all right?"

Anne nodded and got in beside her, and they drove back to the red brick house, Mrs. Murdock talking fluently and irrelevantly, as garrulous on the return trip as she had been silent on the journey down. She did not mention their completed errand again until they drew up at the house. Then she said, reflectively:

"Your father will have to be told. He won't like it."

So when they went into the house, and when Murdock, lying smoking his pipe in the swing on the little porch, asked, "Where have you two been?" Anne told him.

"We went to see Teddy," she answered. "I've — I've broken my engagement, Father."

Murdock took his pipe from his mouth and

knocked out the ashes against the railing.

"I'm not surprised," he answered evenly. "Girls nowadays don't think anything of breaking their promises. Off with the old love, on with the new — that's their game. You'll be sorry for this, Anne. O'Hara's a good boy and deserves better treatment than what you gave him. He's a worker; he has no bad habits; he'll be a success. You'll travel a long road before you'll meet one like him again."

He was unusually controlled, but disturbed. To him, an engagement was next door to a marriage. Girls who entered into vows so lightly, and broke them with an equal ease, were just as apt, he reasoned, to smash all Ten Commandments into a cocked hat. His wife spoke up, as usual, in her child's defense.

"Anne did right," she declared. "I'd rather see her turn at the very altar and run away than talk herself into a marriage she'd regret."

"Oh," her husband said resignedly, "of course you'd take up for the girl."

Anne spoke, miserably:

"I'm sorry you're — upset about it, Father. But I don't love him and I couldn't go through with it."

"I'm not upset," her father denied with some indignation, "and it seems to me that you should have found out you didn't love him before you gave him your word."

Anne's shoulders moved in a little gesture of hopelessness. She turned and went into the house and up to her sweltering hot bedroom, leaving her parents on the porch.

Molly sat down by her husband and touched his hand.

"Anne's unhappy," she said, simply, "don't make it any harder for her, Dad."

He had no immediate answer to that save to pat her lightly on the lean, small shoulder. After a moment he said, his hard thumb ramming down the tobacco in the pipe's bowl:

"I won't. Only in my day a word given was a word kept. I don't understand these young folk, Molly. We have three children. They're as different from us as if we hadn't fathered and mothered them. They're like another race. I guess," he went on slowly, struggling with the unusual need for speech, "it's just because they're the third generation. I remember my people, Molly, and you remember yours. Simple, they were. And we're simple people, too, just a little different from them because of the way we live and the easier money and newspapers and radio and all the rest of it. But our three are further from us than we from our parents. There's nothing simple about *them*." Murdock admitted with a sigh, "headstrong, reckless, greedy children."

Molly said, after a moment, watching him cup his hands and hold the match flare to the pipe:

"At least they're not ashamed of us."

"Why should they be?" he asked in some astonishment. "Haven't we given them everything any father and mother can give children? Food and clothes and a roof over their heads, doctors when they were sick, and the best schooling we could afford? You can't do more for your children, no matter how many times you're a millionaire."

After a while he rose and went heavily into the house. Molly, lax in a creaking wicker chair, fanned herself with her handkerchief and smiled as she heard Murdock mount the stairs.

Murdock thrust his head in at Anne's open door. He asked, gruffly:

"You all right?"

"Yes," Anne answered, and added, "Come in, won't you?"

She was lying on her bed, fully dressed. Murdock went in and sat down beside her and put his hand awkwardly on her hair. He was essentially an undemonstrative man and Anne, knowing him, knew too what agony of embarrassment the gesture cost him.

"Sorry I rode you," he said. "Don't — don't worry. Young bones heal quickly, Annie."

He hadn't called her "Annie" for years — not since she was a small, sparkling child, rebelling at the little nickname. Now it slipped out unawares, and she found herself loving it.

She put her cheek against his shoulder.

"It's all right, Dad," she said. "I made a bad mistake, that's all. And I hate to realize I haven't been on the square."

"You'll come out O. K.," he assured her. "I was worried about you — your fine friends and all — turning your head a little — Kathleen getting away from us —" he went on, snatchily; but Anne understood.

When he left her she undressed and went to bed. She wondered, momentarily, what had passed between Polly and Ted after her departure. She found herself envying the other girl's lack of emotional reticence. She had turned under Anne's eyes from a rather unintelligent, essentially soft and clinging, unimportant little person into a virago, a shrew, a passionate woman battling desperately for — for whom? For a man who did not love her. But he would come to love her, Anne thought, in a flash of prophecy; for she would give him all the demands, answer all the needs of his male nature. She would never give him dreams — and her own dreams would be centered not upon Ted, once she possessed him,

366

but upon Ted's children — but, after all, a man would forget that he had ever wanted dreams.

"He will forget me," thought Anne, with gratitude and relief, and an illogical, wholly feminine sting of wounded vanity.

Well, that was over. That way of escape closed to her. Why, she wondered, had she ever sought it? She faced the answer that she had engaged herself to Teddy in pique — out of hurt pride because Fellowes, under his misapprehension, had cared so little what became of her.

She got up, slender and small in her thin nightgown, and went to the window and looked out over the tops of lonely city trees in whose struggling, dusty branches a star was briefly entangled. She thought of Lawrence Fellowes and she knew that she would not cease to love him until time had worn down her emotional resistance, until her young blood ran cool and her senses starved or were blunted. And she faced that, too, without regret. To have loved wonderfully was worth — all heartache. And now that she had battled through conflicting emotions to a sense of surety, if not peace, to a feeling of roots too deeply planted to be torn up and cast away, she could adjust her life. She would find work; she would make friends; she would be, if not happy, then not unhappy. Somewhere in the world he was alive; somewhere he visioned and achieved and had his being. With that she had to be, if not content, then reconciled.

She fell asleep dreaming that she saw him again, that he held her in his arms, that there were no more barriers, that only love remained.

The days drew out, grew unbearably hot. Jim, who had settled his little family in a Long Island cottage, came to the brick house and observed his mother, flushed and damp, moving slowly about the kitchen, and Anne, white and haggard with the sick pressure of heat, and announced that it was all nonsense and that the two of them must go to Sara's and get some sea air and sound sleep. "Pop can take care of himself," he commented, "and if he can't I'll come out and do it for him."

"Great help you'd be to me about the house," his father answered, "but let the girls go. A rest will do them good."

Jim had been told of the broken engagement. He made no comment except, slangily, "Well, use your own judgment, kid," but his eyes, resting on Anne, were more satisfied, less anxious.

Anne and her mother went out to Sara's by car one Saturday afternoon, Jim and Murdock driving them and returning Sunday. The cottage was a small one, but directly on the ocean, as well situated as the more fashionable neighboring settlement. It was built of weather beaten frame, and the varnished wooden walls were so thin that the proverbial pin sounded like a thunder clap. The two older children, browning and fattening on the beach with Sara's eye upon them, were perfectly happy and comparatively good. The most recent baby thrived and Sara herself, in gingham frocks, and reducing her housekeeping to a minimum, was as happy as they. And when Anne and Mrs. Murdock descended upon her, she foresaw even more leisure. For Mrs. Murdock could not be kept out of the kitchen, or, when she could be, was to be found on the beach in one of Jimmy's oversize, cast-off bathing suits, superintending the marine education of her grandchildren.

As for Anne, she ate and slept, grew tanned and rosy, and the lines went from her face, and the nervousness from her hands; and it seemed to her that she was caught up in a little interlude of peace set to the music of the sea. She would watch it for hours — the broken unity of the waves, the struggle each incoming breaker made to complete the full circle, and the final, foaming frustration.

Life was like that, she thought, buoyant, rushing, striving, always beaten, always rising again, always repeating the endeavor, always falling short — but in beauty — of the full circle, the absolute perfection.

Betty Howard wrote her from New York.

"Ted tells us that your engagement is broken. I'm sorry, Anne, I thought you two youngsters would be happy. But you know best . . . you're wise to find out in time." She went on with news of herself and the boy, her late vacation plans, and concluded, "the office is rather at a standstill since The Chief went away."

So he'd gone. It came to Anne as an absolute shock that Lawrence Fellowes should have left the city, perhaps the country, and she did not know, she who had once known all his plans.

But he had not gone far. The house at Southampton was for sale, and the apartment had been sold. Fellowes was staying at his club, but he found that his work went badly, that he was not sleeping, that he was irritable and cross-grained, that nothing was right; so he did something he hadn't done in years — he took a vacation and went up to Westchester and played golf, and imagined that he was feeling better.

Sanders came up once to see him, and in the course of their business conversation, told him idly:

"The engagement between Anne Murdock

370

and O'Hara is off. No reason given, of course. Just — off."

Fellowes said something, anything, trying to control his amazement and his happiness, his overwhelming, almost painful joy.

"Is she still with Burroughs?" he asked, casually enough.

"No. I heard she'd left some time ago."

Then, thought Fellowes, if she'd given up the other job, now that Linda's divorce had gone through, and the whole stupid affair with the press blown over — perhaps she'd come back.

It seemed to him that he even wanted her back in his office, working beside him, near him, on any terms — on any terms. Just as long as he had her near him again, seeing her every day.

Linda came back to town and wrote him — from the *Ritz*.

"Would you meet me," she asked, "somewhere, quite quietly — here, perhaps, where people are more incurious than one thinks? I want to talk to you Larry."

He went, after some hesitation, and had luncheon with her in the Japanese Gardens. The town was deserted over the week-end. No one they knew saw them except a suave head waiter who marvelled a little, but was accustomed to observing curious *tête-à-têtes*.

Linda looked very lovely. They talked of Europe, of the weather, of people. Then, over her iced tea, Linda stated:

"Dick and I are going to be married — in the autumn. I'm sailing again; we will marry in England and live there indefinitely. I wanted you to know."

He said, aching with that poignant, inescapable regret:

"Thank you, Linda. I — I want you to be happy."

"I shall be. And you?"

"Oh, I don't matter."

"Yes, you do." Abruptly she asked him, "Is Anne Murdock still with you?"

"No — she's engaged — that is, she *was* engaged," he answered, carefully.

"Engaged?"

"To be married. But it's been broken."

"Anne?" Linda's brown eyes were wide. "Had she left the office?"

After a moment, Fellowes explained the surface situation to her — the newspaper gossip, Anne's resignation, his learning of her engagement, his more recent news. Linda listened, exclaimed indignantly, laughed a little, frowned a little more, and then said, thoughtfully, "Poor child!"

Fellowes didn't answer. There was nothing to say. Linda, leaning forward, her big transparent hat tilted over her lovely, kind eyes, said:

"Larry, I must talk to you — for the last time." A little silence fell, and then she went on, simply enough, "It *is* Anne, isn't it?"

"Yes. But when I knew it, it was too late," he answered low.

"You are very blind," she told him. "She's been very much in love with you all along. Can't you see it? This engagement," she flickered her fingers, "camouflage, an issue of unhappiness. Now it's dissolved. She was wise — and in time. Larry, I don't advise — I don't even comment. It wouldn't, perhaps, to your masculine way of reasoning, seem quite decent if I did — but don't make the gravest mistake of your life. Don't."

After a moment he promised, and his gray eyes were shining.

"I won't."

Later, they shook hands and parted, and each went his separate way, the road each of us travels in his or her own fashion, the veiled road upon which we dream we see the signposts to happiness.

Fellowes stayed in town. He went directly to Anne's little flat and found it closed. No, they had no idea where Miss Murdock or her sister were, the janitor told him.

After a time he dug out an address book

and found the street and number of Anne's home. He drove out there through the dusty town, the wheels of his powerful car denting the sickeningly soft asphalt.

The evening had fallen when he arrived — long, golden, summer evening. Murdock was home, puttering around the yard in his shirt-sleeves; and Kathleen was there, too, having arrived unannounced as the road show had closed in the Middle West, the bubble of success pierced and evaporated into thin air.

Fellowes went up on the porch, Murdock, a rake in his hand, following.

He introduced himself and explained his errand.

"Anne's in the country," said her father, and asked bluntly, "What do you want of her?"

Kathleen, who had been presented in a rather informal fashion, listened, watching Fellowes' face.

"I thought," Fellowes answered, smiling, "I might persuade her to return to us. I understand that she and Mr. O'Hara —"

"That's her business," Murdock said, with a rather disarming rudeness.

Fellowes looked at Murdock's sealed but subtly hostile face, at Kathleen's lovely eyes and her lips curved to a smile. He urged, leaning on the porch railing:

"If I could have her address?"

"Of course you can," Kathleen cried, suddenly.

Murdock said, doggedly:

"If she wants to go back to work in the fall — and I suppose she does — she can come to see you later."

Fellowes thought, "What's the use of all this talk and animosity? I can't blame him; she's his child." He looked briefly at Kathleen, then turned a direct gaze to Murdock.

"I'd better be frank," he said. "It concerns you as much as it does me. I love Anne, Mr. Murdock. I wish to find her in order to ask her to marry me."

Stilted the little speech sounded, but the sense was clear enough. Kathleen's breath escaped her in a soft gasp of pure happiness. But Murdock's face was clouded.

"She's not in your class," he said, brusquely.

"Come," answered Fellowes, and smiled, "you don't think that, do you? Not really. You believe, do you not, that she's good enough for any man, and too good for all of them?"

Murdock smiled, reluctantly.

"I do —" he said, and after a moment, held out his hand.

"If she loves you," he told Fellowes, with

genuine dignity, "that's all that matters. I don't approve of mixing the classes, but it happens every day, and I guess it works out. Her mother may be difficult. You are a divorced man, Mr. Fellowes, and Molly has her notions on the subject. The children — they don't think the way she does, they have their own ways of looking at things. I wished them to."

Fellowes took the other man's hand — and held it in a firm clasp, strong and vibrant.

"I'll be good to her," he told Anne's father, in the simplest language of all, the language of the inarticulate heart.

He turned to Kathleen. Murdock, with a nod, went back to weeding his little yard, God knows with what astonishment, speculations and anxieties in his soul. Kathleen said, still breathless:

"I'm so — glad."

"Are you? And shall I be?" he wanted to know.

"I hope so," Kathleen told him, but betrayed no confidence.

"Her engagement —" began Fellowes, a little diffidently.

"You didn't understand that?" she questioned him. "But you will," she said.

And that was all. He arranged to call for her the following morning and take her to

Sara's with him. "My ambassador," he told her, smiling.

He went back to town, to his club, and left, after a practically sleepless night, very early in the morning, to pick up Kathleen and drive her down. Listening sympathetically to her chatter, and thinking — every mile brought him nearer — nearer —

They parked the car in the dune grass back of the cottage, and Kathleen said, mysteriously:

"Wait here, — and if I wave from the porch, go round to the beach. I suppose she'll be there — she spends her time there, she wrote me."

He waited by the car, lighting a cigarette and instantly throwing it away. Wind and water and the grass stirring, and the small wild flowers of the seaside lifting their gallant faces — a blue sky and a blue sea —

He heard the door bang, heard voices, saw Kathleen appear briefly with her mother beside her, saw her wave, saw her turn again, holding Molly's arm firmly.

Fellowes walked around the house, down the few rickety wooden steps to the sand. Anne was lying curled up in the sand by a small, grass-grown dune. No one else was in sight save, not very far off, two little boys who dug busily, building their castles, near enough to the sea to make it thrilling, too far away for danger. He saw their sturdy tanned bodies in the scant suits, heard their little laughter, their wordless speech, intelligible only to each other.

"Anne?"

She looked up — and got somehow to her feet. She wore a plain dark bathing suit, and her round arms and pretty legs were tanned, and the face she lifted bronze and rose. The bright coolie coat she had slipped on until her swim was startingly becoming to her.

"I've come for you," he told her, as still she did not, could not speak.

"For — me —"

Pale, under the tan, now, and her eyes blazing into black. He stretched out his arms in the immemorial gesture of longing.

"I can't get along without you. I love you," he told her. "You'll have to marry me, Anne," he said.

But she did not quite believe it, even when the arms took her, held her, fused into their embrace.

After a little while he released her and asked:

"Why did you run away from me?"

"Because I loved you."

"Why did you engage yourself to O'Hara?"

"Because I loved you," she said again.

"Then, how long have you cared?" he demanded, after the fashion of happy lovers.

"Almost always — ever since I first came into your office. But I didn't know it altogether. You see," explained Anne, facing him, her hands in his, the sea and the wind and the playing children their indifferent audience, "I had you all confused with the work. I loved that, too!"

"And when did you first separate me from your job?" he wanted to know, laughing a little and drawing her down to sit beside him at the sliding sand feet of the dune.

Anne was silent a moment. She knew, deeply, when the first full realization of bitter love had come to her — that night at Hot Springs. But she wished to erase it from her memory. She had nothing but gratitude for Linda and a little wondering, a lack of understanding — how could she, Linda, relinquish anyone as beloved as — Larry? But she had no desire, now, to think of Linda overmuch. So she evaded, with gay tenderness:

"Oh, how can I tell? Suddenly I just knew — that's all."

"I, too," he said, and kissed her again.

After a minute, he told her:

"That night at your flat — hush, I must speak of it, darling — I came to you to ask you to wait until I was free. I — I was driven; I had sworn I would wait until Linda got her decree; I argued that it was best for us both. But when I heard about O'Hara — I had to come, and — ask you if it was true, and if it was not true to tell you that you were mine and I would never let you go."

Anne stared at him, her eyes very dark in her suntanned face.

"What's the matter?" he asked.

But she shook her head and smiled. Better not to tell him. Better that he should never know that his mistake, the word left unsaid, had caused them both so much misunderstanding and suffering. Better that he should never learn that she had not pledged herself to O'Hara before Fellowes had come to her, better that he should never guess that it was for the sake of her own safety, her own escape, that she had done so, eventually, as well as for his sake. Better that he should not dream how tempted she had been to go to him without marriage, without anything but the assurance of his need for her. Better to keep silent, as she had been silent. Better that he should not know this, nor that once upon a time — how very long ago it seemed — she had been willing to accept the half loaf, until she knew she loved him. And then, loving him, had realized that half loaves stale quickly.

He was telling her how he had felt when

he had learned of her broken engagement, he was telling her:

"You never loved him, Anne. Say that you never loved him!"

"No," she answered, "I never loved him. Only you, Larry."

After a long interval, she remembered to ask him:

"How did you find me? How did you come?"

He told her.

"I brought Kathleen with me," he added, "and by the way, your father thinks that your mother may disapprove."

"Not," said Anne, "when she realizes how happy I am." In a little while they must go into the house to be exclaimed over and questioned and made much of. But these few moments, the sweetest, the never-to-be-recaptured, were their own. And Fellowes planned, happily:

"We'll be married — at once. And we'll go away for a little while. Then I must get back to work. We'll find a place somewhere — a house. Wouldn't you like a house, Anne, a little house all your own?"

"I'd adore it!"

"And a camping spot somewhere in the country — not a great barn for you to go to and bury yourself in," he said jealously, "but just a dear place we'll escape to — together."

"And I'll go on being your secretary," Anne announced.

"No," the arm about her tightened, "no, never again."

"Oh, Larry —" She still said his name a little breathlessly — it was so new a name to her lips. "Oh, Larry, why not?"

"Because I love you — too much. Girl, I have to work — you know how hard — and I can't have you near to distract me."

She nodded, after a moment. But she was wounded with a sense of loss. No longer — the Office Wife. Just — Wife. That was better, of course, more wonderful, complete, perfect. Yet —

He said, frowning:

"And getting a new secretary is something I'll have to worry about when we come home again."

Anne asked, instantly:

"Who did your work after I left? Miss Danton? No, she won't do, permanently. Let me see. . . ." She thought a moment and then said, suddenly, "There's a girl — Mr. Power's secretary — a Miss Conner. I knew her very slightly. She's had college and good training. I think she'd do splendidly — and I could break her in for you quickly and easily. She's very capable and quite attractive."

"As if the attractive part mattered!" he protested.

"Oh, but it does." Anne smiled at him wisely, and went on, "You could talk to her — before — before we go away."

"I'll leave it to you," he said, contentedly.

There was a silence, warm and sunny and golden. The ocean beat there, creaming on the wet broad sands, a stone's throw away. A gull flew screaming over the broken blue of the water. On the horizon a boat steamed out to sea, smoke from her funnels rising straight to the sky. They were arched over with azure, bound round with peace. Happiness held them and desire and the radiant promise of fulfillment. The wind marched with the dunes and sang softly in the leaning grasses. There were voices from the house, a little above them, and someone called. Soon they must go in.

"What fun we'll have!" he promised her, softly. "What comrades we'll be!" his voice deepened. "What *lovers!*"

Her heart shook her with an intolerable rapture and the color rose into her throat and face. She tightened her hand in his and looked at him sweetly, gravely, love in her breast, passion on her lips, tenderness in her eyes.

"Of what are you thinking — little Anne?"

"Of you — always of you!"

But she was thinking, briefly, of the distant, unconsciously suddenly important Conner girl — the girl Anne would train to be the perfect office wife; and she was wondering if ever she would be jealous, if ever she would be afraid. She knew, you see, how much a man came to lean on the woman who shared his office hours. She knew. And she herself would be at home — waiting.

Anne tilted her chin in challenge and defiance. No, she was not afraid. She knew that side of him, too. Nothing was sealed to her — nothing was a closed book. No one could usurp her place, no one could threaten her sure position. She held his heart; she knew his mind; she would retain the partnership and be the beloved.

She leaned forward and kissed him.

"We must go in," said Anne, "and tell them our plans."

A caption danced before her mental vision, as on a silver screen: "Employer Marries Secretary."

Well, she knew how to keep her own.

He rose and lifted her to her sandalled feet.

"Dearest —"

Very boyish he was, very young and gay hearted in his unsearching happiness. She felt, raising her lips to his, regardless of the astonished children who, seeing them, suddenly ran staggering and stumbling to their side, how much older she was, how much more wise — with the wisdom of women. And not, she told herself for the last time, not afraid. Never afraid any more.

"I love you," she told him, and there was promise and passion and the dark gravity of unending vigilance in her voice.

They turned, the two little boys flung up to Fellowes' shoulders, and walked to the house — the blue sky overhead, the blue ocean like a pulse-beat in their ears, the sunlight full on their faces, warming the dark, enchanted troubling of their flesh and blood like golden wine.

The employees of THORNDIKE PRESS hope you have enjoyed this Large Print book. All our Large Print books are designed for easy reading — and they're made to last.

Other Thorndike Large Print books are available at your library, through selected bookstores, or directly from us. Suggestions for books you would like to see in Large Print are always welcome.

For more information about current and upcoming titles, please call or mail your name and address to:

THORNDIKE PRESS
PO Box 159
Thorndike, Maine 04986
800/223-6121
207/948-2962